HARDCASTLE'S TRAITORS

A murder in a jeweller's shop proves to be more than meets the eye in Detective Inspector Hardcastle's latest investigation.

It is New Year's Eve 1915 and the Hardcastle family are welcoming 1916 at their home in Kennington, London. But an hour into the New Year, Hardcastle is called to a murder in a jeweller's shop in Vauxhall. In a first for the A Division senior detective, the killers apparently made their escape in a motor car.

As Hardcastle's enquiry progresses, what he believed to be a fairly straightforward investigation turns into one with ramifications extending from Chelsea via Sussex and Surrey to France, close to the fighting on the Western Front, and as is so often the case in wartime, the army becomes involved and so, to Hardcastle's dismay, does Scotland Yard's Special Branch...

Recent Titles by Graham Ison from
Severn House

The Hardcastle Series
HARDCASTLE'S SPY
HARDCASTLE'S ARMISTICE
HARDCASTLE'S CONSPIRACY
HARDCASTLE'S AIRMEN
HARDCASTLE'S ACTRESS
HARDCASTLE'S BURGLAR
HARDCASTLE'S MANDARIN
HARDCASTLE'S SOLDIERS
HARDCASTLE'S OBSESSION
HARDCASTLE'S FRUSTRATION
HARDCASTLE'S TRAITORS

Contemporary Police Procedurals
ALL QUIET ON ARRIVAL
BREACH OF PRIVILEGE
DIVISION
DRUMFIRE
GUNRUNNER
JACK IN THE BOX
KICKING THE AIR
LIGHT FANTASTIC
LOST OR FOUND
MAKE THEM PAY
WHIPLASH
WHISPERING GRASS
WORKING GIRL

HARDCASTLE'S TRAITORS

Graham Ison

Severn House Large Print
London & New York

This first large print edition published 2014
in Great Britain and the USA by
SEVERN HOUSE PUBLISHERS LTD of
19 Cedar Road, Sutton, Surrey, England, SM2 5DA.
First world regular print edition published 2013 by
Severn House Publishers Ltd., London and New York.

British Library Cataloguing in Publication Data

Ison, Graham author.
  Hardcastle's traitors. -- Large print edition. -- (A
  Hardcastle and Marriott historical mystery ; 11)
  1. Hardcastle, Ernest (Fictitious character)--Fiction.
  2. Police--England--London--Fiction. 3. Great Britain--
  History--George V, 1910-1936--Fiction. 4. Detective and
  mystery stories. 5. Large type books.
  I. Title II. Series
  823.9'14-dc23

ISBN-13: 9780727896797

Severn House Publishers support the Forest Stewardship Council™
[FSC™], the leading international forest certification organisation. All
our titles that are printed on FSC certified paper carry the FSC logo.

Printed and bound in Great Britain by
T J International, Padstow, Cornwall.

Glossary

ALBERT: a watch chain of the type worn by Albert, Prince Consort (1819–61).
APM: assistant provost marshal (a lieutenant colonel of the military police).
BAILEY, the: Central Criminal Court, Old Bailey, London.
BARNEY: an argument.
BEAK: a magistrate.
BEF: British Expeditionary Force in France and Flanders.
BENT: crooked *or* stolen.
BLIGHTY: the United Kingdom.
BLIMP: an airship.
BOB: a shilling (now 5p).
BOOZER: a public house.
BULL AND COW: a row (rhyming slang).
CARPET: three months' imprisonment. (The length of time it took to weave a carpet in prison workshops.)
CHOKEY: a prison (ex *Hindi*).
CID: Criminal Investigation Department.
COMMISSIONER'S OFFICE: official title of New Scotland Yard, headquarters of the Metropolitan Police.

COPPER: a policeman.

DARTMOOR: a remote prison on Dartmoor in Devon.

DDI: Divisional Detective Inspector.

DOG'S DINNER, a: a mess.

DPP: Director of Public Prosecutions.

DRUM: a dwelling house, or room therein. Any place of abode.

FENCE, to: to dispose of stolen property.

FENCE: a receiver of stolen property.

FIDDLE-FADDLE: Trifling talk or behaviour.

FIVE-STRETCH: five years' imprisonment.

FLEET STREET: former centre of the newspaper industry, and still used as a generic term for the Press.

FLIM or FLIMSY: a five-pound note. From the thin paper on which it was originally printed.

FLOG, to: to sell.

FOURPENNY CANNON, a: a steak and kidney pie.

FRONT, The: theatre of WW1 operations in France and Flanders.

GAMAGES: a London department store.

GANDER, to cop a: to take a look.

GLIM: a look (a foreshortening of 'glimpse').

GRASS: an informer.

GREAT SCOTLAND YARD: location of an army recruiting office and a military police detachment. Not to be confused with New Scotland Yard, half a mile away in Whitehall.

GUNNERS, The: a generic term to encompass the Royal Horse Artillery, the Royal Garrison

Artillery and the Royal Field Artillery. In the singular, a member of one of those regiments.

GUV or GUV'NOR: informal alternative to 'sir'.

HALF A CROWN or HALF A DOLLAR: two shillings and sixpence (12½p).

HANDFUL: five years' imprisonment.

JIG-A-JIG: sexual intercourse.

JILDI: quickly (*ex* Hindi).

MADAM: a brothel keeper.

MANOR: a police area.

MC: Military Cross.

MI5: counter-espionage service of the United Kingdom.

MOCKERS, to put on the: to frustrate one's plans.

MONS, to make a: to make a mess of things, as in the disastrous Battle of Mons in 1914.

NCO: non-commissioned officer.

NICK: a police station *or* prison *or* to arrest *or* to steal.

NICKED: arrested *or* stolen.

OICK: a cad.

OLD BAILEY: Central Criminal Court, in Old Bailey, London.

ON THE GAME: leading a life of prostitution.

PEACH, to: to inform to the police.

PROVOST, the: military police.

QUEER STREET, in: in serious difficulty *or* short of money.

RAGTIME GIRL: a sweetheart; a girl with whom one has a joyous time; a harlot.

RECEIVER, The: the senior Scotland Yard official responsible for the finances of the Metropolitan Police.

ROYAL A: informal name for the A or Whitehall Division of the Metropolitan Police.

ROZZER: a policeman.

SAM BROWNE: a military officer's belt with shoulder strap.

SAUSAGE AND MASH: cash (rhyming slang).

SCREWING: engaging in sexual intercourse *or* committing burglary.

SCRIMSHANKER: one who evades duty or work.

SELFRIDGES: a London department store.

SHILLING: now 5p.

SIXPENCE: equivalent of 2½ p.

SKIP or SKIPPER: an informal police alternative to station-sergeant, clerk-sergeant and sergeant.

SNOUT: a police informant.

SOMERSET HOUSE: formerly the records office of births, deaths and marriages for England & Wales.

STRIPE, to: to maliciously wound, usually with a razor.

TEA-LEAF: a thief (rhyming slang). (Plural: *TEALEAVES*.)

TOBY: a police area.

TOM: a prostitute *or* jewellery (see *TOMFOOLERY*).

TOMFOOLERY: jewellery (rhyming slang).

TOPPED: murdered or hanged.

TOPPING: a murder or hanging.
TUMBLE, a: sexual intercourse.
UNDERGROUND, The: the London
Underground railway system.
YOUNG SHAVER: a youth or young man.

ONE

The maroons had been detonated at the nearby Renfrew Road fire station at twenty minutes to midnight on New Year's Eve 1915, signalling the onset of yet another air raid by the dreaded Zeppelins. In common with most Londoners, Ernest Hardcastle knew that the alert was invariably sounded when the raiders were crossing the coast. It would take some time, at least an hour, for the giant airships, lumbering along at seventy miles an hour, to reach the capital.

The Hardcastle family was gathered in the parlour of their house in Kennington Road, London. It was the home that Ernest and Alice Hardcastle had moved into immediately after their marriage twenty-three years ago, and was only a few doors away from where Charlie Chaplin, much-loved slapstick star of the silent films, had once lived.

In a corner of the comfortable sitting room stood a decorated Christmas tree. But it bore none of the miniature candles favoured by many families; Hardcastle was only too aware of the fire risk that that would present. Painstakingly made paper chains had been strung from each corner of the room to the electric light fitting in the centre of the whitewashed ceiling.

Hardcastle busied himself spending a few minutes dispensing drinks from a cabinet in the corner.

'A Happy New Year everyone and may it see an end to this wretched war.' On the stroke of midnight, Ernest Hardcastle, his back to a glowing coal fire, raised his glass and took a sip of whisky.

'Amen to that,' said Alice, raising her glass of Amontillado and joining in the toast together with the Hardcastles' two daughters and their son. Kitty and Maud, at nineteen and seventeen respectively, were now old enough for a glass of sherry. But Walter, the Hardcastles' son, whose sixteenth birthday would not occur until the twenty-fourth of January 1916, was only permitted a glass of brown ale, and that as a special treat.

Hardcastle kissed his wife and his daughters and shook hands with Walter.

The war to which Hardcastle alluded had been in progress for the sixteen months since the fourth of August 1914. Despite his pious hope for a swift end to the bloody conflict, there had been nothing but depressing news since the war had started. Nor were there any signs of victory in the foreseeable future; the losses were mounting day after day.

In August 1914, young men had flocked enthusiastically to the Colours fearful that the widely held belief that it would all be over by Christmas would mean missing the 'fun' as they had termed it. But it was a premise that had proved to be well short of the reality. Now, just over a year later, the two opposing armies were firmly entrenched from the North Sea to the Swiss border; and thousands of British, Colonial and German troops lay dead with little but a few yards of blood-sodden ground to show for their sacrifice.

The sight of wounded soldiers and sailors in the streets had become commonplace, and hospitals were overflowing with the seriously injured.

The war no longer seemed like 'fun'. And now that the earlier flood of keen volunteers had started to ebb, Parliament would shortly begin debating the imposition of compulsory conscription to fill the yawning gaps in the ranks of the decimated British Army.

At five minutes past midnight, Hardcastle took his hunter from his waistcoat pocket and flicked open the cover.

'It's time we took shelter, just to be on the safe side,' he said, and conducted his family into the cupboard beneath the stairs, having first instructed Walter to check the blackout curtains and, as an added precaution, to turn out all the lights.

Very soon the menacing heavy throb of

Maybach engines and the spasmodic bark of anti-aircraft guns announced the arrival of the enemy overhead. And occasionally the distinctive sound of British fighters could be heard zooming around the sky in a vain attempt to destroy one of the giant airships. But for the most part they were unable to match the Zeppelins' superior altitude.

Even in the cupboard under the stairs, the Hardcastles were able to hear, somewhere in the distance, the noise of cascading bricks; indication that yet another building had fallen victim to the raiders' bombs.

It was not until one o'clock in the morning that the Hardcastles heard the voice of a cycling policeman shouting 'All Clear', and the family was able to emerge from its makeshift shelter.

'I could do with a cup of tea,' said Alice, stretching her limbs after an hour's confinement in the cramped staircase cupboard.

'Not for me,' said Kitty, 'I'm off to bed. I'm early shift in the morning.' For some months now, Kitty had been working as a conductorette with the London General Omnibus Company. She had taken the job against her father's wishes, but Kitty had always been a headstrong girl. Even so, her excuse that she was releasing a man for the Front had little impact on her father who did not see working on the buses as women's work, whatever the circumstances.

'I'm for bed too,' said Maud, who also worked long hours. For the past few months she had

14

been nursing at one of the big houses in Mayfair that had been converted to hospital accommodation for wounded officers.

Refusing his wife's offer of a cup of tea, Hardcastle was about to pour himself another whisky when there was a knock at the door.

'Surely it's not a neighbour come to wish us a Happy New Year at this hour of the morning,' he muttered, as he pulled open the front door. But it was a jocular comment; he had already anticipated who would be on the doorstep. As the divisional detective inspector of the A or Whitehall Division of the Metropolitan Police he had his headquarters at Cannon Row police station in the shadow of New Scotland Yard. Being the division's senior detective, he was expected to be on call at all hours.

'Mr Hardcastle, sir?' A sergeant from Kennington Road police station was standing on the doorstep.

'What is it, Skipper?' There was a resigned note in Hardcastle's question.

'There's been a burglary at a jeweller's shop in Vauxhall Bridge Road, sir.' The sergeant proffered a message form.

'Why the hell do I need to know that at this hour?' demanded Hardcastle, seizing the form.

'There's been a murder there as well, sir,' said the sergeant, before Hardcastle had finished reading the message.

'God dammit! Best see if you can find me a cab, Skipper. And when you get back to the nick telephone Cannon Row and tell them I want DS Marriott and a couple of detectives at the scene tout de suite.'

'Very good, sir.' The sergeant flicked back his cape and taking his pocketbook from a tunic pocket, made a note. That done, he paused and grinned. 'And a very Happy New Year to you and your family, sir.'

'Some hopes of that,' muttered Hardcastle, donning his Chesterfield overcoat and seizing his bowler hat and umbrella. He took a few paces back into the hallway. 'I've got to go out, love,' he shouted. 'Expect me when you see me,' he added. It was something he always said when called out to deal with a crime.

'You take care of yourself, Ernie,' responded his wife from the kitchen. Having been married to a policeman for twenty-three years, Alice had grown accustomed to her husband being sent for at any hour of the day or night, especially now that he was a senior detective.

The sign over the shop simply read: REUBEN GOSLING. At one end of the fascia a projecting wrought-iron arm bore the three golden balls that were the traditional sign of a pawnbroker.

When Hardcastle arrived, Detective Sergeant Charles Marriott was already there. As a first-class sergeant, he was the officer Hardcastle always chose as his assistant. Marriott lived with his wife Lorna and their two children in police quarters in Regency Street, within walking distance of Vauxhall Bridge Road. Neither Marriott nor his wife was pleased at his being called out so early in the New Year.

Detective Constables Henry Catto and Cecil Watkins were also there, their umbrellas raised. The two DCs, being single men, lived in the police section house at Ambrosden Avenue, and were the ones that Marriott called out in preference to married officers, particularly during festive celebrations such as the New Year.

It was an unseasonably warm night, temperatures having on occasion reached fifty degrees Fahrenheit in late December. But it was raining quite hard.

'What do we know so far, Marriott?' asked Hardcastle, struggling to raise his umbrella as he alighted from his cab.

'Forced entry was made through the shop door, sir.' Marriott indicated a hole in the glass panel. 'A professional job by the look of it: brown paper, treacle and a glass cutter. There was only a Yale rim latch, despite the owner having been advised on several occasions to improve the security. Either the thieves knew that or they struck lucky.'

'More than the victim did,' muttered Hardcastle. 'Where's the body, Marriott?'

'In the front of the shop, sir, near the cash register.'

'Who found it?'

'PC 313A Dodds, sir. He was on this beat and a member of the public called him. Something

17

to do with a car making off at high speed. It was then that Dodds found the broken glass in the door.'

'Where is this PC, Marriott?'

'Here, sir,' said a caped figure. He approached Hardcastle and saluted. 'All correct, sir.'

'I'm glad you think so, lad.' Hardcastle always addressed constables as 'lad' even though they were often his age or even older. 'Sergeant Marriott's given me the brief details, but how exactly did you come across this break-in?'

'I was patrolling my beat in a north-westerly direction, sir—' the PC began.

'Never mind all that fiddle-faddle, Dodds, you're not giving evidence now,' said Hardcastle. 'Just tell me the story.'

'Yes, sir. I was about fifty yards away when I heard someone shouting for police. So I made me way down here a bit swift and come across the broken glass panel in this door, sir, and so I ventured inside.'

'And what did you find when you *ventured* inside, as you put it, lad?' demanded Hardcastle sarcastically. He was always impatient when receiving a report from an officer who prevaricated.

'I saw Mr Gosling's body lying on the floor, sir. I never touched nothing apart from ascertaining that he was dead. Then I shouted for my mate on the adjoining beat, and told him to get assistance from Rochester Row nick, sir. It's only about five minutes away.'

'For God's sake, lad, I know where Rochester Row nick is,' snapped Hardcastle. 'Anything else?'

'Yes, sir, sorry, sir. While I was waiting I had a word with the gent from the outfitters next door. It was him what called me, sir, and he reckoned as how he'd seen a motor vehicle leaving the scene at a fast speed.'

'Did you see this motor vehicle yourself?'

'No, sir. It must've made off in the opposite direction. The opposite direction from the one I come from, if you see what I mean, sir.'

'And who is this man?'

'Mr Sidney Partridge, sir,' said Dodds, quickly referring to his pocketbook.

Hardcastle grunted and turned to Marriott. 'I don't suppose you've had time to find out what's been taken yet. But I presume they didn't leave without helping themselves to the tomfoolery.'

'The glass showcases have been broken into, sir, and they've been emptied,' said Marriott. 'Quite a haul of jewellery, I'd've thought, although they've left some cheap stuff behind, along with all of the stuff that had been pledged, as far as I can tell. It seems as though they knew what they were looking for.'

'We'd better take a glim at this here corpse, then.' Closing his umbrella, Hardcastle pushed open the door with a gloved hand.

The body of an elderly man lay face down in

19

the centre of the shop floor, arms outstretched, his head a mass of matted blood. He was dressed in striped pyjamas, a dressing gown and slippers. An Ever-Ready electric torch – still switched on – lay close to the man's right hand, and a pool of his blood had spread across the linoleum-covered floor. But blood had been splashed everywhere: on the front of the counter, on the walls and on the showcases.

'They must've given him a good whack, judging by the amount of blood, Marriott. Looks like an abattoir,' said Hardcastle, hands in pockets as he glanced around. 'I reckon he disturbed these villains and was bludgeoned on the head for his pains.'

'Yes, sir.' Marriott confined himself to a simple answer, as he always did whenever the DDI stated the obvious. 'I've sent for Doctor Spilsbury, sir,' he said, anticipating the DDI's next instruction.

'That PC said this man's name was Gosling.'

'Yes, sir, Reuben Gosling. He's owned this establishment for nigh on thirty years.' It was Marriott's job to possess such local knowledge. 'He's a jeweller as well as a pawnbroker.'

'I gathered that from the sign outside,' said Hardcastle acidly. 'Is he married?'

'I believe he's a widower, sir. I had heard that his wife died about ten years ago, but I don't know for sure.'

'And he lived over the shop, I suppose.'

'Yes, sir.'

'Where's this witness Partridge, the one that Dodds mentioned?'

'He lives above the outfitters next door, sir.'

'In that case we'll have a word with him while we're waiting for the good doctor to arrive.' Hardcastle turned to the two DCs. 'You wait here for Dr Spilsbury. Have a look round and see if you can find anything of importance, but don't touch it if you do. Understood, Catto?'

'Yes, sir.' Catto was an experienced detective and did not need to be told how to conduct himself at the scene of a murder, but for some reason that Catto had never been able to fathom his abilities were always called into question by the DDI.

The window of the outfitter's shop next to Gosling's establishment contained a number of mannequins attired in the latest men's fashions. Hardcastle looked around the doorway of the shop until he discovered a bell handle high on one side. He pulled at it several times.

Eventually a window on the floor above the door was flung open and a tousled head appeared.

'Who the devil's that at this time of the morning disturbing decent folk when they're trying to get some shut-eye?' The speaker was clearly in a bad mood.

'Police,' said Hardcastle, stepping back from the doorway and looking up.

'Oh, right. Hang on, guv'nor.' The head disappeared and moments later the shop door was opened by a man in a nightshirt over which he wore an overcoat. 'Sorry, I didn't know it was you,' he said. 'You'd better come inside. It's a bit of a dirty night out there.'

Leaving their umbrellas on the step, the two detectives entered the shop and Marriott closed the door.

'You're Mr Sidney Partridge, I understand,' said Hardcastle.

'That's me, sir.' Partridge stood with shoulders slightly rounded and hands clasped together in the manner of the obsequious, mid-fifties, shopkeeper he was.

'I'm Divisional Detective Inspector Hardcastle of the Whitehall Division. Are you the owner of this establishment, Mr Partridge?'

'That I am, sir, and any time I can fix you up with a suit, just say the word. At a discount, of course. I've a very good selection.' Partridge made a sweeping motion with a hand, as if to encompass his entire stock.

'I'll bear that in mind,' said Hardcastle, gazing round at the racks of suits, overcoats and other items of apparel that comprised a gentleman's outfitter's stock-in-trade. 'I understand you have some information that might assist me.'

'Well, I don't know if I've got anything to tell you that might be of any use, sir. Me and Gladys had toasted the New Year on the stroke of twelve and then we chatted for a bit. It must've been about ten past midnight when we decided to turn in. I checked the curtains to make sure they were covering the window, seeing as how the maroons had gone off from the fire station in Greycoat Place about half an hour before. But I knew we had time to spare before those wretched Blimps came right over London. It's always the same, you see, sir. They set off the warning far too early. The curtains were all right, though; being in the trade, so to speak, I can lay my hands on a good quality twill.'

'But what did you see, Mr Partridge?' prompted Hardcastle somewhat tetchily, fearing that the outfitter was on the point of embarking on a lengthy monologue about air raids and curtains.

'Well, like I was saying, I happened to look out of the window and I saw these two men – rough-looking blokes they was – come out of Reuben's shop and jump into a motor car. Then they drove off like the hounds of hell were on their tail. I was pretty sure something had happened, so I opened the window and yelled "Police", and the officer on the beat came running.'

'Do you know what sort of car it was, Mr Partridge?' asked Marriott.

'I don't know much about cars.' Partridge paused, a thoughtful expression on his face. 'But I think the one I saw is called a tourer. It was an open car, but it had a hood that was up; one of those canvas things. Oh, and it had them white tyres.'

'White tyres?' queried Marriott, looking up from his pocketbook.

'Yes, like they have on American cars. You know the sort of thing: painted white round the sides.'

'D'you think it *was* an American car?' asked Hardcastle.

'I don't know, sir. I was watching the two men rather than the car.'

'Motor cars have a number on them. Did you happen to see it?' asked Marriott.

'No, I'm sorry, sir. I never thought of that.'

'What did these men look like?'

'I'm afraid I didn't get a good look at them, what with the street lights being out because of the war. But like I said, they seemed to be rough-looking characters, and they were only wearing jackets and trousers as far as I could see. No overcoats.' Again Partridge paused. 'On the other hand, I think one of 'em had one of them reefer jackets on. And they had something round the bottom half of their faces, a scarf possibly. Oh, and they both had cloth caps on, pulled well down over their eyes.'

'Had you heard anything before you saw these men running away?' asked Hardcastle. 'The sound of someone breaking in, for instance? Or voices?'

'No. As I said, the wife and me had been having a drink and chatting just before I crossed to check on the curtains, and that the windows were closed on account of the air raid.'

Hardcastle failed to see the logic of that, but made no comment in case Partridge returned to the subject of air raids and curtains again. 'Thank you, Mr Partridge,' he said. 'You've been a great help. I'll have an officer call round later in the day to take a written statement from you. Unless you're prepared to make one now.'

'Yes, why not, sir? I doubt I'll get much sleep tonight. But at least I'll have a half-day today, it being a Saturday.'

'Get one of those two officers up here to take a statement from Mr Partridge, Marriott,' said Hardcastle. 'And make it Watkins rather than Catto.'

'Yes, sir.' In Marriott's view Catto was a good detective and he could never understand why the DDI did not share that opinion. But it was probably because Catto appeared to lose his self-confidence whenever he was in Hard-castle's presence.

Returning to Reuben Gosling's shop, Marriott dispatched Watkins to take Partridge's state-ment and then he and Hardcastle began to look around.

'There's quite a lot of blood on this showcase, Marriott,' said Hardcastle. 'It's likely that one of our villains cut himself on the broken glass. And that might mean he wasn't wearing gloves at the time. Be a good idea to get Mr Collins down here to see if he can find any useful fingerprints.'

25

Detective Inspector Charles Stockley Collins was head of the Fingerprint Bureau at Scotland Yard and the comparatively new science of fingerprints had helped to apprehend numerous criminals during the last ten years. Such evidence had first been accepted by the courts in 1905 when the Stratton brothers were convicted of murdering a Deptford oil-shop keeper and his wife.

The door to Gosling's shop crashed open and the tall impressive figure of Dr Bernard Spilsbury, attired in full evening dress, stood on the threshold.

'Good evening, my dear Hardcastle. I understand you have a cadaver for me. Ah, yes, I see it.' Spilsbury glanced at the dead body of Reuben Gosling and rubbed his hands together.

'Indeed I do, Doctor,' said Hardcastle. 'But it looks as though we've interrupted your celebrations.'

'Think nothing of it, my dear fellow,' said Spilsbury, handing his Gladstone bag, top hat, cape, and cane to DC Catto. 'My wife Edith invited all manner of boring people to dinner to celebrate the New Year. To tell the truth, I was delighted to escape.' Although only thirty-eight years of age, Spilsbury was the foremost forensic pathologist of the period. His evidence at the trial of Hawley Harvey Crippen and Ethel Le Neve in 1910 first brought him to the notice of the public, and whenever he now appeared at the Old Bailey to give evidence, the public

26

gallery was usually full if not overflowing. And six months ago, in the case of the Brides-in-the-Bath murders, he was able to demonstrate precisely how George Joseph Smith had killed his three victims, thus negating defence counsel's suggestion of accidental death by drowning.

'There's a bloodstained sash weight over here that I found earlier, sir,' said Catto. 'It had rolled underneath that cupboard,' he added, pointing at a wooden cabinet adjacent to the counter.

'Well done, Constable,' said Spilsbury. 'You have a sharp-eyed man there, Hardcastle.'

'Sometimes,' muttered the DDI.

Spilsbury knelt down to examine the body of Reuben Gosling. 'It was undoubtedly the blow to the head that did for him,' he said, turning his head to address Hardcastle. He pulled an envelope from his inside pocket and rested it on the floor. Using a silver propelling pencil, he made a few notes. 'Well, that's all I can do for the time being.' He stood up and brushed the knees of his trousers.

'There's a blood stain on one of the showcases, Doctor,' said Hardcastle. 'I was wondering if it belongs to one of our killers.'

'I'll take a sample and analyse it for you,' said Spilsbury. Taking the necessary equipment from his bag, he scraped a little of the blood on to a slide and placed it in a small glass jar. 'Get the cadaver to St Mary's at Paddington, Hardcastle, there's a good chap, and a prosperous New Year to you and your good lady.'

'And to you, Doctor.' Hardcastle crossed the shop and opened the door. 'Catto, the doctor's hat and cane. Quickly now.'

'Yes, sir.' Catto handed the items over and half bowed.

'Well, here's a pretty kettle of fish, Marriott,' said Hardcastle, sitting down on one of the bentwood chairs that were provided for Gosling's customers. 'A couple of burglars who use a car to get away from the scene of their crime. I don't know what the world's coming to.'

'It looks as though they used the air raid to cover the burglary, sir,' suggested Marriott.

'Just what I was thinking, Marriott,' said Hardcastle, who had not thought of it until Marriott had mentioned it. 'And you know what that means, don't you? It means that they're probably local. I doubt that anyone would come from out of town on the off chance there was going to be a raid.'

'It might've been a coincidence, sir,' suggested Marriott, changing his mind. But before Hardcastle was able to reply, Watkins reappeared.

'I've got Mr Partridge's statement, sir.'

'I should hope you have, lad. That's what I sent you up there for. Has he said any more than he told me, I wonder.' Hardcastle took the statement and glanced through it. 'Not much good, really, Marriott. He saw a car he couldn't identify, and the description of the two men he saw could've been any one of a hundred.' He handed the statement back to Watkins. 'Catto, get hold of a paper bag and wrap up that sash weight. We might get lucky if Mr Collins can find some prints on it.'

'Where can I get a paper bag, sir?' asked Catto.

'You're a detective, Catto, find one, and don't bother me.' Hardcastle turned back to Marriott. 'Now all that's left for us to do is to get the body up to Dr Spilsbury's room at St Mary's.'

'There's a telephone here, sir. I'll get on to the nick to send a van.'

'Oh, that thing,' muttered Hardcastle dismissively. In common with his contemporaries, he regarded the telephone as a new-fangled device that, like many other innovations introduced by the hierarchy at Scotland Yard, would not last. 'And while you're about it speak to Rochester Row and tell them to send a couple of constables to relieve Catto and Watkins and guard this place until it's properly secured.' He glanced at the empty showcases. 'Not that there's much left to nick.'

Marriott returned minutes later. 'Van's on its way, sir,' he said, having completed his call.

'Good. Catto, I want you and Watkins to secure the premises and wait until the uniforms get here to keep an eye on it. Then the pair of you can escort the body to St Mary's. When you've done that I want the pair of you to get round the local hospitals.'

'What for, sir?' Catto visualized not seeing his

bed again until that evening.

'Good God, man, to see if anyone, like one of our murderers, has turned up with a cut hand,' said Hardcastle impatiently. 'If he has, find out who is he and where he is. You got that, Catto?'

'Yes, sir.'

'Good. And when you've done that, call on all the local pawnbrokers and jewellers and see if anyone's tried to unload any bent tom.'

'Yes, sir,' said Catto.

'We'll come back here later today, Marriott,' said Hardcastle, 'and have a look round when there's more light.'

'I'll arrange for Mr Collins to be here as well, sir.'

Hardcastle and Marriott stepped into the street and were fortunate enough to sight a cab immediately, despite it being New Year's Day.

'Scotland Yard, cabbie,' said Hardcastle, and turning to Marriott, added, 'Tell 'em Cannon Row and half the time you'll finish up at Cannon Street in the City.'

'So I believe, sir,' said Marriott, sighing inwardly. It was a piece of advice he received every time he and Hardcastle returned to their police station by taxi.

TWO

'All correct, sir.' Surprised at the unexpected arrival of the DDI so early in the morning of New Year's Day, the station officer stood up so quickly that he caught his knee on the underside of his desk.

'That's a matter of opinion, Skip.' Hardcastle was always irritated by the requirement for such a report to be made to a senior officer, whether everything was all correct or not. 'Anything happening I should know about? Apart from a murder in Vauxhall Bridge Road,' he added wryly.

'We've had a fair few arrests off of Trafalgar Square, sir, even though there was an air raid on. The cells here is full to overflowing and Inspector Joplin's still taking the charges. And I heard tell there's just as many off of Piccadilly Circus up at Vine Street nick an' all. We've got a couple of pickpockets in, but for the most part it's young gents what'd had more champagne than was good for 'em while they was celebrating the New Year. Two of 'em had their collars felt for nicking a copper's helmet.'

'Spoilt toffs like that should be in the bloody

army.' Hardcastle glanced through the glass panel into a charge room crowded with drunken young blades attired in full evening dress. 'Still, they'll be in the trenches once Lord Derby's caught up with 'em.'

Once in his office, Hardcastle took the unusual step of inviting Marriott to take a seat. 'Well, m'boy,' he said, lapsing into a rare informality, 'I don't suppose you and Mrs Marriott had much time to celebrate the New Year before you got called out.' He took a bottle of Scotch and two glasses from a drawer in his desk and poured a substantial amount into each.

'Your good health, guv'nor, and a Happy New Year to you and Mrs H,' said Marriott, following his chief's familiarity of address, and took a swig of whisky.

'And to you and Mrs Marriott,' said Hardcastle, taking a sip of his Scotch. 'Now, m'boy,' he continued thoughtfully, placing his glass in the centre of the blotter, 'we've got to work out how we're going to catch two murdering tea-leaves who've taken to using a motor car to get away from the scene of their crime.' Taking out his pipe, he began to fill it with his favourite St Bruno tobacco. 'These young villains have got no respect for the law, that's the trouble. If things go on like this the police will have to get some motor cars of their own to chase 'em with.' He chuckled at such a preposterous idea. 'Which reminds me,' he continued, 'we'd better find out what we can about the car that Partridge saw them driving off in.'

'Bit of a long shot, sir, given that we don't have a description of it.'

'Ah, but we do...' Hardcastle paused to light his pipe. 'According to Partridge it was an open tourer with a hood and white-sided tyres. There can't be too many of them about. That'll do for a start. Best send a message to all stations just in case they're wide enough awake to have seen a car with tyres what's painted white.' But by the tone of his voice it was apparent to Marriott that the DDI held out little hope for achieving such a profitable result.

'I'll get on to it, immediately, guv'nor,' said Marriott, and returned to his office where he spent ten minutes drafting a message about the car that Sidney Partridge had seen. He took it downstairs to the constable responsible for sending teleprinter messages and stood over him while he transmitted it to all the stations in the Metropolitan Police District.

It was getting on for ten o'clock that morning when Hardcastle and Marriott returned to Reuben Gosling's shop in Vauxhall Bridge Road.

'All correct, sir.' The policeman posted at the premises drew himself to attention and saluted.

'I should hope so, lad,' muttered Hardcastle, but as he and Marriott were about to enter the shop the DDI was approached by a man in a shabby raincoat and a soft felt hat. Accompanying him was a younger man carrying a box camera with a flash attachment and a tripod.

'Charlie Simpson, Mr Hardcastle, *London Daily Chronicle*.'

'Yes, I thought I recognized you, Simpson. What can I do for you? It didn't take you very long to sniff out a juicy murder.'

'It's what I'm paid for, guv'nor. Are you close to making an arrest for Reuben Gosling's murder?'

'You know me well enough to know I'm always close to making an arrest, Simpson, but right now I'm not sure just how close I am.'

'Any chance of getting a few photographs?' asked Simpson, as his colleague set the camera down on the pavement and stood his open umbrella over it to keep it dry.

'No,' said Hardcastle firmly.

'Well, can you at least tell me what happened?'

'The body of Reuben Gosling was found in the shop just after midnight, Simpson. He'd been bludgeoned to death and a quantity of jewellery was stolen.'

'But—'

'But now you know as much as I do,' said Hardcastle, as he and Marriott entered the shop leaving a disappointed reporter and his photographer outside in the rain. 'Having the bloody press nosing about my murder scene and getting in my way is all I need,' he muttered.

The DDI hung his hat, coat and umbrella on a

hatstand in the corner of the shop, and he and his sergeant began a careful search of the immediate area.

'There's a footprint here, sir,' said Marriott, pointing to the impression in Reuben Gosling's blood, near where the jeweller's body had been discovered. 'Might be useful.'

Hardcastle crossed to where Marriott was standing and examined the print. 'See if that reporter and his mate are still outside, Marriott. If they are, bring 'em in.'

Moments later, Marriott returned with Charlie Simpson and the photographer.

'I'll make a deal with you, Simpson,' said Hardcastle. 'You can have a few pictures for your paper, but I want you to take some for me.'

'Just say the word, guv'nor,' said Simpson. The photographer set up his tripod and moved his camera into position.

'But any that you take for me aren't to appear in your rag. Is that understood?'

'What's in it for me, guv'nor?'

'You get your pictures, and seeing as how you're the only reporter who's bothered to turn up here, you'll be the first to know about anything important I come across.'

'Seems fair enough,' said Simpson.

'Good. So long as we understand each other.'

'Where d'you want me to start?'

'I want a picture of this here footprint, a nice clear one mind, and I want an enlargement of it delivered to Cannon Row police station tout de suite. All right?'

'Good as done, Mr Hardcastle,' said Simpson. The photographer adjusted the tripod's position so that his camera covered the bloody footprint and took several close-up shots. 'All right for him to take a few of the interior now?' he asked.

'Go ahead,' said Hardcastle. 'You can have a general one of the shop, one of where the body was found, and a few of the showcases that have been broken into. You can publish all of those, and you can let me have a copy of the showcase pictures.'

'Done,' said Simpson, and signalled to his colleague to start taking his photographs.

Once Simpson and the photographer had departed in a cab for Fleet Street, Hardcastle and Marriott resumed their search.

'There's a button here, sir,' said Marriott, pointing at the item near one of the burgled showcases.

'I wonder why Catto didn't find it,' muttered Hardcastle, as he joined his sergeant.

'It was very dark in here when we first arriv-ed, sir,' said Marriott, attempting to counter what he thought was another of the DDI's unfair criticisms of Catto.

'Seems an ordinary sort of button.' Ignoring Marriott's comment, Hardcastle picked it up and examined it closely. 'We might be lucky and find the owner of the coat it came off of,' he said hopefully. 'Bring it with you,' he added, handing the button to Marriott.

There was nothing further to be found in the shop and the two detectives opened a door marked 'Private' and mounted the staircase.

The jeweller's living quarters consisted of a sitting room, a bedroom and a kitchenette; each was untidy enough to indicate that Gosling led a bachelor existence. At the rear of the first floor there was a third room, the door of which was locked.

Entering the bedroom, Hardcastle made straight for the wardrobe. After searching various items of clothing he eventually found a bunch of keys in a pocket of an overcoat.

'Take these keys, Marriott, and see if any of 'em will open that locked door.'

It took only a few seconds for Marriott to find the correct key. 'It looks like a storeroom, sir,' he said, pushing open the door.

'So it does, Marriott, so it does.' Hardcastle entered the room and gazed around. There were two locked cupboards. 'Have you got keys for them on that ring?' he asked.

'Bound to be among this lot, sir.'

The cupboards that Marriott eventually unlocked proved to be Gosling's reserve stock of jewellery. There were rings on trays, watches – including the new wristwatches that the DDI dismissed as modern frippery – a collection of pearl necklaces, brooches and a selection of gold alberts.

'I'll wager our two killers never knew that lot was here, Marriott,' said Hardcastle. 'They'd likely have doubled their haul if they had.'

'D'you reckon there *were* two killers, sir?'

'According to what our friend Partridge next door said, he saw two men making off in a car. For the time being, I'm assuming they were the ones that done the deed. It's hardly likely that they came across Gosling's open door and his dead body and decided to take advantage of the situation. If I know anything about villains, Marriott, and I know quite a lot, they'd've run a mile.'

A PC appeared at the top of the stairs. 'Mr Collins is here, sir.'

'Right, tell him I'm coming down.'

'Good morning, Ernie, and a Happy New Year to you,' said Detective Inspector Collins, as he hung up his coat and hat.

'And to you, Charlie, but right now it's not shaping up too well.' Hardcastle described what was known of the murder of Reuben Gosling. 'One of 'em seems to have cut himself on one of the showcases, Charlie, so I suspect he wasn't wearing gloves.'

'I'll see what I can do, Ernie.' Collins opened his case and withdrew a magnifying glass. 'I'll let you know if we find anything worthwhile.'

Within minutes of Hardcastle and Marriott returning to Cannon Row police station, Marriott was surprised to find a constable appearing in his office with news of the missing motor car. 'A telegraph message from Chelsea nick, Sergeant,' he said, handing the form over.

Marriott scanned the brief details and crossed the corridor to the DDI's office. 'It would appear that a car was stolen on Chelsea's manor, sir.'

'Does it fit the description?' asked Hardcastle.

'Yes, sir. An open tourer with what the loser describes as white-walled tyres. According to the message, the vehicle disappeared between eight o'clock last night and seven o'clock this morning, sir. It was an American car called a Haxe-Doulton, manufactured in 1915 and imported from Detroit in Michigan.'

'If that's the car we're interested in, Marriott, I think we can narrow the time down to between eight o'clock yesterday evening and shortly before midnight. Where was it nicked from?'

'From outside a house in Flood Street, sir.'

'What's that, a couple of miles from Vauxhall Bridge Road? Sounds promising, Marriott. Who reported it lost?'

'A man by the name of Sinclair Villiers, sir.'

Hardcastle took out his hunter and stared at it. Briefly rewinding it, he dropped it back into his waistcoat pocket. 'Time for lunch, Marriott, and then we'll have a chat with this here Sinclair Villiers. We'll make it four o'clock; that'll give Mr Villiers time to sleep off the New Year festivities.'

'Very good, sir,' said Marriott with a grin. Lunch for the DDI consisted of a couple of pints of best bitter and a fourpenny cannon in the downstairs bar of the Red Lion public house, immediately outside the west gates of New Scotland Yard.

As the two detectives were about to leave the police station, a constable presented Hardcastle with a large envelope.

'This just arrived in a cab for you, sir.'

Hardcastle took the proffered letter and opened it. 'Ah, the photographs of the footprint and the showcases that Simpson took, Marriott. They're pretty good, too.' He turned to the PC. 'Leave them on my desk, lad.'

Alighting from their cab, Hardcastle and Marriott mounted the steps of the three-storied house in Flood Street, Chelsea.

Hardcastle hammered on the knocker. 'Looks like there's a bit of sausage and mash here, Marriott,' he said.

'It certainly looks as if it's worth a few pounds, sir.'

'Yes?' A butler opened the door. Sensing that the two detectives were not the usual sort of visitors his master received, he looked down his nose with an air of disdain.

'I'm here to see a Mr Sinclair Villiers,' said Hardcastle.

'Do you have an appointment?'

'No, I don't have an appointment,' snapped Hardcastle, 'but perhaps you'd tell your employer that the police wish to speak to him.'

'Step inside,' said the butler. 'I'll enquire if the master is at home.'

'Why are butlers always toffee-nosed flunkeys, Marriott?' muttered Hardcastle, while they waited for the butler to make his enquiries. 'Mind you, if this conscription business is brought in, he'll be off to the Colours a bit tout de suite. That'll take the edge off of him.'

'If you come with me, the master will see you in the drawing room.' The butler sniffed and turned to lead the way. His very demeanour gave an impression of surprise that his employer had yielded to Hardcastle's request for an interview.

'I'm Sinclair Villiers, gentlemen. What's this about?' The tall silver-haired man standing in front of a blazing fire was about fifty, and was attired in a maroon smoking jacket. In his right hand he held a cigarette in an amber holder.

'I'm Divisional Detective Inspector Hardcastle of the Whitehall Division, sir, and this here is Detective Sergeant Marriott.'

'Take a seat, gentlemen.' Villiers glanced at the butler. 'Bring a decanter of whisky, Henwood.'

'Very good, sir.'

'I imagine you've come to see me about my stolen motor car, Inspector.'

'Indeed, sir,' said Hardcastle cautiously. 'If it is your vehicle, I believe it might have been taken in order to carry out a robbery.'

'Good grief!' exclaimed Villiers. 'Where was

this?'

'At a jeweller's establishment in Vauxhall Bridge Road.'

'Was much taken?'

'Very likely, sir, but we don't know for sure yet,' said Hardcastle. 'However, that don't really concern the police so much as the fact that the owner, a man by the name of Reuben Gosling, was murdered in the course of the robbery.'

'Good grief!' exclaimed Villiers again. 'It's this damned war, you know, Inspector. Decent common standards seem to have gone out of the window. Have you caught the murderer yet?'

'Not yet, sir,' said Hardcastle, 'but you can rest assured I'll have him standing on the hangman's trap before long. Or, I should say, have *them* waiting for the drop.'

'There was more than one, then?' Villiers assumed an air of surprise.

'According to a witness at the scene, two men were involved.'

'Have you any idea—?' Villiers broke off as the butler entered the room bearing a whisky decanter, a soda siphon and three crystal tumblers on a tray. 'Just put it down over there, Henwood. I'll deal with it.' He turned to Hardcastle. 'I dare say you gentlemen wouldn't be averse to a dram to celebrate the New Year, eh, Inspector?'

'Most kind, sir,' murmured Hardcastle, grateful that Villiers had not made the usual fatuous comment about policemen not being permitted to drink on duty.

'I don't suppose you've found my car yet, have you?' enquired Villiers, as he handed round the whisky.

'Not yet, sir, but I've no doubt it'll turn up. Thieves of this sort usually abandon a car they've used once it's served its purpose.' Hardcastle had never before dealt with a murder involving a car, but made the comment as though fully conversant with such a situation. 'And with any luck, we'll find that they've left their fingerprints all over it.'

'I just hope they haven't damaged it,' said Villiers, taking a sip of his Scotch. 'It's a valuable motor car, a Haxe-Doulton.'

'So I believe,' murmured Hardcastle, sampling Villiers's excellent whisky. 'This is a very decent malt, if I may say so, sir,' he said.

'I have it sent direct from Islay,' said Villiers, waving a deprecating hand in response to the compliment. 'I imported the car from America just before the war and it cost me over seven hundred pounds plus the cost of having it brought over,' he said, confirming Hardcastle's view that the car's owner was an exceedingly wealthy man.

'Where do you normally keep the car, sir?' asked Marriott, even though the message from Chelsea had stated that the vehicle had been taken from outside Sinclair Villiers's house.

Villiers appeared surprised by the question.

'Outside in the street,' he said, as though it were an obvious place to park a car. 'I told the sergeant at Chelsea police station that that's where it had been left.'

'And you last saw it when?' queried Hardcastle. He knew that that information had also been contained in the message.

'At eight o'clock last night,' said Villiers. 'But, look, Inspector, I told the chap at Chelsea all this.'

'I presume you didn't go out to celebrate New Year's Eve, then.' Hardcastle ignored Villiers's mild protest; he knew that the information about the car's theft had been given to the police at Chelsea, but always wanted to hear it first-hand.

'I'm getting a bit too old for that sort of revelry, Inspector. I went to bed at about eleven, read for twenty minutes or so, and didn't wake up until just gone seven when Henwood brought me my morning tea. He opened the curtains and stared down into the street. Then he turned to face me and told me that the car wasn't outside. That was the first I knew that it had gone.'

'Does anyone else in the house have permission to drive your car, sir?' asked Marriott.

'No, I'm here alone, apart from the servants. My wife doesn't live with me any more. She's got her own place in Prince of Wales Drive in Battersea,' said Villiers, without enlarging on the reason. 'But I do allow Haydn to use it

44

when he's on leave, but he's in France at the moment.'

'Haydn, sir?'

'Yes, he's my son. He's a captain in the Royal Field Artillery. But he spends what little furlough he gets with Hannah – that's my wife – although most of the time I suspect he's in the West End enjoying himself. With some young ragtime girl, if he's got any sense. Frankly, I don't see much of him, but you can't blame these young officers for letting their hair down when they get the chance. From what I've heard of it, it's pretty bloody out there, in more ways than one.'

'So I believe, sir,' murmured Hardcastle.

'Is it possible that your son is on leave at the moment, but that you don't know, sir?' asked Marriott. 'I was thinking that he might've borrowed the car without telling you.'

'Definitely not, Sergeant. He wouldn't have taken it without asking my permission,' said Villiers. 'He always makes a point of coming to see me, if only briefly, so I can assure you he's not on leave. My son and I get on extremely well, even though Hannah and I no longer see eye to eye,' he added, allowing his guard to drop for a brief moment. 'In fact, I had a letter from Haydn only two days ago.'

'I think that's all you can help me with at the moment, sir,' said Hardcastle, as he and Marriott rose to their feet. 'I'll let you know if we find your motor car.'

'I'd much appreciate getting it back, Inspector,' said Villiers. 'I was thinking of having a run to Worthing tomorrow.' He crossed the room and tugged at a bell pull. 'Henwood will see you out, gentlemen.'

'Thank you for the whisky, sir,' said Hardcastle. He did not say that if the vehicle was found, it was unlikely to be returned until DI Collins had been given the chance to examine it thoroughly.

The butler stepped ahead of Hardcastle and opened the front door.

'Were you at home here all last night, Henwood?' Hardcastle asked.

'I most certainly was.' The butler assumed a pained expression.

'And your master?'

'Mr Villiers was here all night. Will that be all ... Inspector?'

'Thank you, Henwood.'

'What d'you think, sir?' asked Marriott, as he and the DDI walked down Flood Street in search of a taxi.

'Damn silly place to leave an expensive motor car, Marriott, that's what I'm thinking,' said Hardcastle. 'I'd've thought that a man with that much money could've found an empty coach house nearby where he could've kept the thing. Not that it's the sort of problem that's ever likely to worry me,' he added, finally sighting a cab.

THREE

It was not long before Hardcastle was given further news of Sinclair Villiers's stolen motor car. At six o'clock, a constable appeared in the DDI's office holding a message form.

'What is it, lad?'

'A message from Wandsworth about a Haxe-Doulton car that's been found, sir.' The PC handed Hardcastle the telegraph form.

'Ask Sergeant Marriott to step across,' said the DDI as he scanned the message.

'I understand the car's been found, sir,' said Marriott, buttoning his jacket as he entered Hardcastle's office.

'Yes, it has, Marriott. It's a Haxe-Doulton, and the number plate matches the one that Mr Villiers gave the Chelsea police when he reported it stolen. It's at Wandsworth nick. I just hope that whoever took it in was wearing gloves.'

'So do I, sir. When I sent the message to all stations, I directed that caution should be taken because of the possibility of fingerprints being found.'

'And I suppose they might even have read it,' complained Hardcastle caustically; he had no great faith in the scholarship of policemen. 'Go across to the Yard and ask Mr Collins if he can attend, or if he's not available to send one of his people.'

'Very good, sir.'

'And tell him we'll meet whoever it is at Wandsworth.'

'Yes, sir,' said Marriott, hiding the disappointment from his voice. His hopes of spending the evening of New Year's Day with his family had just been dashed by the DDI.

'Can I help you, sir?' An elderly station sergeant crossed from his desk to the counter as Hardcastle and Marriott entered the front office of Wandsworth police station.

'I'm DDI Hardcastle of A, Skipper, and this is DS Marriott. Your officers have recovered a stolen motor car, I believe.'

'Yes, they have, sir, it was found abandoned in Wandsworth High Street. The vehicle in question is in one of the empty stables. I'll show you the way.'

'Haven't you got any horses here, then?' asked Hardcastle.

'Most of 'em have been took by the army, sir,' said the station sergeant, as he lifted the flap in the counter and led Hardcastle and Marriott out of the back door and into the station yard.

Sinclair Villiers's Haxe-Doulton, shrouded in a tarpaulin, was standing in the centre of one of the stables.

'We thought it would be a good idea to cover it up, sir, what with the dust and bird droppings and that what comes off of the rafters.'

'Help the station sergeant get that tarpaulin off, Marriott,' said Hardcastle, standing back and lighting his pipe.

Once Villiers's car was uncovered, Hardcastle walked slowly round it. It was mud bespattered but apparently undamaged. The DDI, however, made no attempt to search it immediately.

'We'll wait for the fingerprint officer to examine it before we see if we can find anything in it that might help, Marriott.'

'Yes, sir.' Not knowing how long it would be before DI Collins or one of his men arrived at the police station, Marriott made no comment about the prospect of not getting home before midnight, by which time he would have been on duty for a good twenty-three hours. But that was the lot of a CID officer, particularly one who had aspirations for further advancement in the Force. And Marriott hoped, one day, to be an inspector or even more.

It was almost nine o'clock before Charles Collins arrived.

'I thought I'd come myself as it's a murder job, Ernie.'

'Very good of you, Charlie. We haven't touched it beyond taking off the tarpaulin.'

DI Collins spent the next thirty minutes closely examining every surface on the outside and inside of Villiers's motor car, occasionally muttering to himself while dusting certain parts of the vehicle with grey fingerprint powder. Finally, he produced a camera from his case and began taking photographs.

'I've got a few prints, Ernie,' he said, as he began packing away his equipment. 'I'll let you know if they match any in my records. Incidentally, there's a bloodstain on the steering wheel. Looks as though whoever was driving it might've injured himself.'

'Might be a match for the blood on the showcase, sir,' suggested Marriott.

'Possibly, Marriott, possibly,' said Hardcastle. 'How soon can you give me a result, Charlie?'

'It'll take a day or two,' said Collins, 'even after I've classified them into arches, loops, whorls or composites.'

'I suppose that all means something,' muttered Hardcastle, who had no great knowledge of the finer points of fingerprint classification. But he knew he had to be satisfied with Collins's decision, having long ago discovered that experts were not to be rushed.

'I'll let you know if I come up with a match, Ernie,' said Collins.

'We'll see if we can find anything useful in this here motor car, Marriott,' said Hardcastle, once Collins had departed to make his way back to Scotland Yard.

But the detectives' search proved disappointing, apart from a scarf that Marriott found on the floor of the vehicle.

'Ah, and there's this, sir,' said Marriott, producing a gold albert from beneath the driver's seat.

'Bring them with you, Marriott,' said Hardcastle. 'They might belong to one of our killers. On the other hand, they might belong to Sinclair Villiers. Although I doubt that Villiers would've left an albert in his precious motor car.'

'Could be part of the villain's haul, sir. Either way up, it doesn't look as though Villiers will be able to have his run to Worthing tomorrow.'

'Hard luck!' said Hardcastle, who was not greatly concerned about the pastimes of people he described as the idle rich.

Despite their late finish on the Saturday evening, Hardcastle and Marriott were back at Cannon Row police station on the Sunday morning. But with an uncharacteristic act of charity, Hardcastle had told Marriott that he need not arrive until nine o'clock.

'We'll pay Mr Villiers a visit, Marriott,' said Hardcastle, glancing at his watch, 'and give him the glad news about his car. We'll also ask him if he knows anything about the scarf and the albert we found in it.'

'I hope you've come to tell me that you've found my car, Inspector,' said Villiers, as the butler showed Hardcastle and Marriott into the parlour in Flood Street. His tone was such as to indicate that he expected nothing less.

'Yes, we have, sir,' said Hardcastle.

'Splendid,' said Villiers warmly. 'Have you brought it with you?' He took a step towards the window and peered out.

'No, Mr Villiers, we haven't. It's at Wandsworth police station waiting for you to collect it at your convenience.'

'But surely, the least the police could have done was to bring it back to me.' Villiers turned from the window, his eyebrows raised.

'I'm afraid not, sir,' said Marriott. 'Police regulations don't allow it. If there was an accident, the Commissioner would be liable for any damages that might be incurred, you see.' He was unsure whether this was the case, but it seemed a good reason for not providing such a service to the careless owners of expensive motor cars that they left in the street.

Hardcastle nodded his approval at his sergeant's initiative. 'What my sergeant says is quite correct, sir.' Not that such an excuse would have occurred to the DDI; and he did not even know whether it was true.

'That's a damn' nuisance,' said Villiers. 'As I told you yesterday, I was hoping to go to Worthing today.' He paused. 'Was the car damaged in any way?'

'Not as far as we could see, sir,' said Hardcastle, 'although there's a goodly amount of mud on it.'

'Have you seen this scarf before, sir?' asked

Marriott, producing the item of clothing that he had found behind the driver's seat in Villiers's car.

Villiers took the scarf and examined it. 'No, it's certainly not mine. In fact I've not seen it before,' he said, but it did not escape Hardcastle's notice that Villiers had hesitated before answering, more than he thought was necessary. He was certain that he would know what his own scarves looked like and it would be an instant decision to say whether one was his.

'And give Mr Villiers a glim of the button, Marriott,' said the DDI.

'Have you seen this before, sir?' Marriott handed over the button.

Villiers took some time examining it before returning it. 'No, I'm sorry.'

'Or this?' asked Marriott, producing the albert.

Villiers took the item and ran it through his fingers, studying it closely. 'No, Sergeant,' he said, returning it. 'It looks to be a rather cheap watch chain. Not the sort of thing I'd wear, or even possess. It's gold plate; not the real thing at all.'

'The police station is in Wandsworth High Street, Mr Villiers,' said Hardcastle helpfully, 'just at the foot of West Hill. It would be as well if you took some proof of your ownership of the vehicle with you.'

'Thank you, Inspector.' Villiers did not seem at all happy at having to traipse all the way to

Wandsworth to get his car back. Although he said nothing to Hardcastle, it crossed his mind to pen a letter of complaint to the Commissioner.

'By the way, sir,' said Hardcastle, 'there was a bloodstain on the steering wheel. Was it there when you last saw the vehicle?'

'*A bloodstain?*' Villiers spoke sharply, his voice expressing horror as though any suggestion that his beloved car might not be immaculate was tantamount to a personal insult. 'It's certainly nothing to do with me. Where did it come from?'

'Probably from one of the men who stole your car in order to commit a murder, sir.'

'I hope you catch them, Inspector.'

'Oh I will, sir,' said Hardcastle. 'Rest assured that early one morning the hangman will be stretching their necks as they mark time in thin air. And if I have anything to do with it, it'll be sooner rather than later.'

'Yes, quite so.' Villiers wrinkled his nose with distaste at Hardcastle's bloodthirsty language.

'How d'you start your car, Mr Villiers?' asked Marriott, who was more familiar with motor vehicles than his DDI.

'You pull out the choke and press the starter,' said Villiers, as though such a course of action was obvious. 'And then let the choke in slowly as the revs pick up.'

'Isn't a key required to start it, then? Or to lock the vehicle with?'

'No, but then one doesn't expect people to go about stealing cars, does one?'

'I do,' commented Hardcastle drily.

'Yes, I suppose so,' said Villiers, and rang for the butler to show the detectives out.

Hardcastle and Marriott strode along Flood Street towards King's Road in search of a cab. 'That there Sinclair Villiers seemed to make a bit of a meal out of deciding whether that scarf was his or not, Marriott,' said Hardcastle.

'It certainly wouldn't have taken me that long, sir,' agreed Marriott. 'But then I've only got one scarf and as Lorna knitted it for me, I'd've recognized it straight off.'

'I'm just wondering whether that Villiers knows more than he's telling,' said Hardcastle, finally spotting a taxi.

'You surely don't think he had anything to do with this murder, do you, sir?' Once again, Marriott was astounded at what he secretly called 'one of the guv'nor's flights of fancy'.

'You've known me long enough to know that I always keep my options open, Marriott,' said Hardcastle mysteriously. 'I've known of a few toffs who've committed murder over the years.'

'But the butler was adamant that he and Villiers were at home all night, sir.'

'Of course he was, Marriott,' said Hardcastle. 'Of course he was. Unless it was the butler what nicked Villiers's precious motor car. So far, all they've come up with is what you might call mutually compensating alibis.' He chuckled at what he thought was quite a clever turn of phrase.

On their return to Cannon Row police station, Hardcastle spent a few minutes in the front office examining the crime book. Satisfied that there was nothing to demand his immediate attention, he ascended the stairs to the detectives' office.

Pushing open the door, his gaze lighted on DC Catto.

'What have you done about those enquiries I gave you and Watkins, Catto?'

'We checked with the hospitals, sir. Westminster, Charing Cross, Saint Thomas', Saint George's—'

'All right, all right, Catto, I know which they are. You checked them all within, say, a five-mile radius, I hope.'

'Yes, sir.' Catto knew that for him to have done otherwise would have incurred the DDI's wrath. 'There was no record of anyone attending after midnight on Friday with an injury like a cut hand.'

'Did you try Putney hospital?'

'Putney, sir? No, sir.' Catto was clearly puzzled by the DDI's question.

'Why not? The car was found in Wandsworth.'

'I'll get on it straight away, sir.'

'What about jewellers and pawnbrokers?'

'We checked all those on the list, sir, and

nothing has been taken in yet.' Catto was alluding to the list that each police station held of all such establishments in its area. 'Some of them won't open until tomorrow morning though.'

'Well, I hope you'll be on their doorsteps waiting for them to turn up,' said Hardcastle, and returned to his office, leaving Catto wondering how he could be in more than one place at the same time.

'Better send a message to surrounding stations, Marriott, asking for checks to be made in case our villains have been trying to fence their ill-gotten gains further afield.'

'Very good, sir.'

'And then, Marriott, I think we'll call it a day. There ain't much we can do until tomorrow morning. My regards to Mrs Marriott.'

'Thank you, sir, and mine to Mrs H.'

The clattering of the letter box signalled the arrival of the morning newspaper. Hardcastle stood up from the kitchen table and walked through to the hall. Picking up the *Daily Mail*, he began scanning the headlines as he returned to start his breakfast.

'Anything in the paper, Ernie?' Alice posed the same question every morning. She placed a plate of eggs, bacon, a sausage and fried bread in front of her husband, and poured him a second cup of tea. It was the breakfast that Hardcastle consumed every morning and without which he claimed he could not face a day's work.

He never enquired how his wife was able to produce such a hearty breakfast every day despite the shortages brought on by the war; he just assumed that the grocer was generous because Hardcastle was a senior police officer.

'It says here that last Thursday the P&O liner SS *Persia* was torpedoed in the Mediterranean.' Hardcastle propped the newspaper against a tomato ketchup bottle. 'Over three hundred passengers were drowned, including two Americans. And one of them was a diplomat. It's things like that that'll bring the Americans into this war, my girl, you mark my words.'

'It's shocking what the war is doing,' said Alice, sitting down opposite her husband. 'People murdering people all the time.'

'I know,' said Hardcastle. 'I'm in the trade.'

'You know what I'm talking about, Ernest,' responded his wife. She only ever called him by his full name by way of reproof or in moments of exasperation.

'And that's not all,' continued Hardcastle between mouthfuls, as his eye lighted upon another item. 'It seems that on the same day HMS *Natal* blew up in Cromarty harbour in the North Sea. Over three hundred killed. It says here that there was a children's party going on and the captain, a man called Eric Back, and his wife and all the children were killed.'

Alice Hardcastle put a hand to her mouth. 'Oh, those poor children,' she said. 'The Germans have got a lot to answer for, Ernie.'

'According to the paper, the Admiralty are saying it was an accidental explosion.' Hardcastle looked at his wife. 'And if you believe that, you'll believe anything,' he said. 'That'll be the censor's doing, saying that. They don't want to alarm people, you see, my girl.' He folded the newspaper and stood up. 'But the people of this country aren't stupid. They know what's going on, and they'll have worked out that somehow or other a German submarine got right into Cromarty harbour.'

After what seemed an interminable wait, Hardcastle eventually caught a crowded tram, and arrived at his office at half past eight.

'Good morning, sir,' said Marriott, as he followed Hardcastle into the DDI's office.

'I've decided that we'll pay a visit to Mrs Villiers,' said Hardcastle, without returning his sergeant's greeting, but Marriott was accustomed to the DDI ignoring the common courtesies.

'What do we hope to learn from her, sir?' Once again, Marriott was baffled by the course of action the DDI was suggesting. But he knew Hardcastle well enough to know that he frequently embarked on a seemingly pointless enquiry only to see it bear fruit.

'Won't know till we ask,' said Hardcastle. 'According to Sinclair Villiers, Hannah Villiers lives in Prince of Wales Drive, Battersea. Where exactly?'

Marriott had known that the question would be asked sooner or later, and the previous day had dispatched a detective to find out. 'It's one of the mansion flats, sir. I've got the details.'

'We're police officers, lass, and I'd like to speak to Mrs Villiers,' said Hardcastle, when a young housemaid answered the door. 'But tell her there's nothing to worry about.' Early on in the war the DDI had learned that families with men at the Front always feared the worst when the police arrived at their door. And Sinclair Villiers had told him that their son, Haydn Villiers, was a captain in the Royal Field Artillery serving with the BEF.

'If you'll step inside, sir, I'll see if the mistress is at home.' Having made that formal response, the housemaid conducted the two detectives into the hall, and disappeared into a room on the right. Moments later, she returned. 'Come this way, please, sir.'

'Elsie, my maid, tells me you're from the police.' Hannah Villiers was a tall, elegant and attractive woman. Given that she had a son who was a captain, she must have been at least forty-five, but looked a good ten years younger. Crossing the room with a swish of her silk dress and a waft of Attar of Violets, she shook hands with Hardcastle. 'Please take a seat, gentlemen, and tell me how I may help you,' she added, waving a hand at a sofa.

'I'm Divisional Detective Inspector Hardcastle of the Whitehall Division, madam, and this is Detective Sergeant Marriott.'

'From Whitehall, eh? How intriguing. Would you care for some tea? I was about to have some myself.'

'Most kind,' murmured Hardcastle, taking a seat opposite the woman.

'Now tell me what this is all about,' said Mrs Villiers, once Elsie had been dispatched to make the tea. She briefly touched her upswept brown hair.

'I'm investigating a murder that took place during a robbery in Vauxhall Bridge Road, madam,' Hardcastle began. 'It was a murder in which we believe Mr Sinclair Villiers's car was involved.'

Hannah Villiers threw back her head and emitted a gay, tinkling laugh. 'D'you mean someone stole his precious Haxe-Doulton motor car to carry out this murder? Did they wreck it?'

'No, Mrs Villiers,' said Marriott. 'There wasn't a scratch on it.'

'Oh, what a shame. Speaking frankly, Sergeant, my estranged husband loved that car more than he loved me. But why have you come to see me? I no longer live with him, as I'm sure he must have told you.'

'So I understand, madam,' said Hardcastle.

'It must've hurt his ego when I upped sticks and left him just before the war started,' continued Hannah Villiers in matter-of-fact tones.

'But Sinclair always liked to be in control. He insisted on the household being kept in a certain order and would carry out inspections, and re-organize things. It really was most intolerable. Apart from that, he ignored me ... in every way. I'm sure you know what I mean, Inspector; to him, bed was a place for sleeping in.' She paused to stare directly at Hardcastle as she fingered the Star of David that hung from a silver chain at her neck. 'It was really too much, so I left him. However, you still haven't told me how any of this concerns me.'

Once again, Hardcastle was surprised at how often women were prepared to share the most intimate details of their married life with a complete stranger. But, paradoxically, rarely spoke of it to their closest friends.

'Mr Villiers told me that your son, Captain Villiers, stays with you when he is on leave.'

'That's correct. In fact he's here now. But surely he can't help you with this murder, can he?'

However, further conversation on the subject was interrupted by the arrival of the tea.

'Just put it down over there, Elsie,' said Hannah. 'I'll deal with it.' And she spent the next few minutes pouring the tea and handing it round.

'You say your son is here now, Mrs Villiers,' said Hardcastle. 'Mr Villiers told me that he was still in France.'

'Well, Sinclair doesn't know everything,

despite what he might think. Haydn's not here at this precise moment, but he is staying with me. I think he's due to go back to France on Friday. He was lucky enough to get leave for Christmas and actually arrived late on Christmas Eve. But I don't really see how he can help you, Inspector.'

'Nor can I, madam,' said Hardcastle disarmingly, 'until I speak to him. According to Mr Villiers, your son had permission to use the car, and I was wondering whether he had taken it and perhaps left it somewhere, and that it was stolen from there rather than from Flood Street.' He did not think that at all, but was wondering whether Haydn Villiers had actually been involved in a robbery that had culminated in murder.

'I see. Well, he'll probably be back in time for luncheon. He wasn't here last night, and I've no idea where he's been.' Hannah Villiers paused and gave a wry smile. 'But I could hazard a guess at *what* he was doing.'

Hardcastle took out his hunter and stared at it. Giving it a brief wind, he dropped it back into his waistcoat pocket and stood up. 'I wonder if you'd be so good as to ask him to call in at Cannon Row police station at his convenience, madam. Then I can clear this matter up for once and all.'

'Of course, Inspector.' She picked up a small bell and rang it. Seconds later, the housemaid appeared. 'These gentlemen are leaving now,

Elsie. Perhaps you'd show them out.'

'Yes, ma'am.' Elsie bobbed a brief curtsy and waited.

'I hope you catch your murderer, Inspector.' Hannah Villiers smiled, but the smile was directed at Marriott rather than Hardcastle.

'I will, madam,' said Hardcastle. 'You may rest assured of that.'

FOUR

At two o'clock that same afternoon a constable appeared in Hardcastle's office.

'There's a Captain Villiers downstairs, sir. He says as how you want to see him.'

'Yes, I do. Show him up, lad, and on your way out tell Sergeant Marriott to come in.'

Haydn Villiers, a man in his early twenties with a neatly trimmed moustache, was immaculate in every respect. His service dress was well-tailored and his Sam Browne and riding boots were polished to perfection. His tunic bore three stars on each cuff, the ribbon of the Military Cross and grenade badges on the collar. His squarely placed cap displayed the distinctive cannon insignia of the Royal Artillery.

'Inspector Hardcastle? I'm Haydn Villiers,' the youthful gunner said smoothly, and saluted: a courtesy rather than an obligation.

'Please take a seat, Captain Villiers. This is Detective Sergeant Marriott.'

Villiers nodded briefly in Marriott's direction. 'My mother told me that you wanted to speak to me. Something about my father's car?' He placed his cap on the edge of Hardcastle's desk, and took out a gold cigarette case. 'D'you mind?' he enquired, holding a cigarette in the air.

'Not at all,' said Hardcastle, reaching for his pipe. 'I have spoken to your father and he told me that you have permission to use his car, Captain Villiers. Is that correct?'

'Yes, but I don't see what this has to do with me, Inspector.'

'I presume your mother told you about the murder I'm investigating,' said Hardcastle, having eventually got his pipe alight to his satisfaction. 'A murder that we believe your father's Haxe-Doulton was involved in.'

'She did, but I still don't see what that has to do with me.' Despite repeating that disclaimer, Villiers appeared to be a little anxious, as though unsure where Hardcastle's line of questioning was leading.

'Let's get down to brass tacks, then, Captain. Have you used your father's car at any time since coming home on Christmas Eve?'

'No, I haven't. I admit I've used it in the past, but only with the guv'nor's permission. As a matter of fact, I haven't been to see him this time round.'

'But he told us that he received a letter from you only two days ago. And that led him to believe you were still in France.'

'It's probably the one I wrote to him a fortnight ago,' said Villiers. 'The army postal service is a bit hit and miss. It can sometimes take days if not weeks to get the troops' mail moving across the Channel. And vice versa,' he added.

'Is there a particular reason why you haven't visited him on this occasion?' enquired Hardcastle.

'I'm afraid that he and I don't always see eye to eye,' said Villiers. 'Not to put too fine a point on it, my father is a bully.'

Haydn Villiers's mother had mentioned that Sinclair Villiers enjoyed being in control, and it was probably that that caused his son to be disinclined to visit his father.

'Where were you on New Year's Eve, Captain Villiers?' demanded Hardcastle, getting straight to the point.

'With respect, I don't see that that's any of your business, Inspector.' From the way he replied, the young officer was clearly irritated at what he saw as an unwarranted intrusion into his private life.

'I would remind you that I'm investigating a particularly brutal murder, Captain,' said Hardcastle sharply. 'Perhaps you'd be so good as to answer the question.'

'I was with a lady.' Villiers brushed at his moustache and smiled.

'What's the lady's name, Captain Villiers?' asked Marriott, opening his pocketbook and taking out a pencil.

'I'm sorry, but I'm not prepared to tell you. It's a rather delicate situation, don't you know.'

'In other words, you're not willing to tell me

where you were.' Hardcastle placed his pipe in the ashtray and leaned forward linking his hands on his desk, and fixing Villiers with a steely gaze. 'You appreciate that your refusal to name this lady makes me suspicious.'

'Then you'll just have to be suspicious, won't you, Inspector? I do have the lady's reputation to consider.' A faintly supercilious expression crossed Villiers's face. 'Now, if there's nothing else, I do have an appointment.'

'Thank you for calling in, Captain Villiers.' Hardcastle paused. 'I understand that you're returning to France on Friday.'

'Yes, that's correct.'

'Keep your head down,' said the DDI.

'You've no need to worry about that, Inspector. Being at the Front tends to develop one's innate ability to sense danger.' It was an enigmatic statement that was not lost on the DDI.

'I may have to see you again, Captain Villiers.' Hardcastle did not think that to be the case, but merely said it to see Villiers's reaction.

'You'll have to come to Neuve Chapelle, then.' And with that pithy rejoinder, Captain Villiers put on his cap, turned abruptly and left the office.

'Our young captain seemed more than a little anxious when I was asking him about his father's car, Marriott.'

'I suppose he could've been involved, sir. Either that or he's bedding a married woman.'

'Or he's got something else to hide,' said

68

Hardcastle. 'Fetch Catto in here.'

Seconds later, Henry Catto hovered nervously in the DDI's doorway, apprehensive as always in the DDI's presence.

'You wanted me, sir?'

'I've got a following job for you and Watkins, Catto.' For a moment or two, Hardcastle studied the junior detective, wondering whether he had made the right decision in selecting him for the job he had in mind. 'Captain Haydn Villiers has just left my office. He said that he spent New Year's Eve with a lady. I want you to find out who she is.' He picked up his pipe. 'Although I've got my doubts that such a lady exists.'

'Do we know where this Captain Villiers lives, sir?' Catto was taken aback at the enormity of the task that the DDI had just set him and Watkins.

'He's staying with his mother in Battersea while he's on leave, Catto. Sergeant Marriott will give you the address and a description of the man. But he was away from that address last night, and he claimed that he was with a lady. If that was the case, it's an odds-on chance that he'll be there again tonight. Follow him. Discreetly.'

'What time d'you want us to start the observation, sir?'

'In time to make sure you're bloody well there when he sets off, Catto.' Hardcastle waved an impatient hand of dismissal.

'Yes, sir.' The DDI's reply left Catto with a dilemma. If he and Watkins arrived too early, there was a good chance of them being seen loitering; and they did not want to arouse suspicion. To arrive too late might mean missing the captain altogether.

'And don't make a Mons of it, Catto.'

'No, sir.'

Marriott followed Catto out of Hardcastle's office and into the detectives' office opposite.

'Catto.'

'Yes, Sarge?' An unhappy Catto turned to face Marriott.

'You and Watkins take up the observation at six o'clock, and if that turns out to be too late, you can tell the guv'nor that was when I told you to take it up.' Marriott had much more faith in Catto than did Hardcastle. He knew that he was a good hard-working detective, and only ever lost his self-confidence when confronted by the DDI. Apart from which, he was irritated that the DDI had not given Catto specific instructions. Not that he would say as much to a junior officer. Before dismissing the detective constable, Marriott gave him a description of Haydn Villiers and drew a rough sketch of the cap badge that the army officer wore.

'Thanks, Sarge,' said a relieved Catto.

'And the rank is sergeant, not sarge, Catto,' said Marriott, and returned to the DDI's office.

Hardcastle glanced at his watch, briefly wound it and dropped it back into his waistcoat pocket. 'Time we were getting up to Padding-ton, Marriott. Dr Spilsbury's conducting the post-mortem on Gosling this afternoon.'

'I've just finished, Hardcastle.' Spilsbury took off his rubber apron and tossed it on to a side bench. 'I haven't found anything that you don't know already, my dear fellow. And that is that Gosling died as a result of several severe blows to the head causing multiple cranial fractures of the skull associated with contusion of the brain. I found six lacerated wounds on the scalp show-ing dents from one to two inches long, some on the front and some on the back of the head.' The pathologist paused. 'I would say that your attackers intended to kill the poor man.'

'D'you think it was the sash weight we found that did for him, Doctor?'

'Almost certainly,' said Spilsbury. 'If you care to let me have the weight, I'll be able to tell you for sure. I've also analysed the blood sample that was found on the showcase, but I'm sorry to have to tell you that it was blood group O-plus.'

'Is that no good, then?' Hardcastle was not too well versed in medical matters.

'I don't think that it will be of any assistance to you. It's the most common blood group there is. Probably forty per cent of the population have it running through their veins.' Spilsbury paused, smiling. 'And their arteries of course.'

'If he used a sash weight, he must've brought

it with him,' said Hardcastle. 'And that, to my mind, shows intent to murder.'

'Very likely,' said Spilsbury, 'but that's your province rather than mine, Hardcastle.'

It was a tortuous journey from Whitehall to Battersea by public transport, but Henry Catto and Cecil Watkins knew that they would not be reimbursed for a cab fare just to get there. To make matters worse it had started to rain by the time the two detectives arrived at Prince of Wales Drive, and a quite sharp breeze was blowing across from Battersea Park.

Dispirited, they hunched their shoulders beneath their overcoats and began to amble up and down trying to appear inconspicuous. There was no cover and no shop doorways in which they could shelter and be hidden from any curious eyes that might be watching them from the mansion flats. But at least their umbrellas shielded their faces. For what good that was.

For an hour and a half the two detectives wandered disconsolately up and down the street, grateful that it was now dark and that, thanks to wartime restrictions, some of the street lamps were unlit; those that were alight had been dimmed.

Their enforced patience was rewarded at half past seven when they saw an army officer emerge from one of the grand entrances.

'D'you think that's him, Henry?' asked Watkins.

'I hope so, Cecil. Is he a captain?'

'Yes, he's got three pips on the shoulder straps of his greatcoat and what looks like an artillery badge on his cap, but I can't see it clearly. But it looks a bit like the one that Sergeant Marriott drew for you.'

'He certainly fits the description that the skipper gave me.' Not that that was any great help; to Catto and many other civilians, one army officer looked much like another.

Fortunately for the watching detectives, two cabs came along Prince of Wales Drive one after the other. The army officer hailed one, and Catto hailed the following one.

The gunner officer's cab crossed Albert Bridge, turned into King's Road, Chelsea, and finally stopped outside a three-storied dwelling in Elm Park Gardens.

Catto and Watkins remained in their cab until they saw which house the army officer had entered.

'I hope to God that was him,' said Watkins.

'So do I,' said Catto. He paid the cab driver and took a note of the plate number without which details the DDI would disallow his claim. It was not unknown for the Receiver's clerks to question cab drivers about particular fares, but they almost always confirmed them. Cabbies had no wish to upset the police officers who used them. And might use them again. The police and cab drivers were never good friends, even at the best of times.

'What do we do now, Henry?' asked Watkins. 'Do we wait?'

'If Villiers has gone there for what the guv'nor thinks he's gone there for, he won't be out until tomorrow morning, Cecil. No, we'll pack it in and hope for the best.'

'I s'pose we'd better find a bus that'll take us back to the nick, then, Henry.'

At eight thirty on the Tuesday morning, Marriott stepped into Hardcastle's office. 'Catto and Watkins seem to have done a good job, sir,' he said.

'Remains to be seen,' grunted Hardcastle, unwilling to offer praise to detectives who were only doing their jobs. 'Do we know who lives at this Elm Park Gardens address?'

'I got Carter to do a check on the burgesses' register last night, sir, and there appears to be only one eligible voter there. His name's Valentine Powell. It could be his wife that Villiers has been visiting, but of course she's not shown on the register.'

'She wouldn't be, Marriott,' said Hardcastle testily. 'Women don't have the vote. Good God, you've seen enough of those damned suffragettes to know that.'

Marriott did know that, only too well, but he knew better than to reply to the DDI's observation; it would set him off on one of his diatribes about votes for women. 'Valentine Powell's shown as an absentee voter, sir.'

'Probably in the army or the navy, I suppose,' suggested Hardcastle. 'One way to find out: we'll go and speak to whoever is there now.'

'But what do we hope to achieve, sir?' Once again Marriott was mystified by the DDI's proposed course of action; an action that seemed to be straying from the main thrust of the murder enquiry. Nevertheless, he knew from previous experience, how often Hardcastle's 'flights of fancy', as he called them, produced a useful result.

'To find out whether the bold Captain Villiers is lying to us, Marriott,' said Hardcastle. 'Or whether he really was there on New Year's Eve. Or perhaps he was somewhere else,' he added significantly.

'You surely don't think he had anything to do with Reuben Gosling's murder, do you, sir?'

'You know me, Marriott. Everyone's a suspect until I have evidence to the contrary.'

The cab set Hardcastle and Marriott down in Elm Park Gardens at a little after eleven o'clock, Hardcastle having decided that Captain Villiers would have left by then. Assuming, of course, that it was Villiers whom Catto and Watkins had followed, and if it was Villiers that he *had* spent the night in Mrs Powell's bed.

The door was opened by an attractive woman, probably in her early thirties. To Hardcastle's surprise, she was wearing a Japanese silk kimono and satin slippers. Her long jet-black hair

tumbled around her shoulders and she displayed not the slightest embarrassment at being in a
state of comparative undress.

'Mrs Powell?' asked the DDI, certain that a
housemaid would not be dressed with such
casual elegance as the woman now facing him.

'Yes, I'm Annabel Powell.' The woman gazed
enquiringly at the two detectives. 'Who are
you?'

'Divisional Detective Inspector Hardcastle of
the Whitehall Division, madam, and this here's
Detective Sergeant Marriott.'

'Oh my God!' Mrs Powell put a hand to her
mouth. 'Is it about Valentine?'

'Valentine, madam?' queried Hardcastle, pretending innocence.

'Colonel Powell, my husband. Has he been
killed?'

'Not to my knowledge,' said Hardcastle,
somewhat piqued at being obliged to carry on a
conversation on the doorstep. 'It's certainly not
what I've come about.'

As if sensing Hardcastle's irritation at her
discourtesy, Mrs Powell hurriedly invited the
two detectives into the house and led them into
the drawing room. Waiting until she had settled
herself in an armchair, Hardcastle and Marriott
sat down on a sofa facing her.

'What have you come here for if it's not about
my husband?' Perfectly relaxed, the woman
focused her deep brown eyes on Hardcastle.

'I understand that a Captain Haydn Villiers

spent the night with you on New Year's Eve, Mrs Powell.'

Marriott was astounded by the bluntness of his DDI's assertion, and that he had made it without having the slightest evidence that that was indeed the case.

'*What?*' Annabel Powell shot forward in her chair, the cool reserve that had possessed her thus far vanishing in an instant. 'Is that what the damned fellow told you, Inspector?' Clearly outraged, she almost spat the words.

'So you do know him,' said Hardcastle, allowing the colonel's wife to draw, what to her, must have seemed the only logical conclusion: that Villiers had offered up her name as an alibi.

'Yes, I do know him. He's in my husband's brigade, but he certainly did not spend the night with me. It's a monstrous thing for him to have said.' Mrs Powell quickly recovered her equanimity, and spoke in matter-of-fact tones. 'My husband is a regular officer commanding a brigade of the Royal Field Artillery in France, somewhere near Neuve Chapelle, I believe. He's often critical of the quality of young men who are being commissioned today. In fact, he describes them as "oiks", whatever that may mean, and it would seem that Haydn Villiers is one of them. But, despite that, I found him to be a very personable young man, even if he has turned out to be a bounder.'

'Would I be right in assuming that Captain Villiers is one of your husband's battery commanders, Mrs Powell?' There was a good reason why Marriott had made it his business to learn about the way in which the British Army was structured. His DDI possessed but a sparse knowledge of it, and displayed no interest in furthering that knowledge, even though being involved often with military matters. Marriott, however, was doubtful that Colonel Powell commanded a brigade; as far as he knew that would be a brigadier general's command.

'That's correct. However, what has any of this to do with the police?'

Hardcastle explained in some detail about the Vauxhall Bridge Road murder, stressing the fact that Haydn Villiers's father's car was most likely to have been used in its execution. And that it had taken place on New Year's Eve.

'Captain Villiers has been known to drive the car in the past, Mrs Powell, but he claimed that he had nothing to do with the murder, and told me that he'd spent the night with you.' Hardcastle avoided saying that Villiers had not mentioned her by name, rather than to reveal details of the observation that he had ordered two of his officers to conduct.

'I'm not denying that Haydn Villiers was here, Inspector, but he certainly did not spend the night with me. The idea is preposterous. He merely called to give me a letter from my husband, and to assure me that he was in good health and safe.' Annabel glanced momentarily at her satin-slippered feet. 'Mind you, Haydn

78

did make me a gift of some French perfume that it's almost impossible to obtain in England since the war started, so I suppose he's not all bad.'

'What time did Captain Villiers leave here, madam?' asked Marriott.

Annabel Powell paused, long enough for the detectives to know that whatever she said, it would not be the truth. 'About nine o'clock, I suppose,' she said eventually, having decided that it was a little later than courtesy demanded, but not too late to raise doubts about her morality.

'And was that the only occasion Captain Villiers called on you?' asked Hardcastle.

'Yes, it was.'

'Thank you, Mrs Powell,' said Hardcastle, as he and Marriott rose to their feet. 'We'll see ourselves out.'

Leaving the house, the two detectives walked through to King's Road in the hope of finding a rare cab.

'Well, what d'you think of that, Marriott?'

'Judging by the way Mrs Powell was dressed, sir, it wouldn't surprise me if young Villiers was upstairs in her bed while we were talking to her.'

'Nor me, Marriott. She certainly looked as though she'd just tumbled out of her four-poster.' Hardcastle always assumed that the moneyed classes slept in a four-poster bed. 'But I'll tell you this much: I'd put money on it being the last time the bold captain sees the inside of Annabel Powell's bedroom.'

'D'you think she was lying, sir?'

'I'm sure she was, Marriott. It certainly took her long enough to come up with a time that Villiers was supposed to have left her. Mind you, I wouldn't have expected the colonel's lady to admit having had a bit of jig-a-jig with one of her husband's virile young officers. Even so, we'll have another word with Captain Villiers.'

'Shall I get one of the DCs to send for him, sir?'

'Yes, and sooner rather than later, Marriott.'

In the event, Marriott's intention to send for the young army captain proved to be unnecessary.

At two o'clock that afternoon, an irate Haydn Villiers was shown into Hardcastle's office. He was red in the face and bore all the signs of being incandescent with rage.

'I take it that Annabel Powell's been in touch with you, Captain Villiers,' observed Hardcastle mildly, before Villiers had a chance to speak.

'Damn' right, she has. What the hell d'you think you were doing, going to see her? And how the devil did you know where to find her?'

Hardcastle declined to answer that question. 'I'm dealing with a vicious murder, Captain Villiers, and I was checking your alibi. Had you furnished me with the lady's name, I would have acted discreetly, and quite possibly accepted your word for it,' he said, not that he would have let it go at that. 'As it is, you wouldn't name the lady and I suspected that you weren't telling me the truth. And it seems I was right. Mrs Powell denied that you spent the night with her.'

'Of course she did. She's my colonel's wife for God's sake.'

'So she said.' Hardcastle spent a few moments filling and lighting his pipe, further frustrating Villiers. 'Perhaps you'd better give me your side of the story, then,' he said.

'Colonel Powell granted me leave for Christmas and the New Year,' began Villiers, by now a little calmer than when he had arrived. 'He asked me to call on his wife, to assure her that he was safe and well, and to give her a letter and some perfume he'd bought for her.'

'Mrs Powell seemed to be under the impression that the perfume was a gift from you, Captain Villiers,' said Marriott, 'rather than from her husband.'

Villiers was obviously embarrassed by that revelation. 'Well, I didn't think there was any harm in letting her think it was from me,' he said. 'Particularly in view what happened later.'

'When did you first call on Mrs Powell?' asked Marriott.

'On Boxing Day, in the evening.' Villiers paused, and then decided to tell the whole story, secure in the knowledge that, thanks to Hardcastle's intervention, he was unlikely ever to enjoy Annabel Powell's favours again. 'Right from the moment I arrived she made it quite obvious that she wasn't averse to having a little fun, if you know what I mean.'

'By which you mean she was up for a screwing, I suppose,' said Hardcastle bluntly.

'That's not quite how I'd've described it,' responded Villiers acidly, irritated by the DDI's description of what Villiers saw as a romantic tryst.

'Matter of opinion,' commented Hardcastle quietly.

'However, in no time at all she was telling me how lonely it was for a girl to be left on her own. She actually described herself as "a girl", despite the fact that she must be at least ten years older than me. What's more, she said her husband was a bully who had no interest in her. I could certainly vouch for Colonel Powell being a strict disciplinarian, but it seems he was when he was at home as well as with the brigade. Annabel made it quite obvious that she was up for a bit of fun and it was too good an offer to refuse. As a result, I've spent every night with her since.'

'I hope your colonel doesn't find out, Captain Villiers,' said Hardcastle.

'Ye Gods!' exclaimed Villiers. 'So do I. I hope you don't propose speaking to him.'

'I might be a thorough detective, Captain Villiers, but I'm damned if I'm going to France just to shop you to your colonel.'

'Captain Villiers, is there anyone you've made an enemy of recently? Apart from Colonel Powell, of course,' said Marriott quietly. 'Not that he knows he's an enemy. Yet.'

Villiers leaned back against the hard chair and lit a cigarette, this time without asking Hardcastle's permission. 'As a matter of fact there is, although I don't see that it has any bearing on your enquiries. He's a new subaltern in my battery. Soon after his arrival, I learned that he was in debt to quite a substantial amount. Most of the young officers take to the bottle, but Tindall has started gambling. One of the other officers mentioned it to me and said that he'd heard that Tindall owed money all over London. I took him to task and told him to settle up and stop gambling or I'd have him court-martialled and thrown out. As a matter of fact, I gave him a bloody good dressing down and he let fly with a string of abuse, so much so that I threatened to have him up in front of the colonel for insubordination. He even suggested that I shouldn't turn my back on him in the heat of battle. But I put that down to the stress of warfare. People out there often say things they don't mean.'

Hardcastle suddenly realized why Marriott had posed the question. 'You say this officer's name is Tindall, Captain Villiers, and he's in the Royal Field Artillery?'

'I'm sorry to say he is, God help us. Second

Lieutenant George Tindall, a hostilities-only officer, so I believe. He's in his twenties, I'd think, and with the present drain on subalterns I don't suppose he'll last more than a few weeks, but that's no excuse for his behaviour. Trouble is that new officers these days aren't out of the top drawer, so to speak, and even worse, I'll probably find that he went to a grammar school.'

It was a remark that did little to endear Villiers to Hardcastle who had been the doubtful beneficiary of a London County Council elementary school education.

'Is this here Tindall still in France?' asked Hardcastle.

'I imagine so, but there again he might be dead,' commented Villiers, revealing the pessimistic fatalism of those soldiers who prosecuted the war from muddy rat-infested holes in France and Flanders.

'As a matter of interest, why *didn't* you report any of this to Colonel Powell?' asked Hardcastle.

'I thought I'd sort it out myself,' said Villiers. 'As I said just now, if I'd placed the matter before the colonel, he'd have had no alternative but to have a summary of evidence taken, with a view to court-martialling Tindall.'

'Thank you for calling in again, Captain Villiers. I doubt that I'll need to speak to you again.'

'I hope not,' said Villiers. He paused at the

door. 'You didn't tell me how you found where Annabel lived, Inspector.'

'No, I didn't,' said Hardcastle.

FIVE

Later that afternoon, Hardcastle was seated in his office, contentedly smoking his pipe and thinking. Occasionally, he would stand up and pace the office, sometimes stopping to stare unseeing at the Underground station below his window. After fifteen minutes of this deliberation he sent for Marriott.

'I've been wondering about this here Second Lieutenant George Tindall of the Royal Field Artillery, Marriott.'

'What about him, sir?'

'It's possible that he was being a bit clever in getting his own back on Villiers.' Hardcastle had almost convinced himself that Tindall was Reuben Gosling's murderer. Or one of them. 'Supposing he stole Sinclair Villiers's expensive motor car and carried out the murder to throw suspicion on Captain Villiers?'

'How would he know where Sinclair Villiers lived, sir?'

'I'd think he could've got that from the records at the unit where they were both serving?' suggested Hardcastle. 'But you seem to know more about the army than I do,' he added

86

archly. 'Is it possible?'

'I suppose so, sir,' said Marriott, surprised that for once the DDI was deferring to him. 'But if Tindall had wanted to kill Villiers, it would've been easier for him to do it in Flanders, surely? According to Villiers, Tindall told him never to turn his back on him. My brother-in-law Frank reckons that quite a few sadistic NCOs have got a bullet in the back out there.' Frank Dobson was a sergeant-major in the Middlesex Regiment, and had told Marriott the tale of one or two vindictive sergeants who had met their end at the hands of their own men. In the absence of any evidence to the contrary, their deaths were put down as 'killed in action'. 'Mind you, sir,' continued Marriott, 'I don't really see that Tindall would have such an opportunity; RFA officers don't go over the top like the infantry.'

'Yes, but even so, that wouldn't have paid off his debts, Marriott, would it?' Hardcastle sat back, a satisfied smile on his face. 'But a handful of tomfoolery might've done. And, like I said, using Sinclair Villiers's car to do it would have thrown suspicion on Haydn Villiers.'

'But do we know if anyone else knew about the debts, sir? It might just be a tale that Haydn Villiers put about because he didn't like the man.'

'One way of finding out,' said Hardcastle. 'First of all we'll have a word with the military police, and maybe have another chat with young Villiers.'

'But is there any indication that Tindall is our man, sir?' Once again, Marriott thought that the DDI was taking the investigation off at a tangent.

'If he's not, we'll have eliminated him from the enquiry, Marriott,' said Hardcastle, as if his sergeant should have known that.

Hardcastle and Marriott made their way down Whitehall to Horse Guards Arch.

Hooking his umbrella over his left arm, Hardcastle solemnly raised his bowler hat in acknowledgement of the unwarranted salute accorded him by the Life Guards dismounted sentry. Household Cavalry sentries tended to salute anyone wearing a bowler hat, just to be on the safe side.

'Good morning, Inspector.' Sergeant Cyril Glover was chief clerk to the assistant provost marshal, Lieutenant Colonel Ralph Frobisher of the Sherwood Foresters.

'Good morning, Sergeant Glover,' said Hardcastle. 'Is the colonel in?'

'Yes, he is, Inspector. Go through.'

'Good morning, Mr Hardcastle.' Frobisher stood up, skirted his desk and shook hands with the DDI and Marriott. 'I take it you have another problem for me to solve,' he said, with a smile. The DDI usually presented him with a difficult problem. 'Please take a seat, gentlemen.'

'Indeed I have, Colonel.' Hardcastle rapidly outlined details of the murder he was investigating and related what Haydn Villiers had told him about George Tindall.

Frobisher pursed his lips. 'This is a very serious matter, Mr Hardcastle. For an officer to incur debts is contrary to the Army Act. It's called conduct unbecoming an officer and a gentleman. He could be cashiered.'

'Really?' Hardcastle was unimpressed by this piece of military legalese. 'In the Metropolitan Police we'd just sack the man.'

Frobisher smiled. 'That's what the army means by cashiering an officer, Inspector. Although it might sound like it, "cashiering" doesn't mean we'd pay off his debts, either.' He drew a writing pad across his desk. 'What was his name again?'

'Give the colonel the details, Marriott.' Hardcastle, mildly piqued by Frobisher's gentle joshing, spoke sharply.

'Second Lieutenant George Tindall of the Royal Field Artillery, sir,' said Marriott. 'I don't know which battalion, but his commanding officer is Lieutenant Colonel Valentine Powell and we've been led to believe that they're somewhere near Neuve Chapelle.'

'It's not a battalion, Sergeant Marriott. A lieutenant colonel's command in the artillery is called a brigade. However, he shouldn't be too difficult to find,' said Frobisher, scribbling down the details. 'But how can I help you in this matter, Mr Hardcastle?'

'It would greatly assist me if you were able to tell me whether Tindall was on leave in London over New Year's Eve, Colonel,' said Hardcastle.

'D'you think he might've had something to do with this murder?' Frobisher appeared concerned at the prospect of an officer being suspected of murder.

'It's a possibility I'm considering,' said Hardcastle. 'I suppose you'd cashier him for that, too,' he added impishly.

Frobisher burst out laughing. 'No, Inspector, I think the army would let the civil authorities deal with that. And *then* we'd cashier him. I'll let you know as soon as I hear anything. I must warn you, however, that it might take time. I'll have to find out where Powell's brigade is at the moment, and then get a signal off to him. Provided we can find the brigade in the first place. It might've moved, you see.'

Hardcastle nodded. He had become accustomed to the complaints of the military about the difficulties involved in tracking down entire units, let alone individuals. He kept to himself his opinion of what he regarded as inefficiency, but he had no idea of the difficulties faced by the British Expeditionary Force.

'I shall need to interview Captain Villiers,' continued Frobisher. 'As he seems to have been aware of this matter and failed to report it, then he too will be guilty of an offence. Are you able to give me his address here in England?'

'Certainly, Colonel, but I'd be grateful if you could leave that until I'm satisfied that he had nothing to do with this here murder of mine.'

'Of course,' said Frobisher. 'And if the worst comes to the worst it could always be dealt with once he returns to his brigade.'

Hardcastle laughed. 'Then you'd better not mention that he's having an affair with his colonel's wife.'

'*What?*'

'It's only a rumour, Colonel.' Hardcastle decided not to repeat what Haydn Villiers had told him, not knowing what penalties the military might impose for adultery. As far as he was concerned, such behaviour was commonplace, and he could not bring himself to damn an officer who was prepared to give his life for his country.

'While we're waiting for the good colonel to find out about this here Tindall, Marriott,' said Hardcastle, once they were back at the police station, 'I think we'll have a closer look at Reuben Gosling's background.'

'It's possible that Tindall had nothing to do with it, sir.' Marriott was pleased that the DDI appeared to be veering back to the victim, rather than pursuing one of the tenuous theories of which he was so fond.

'Maybe, but we'll have to wait and see. Get one of the men working at Somerset House. I want to know all there is to know about Reuben Gosling. Better put Wood on it. He's reliable.' Detective Sergeant Herbert Wood was one of those diligent officers who took a pride in his work, but who had no interest in further promotion.

'Yes, sir.'

'And I think we'll have another word with that chap who keeps the clothing shop next door. What was his name again?'

'Sidney Partridge, sir. Gents' outfitter.'

'Yes, that's the fellow.'

It was two o'clock in the afternoon of the Wednesday following Reuben Gosling's murder when Hardcastle and Marriott arrived at Sidney Partridge's shop in Vauxhall Bridge Road. Partridge, clad in a waistcoat, but without a jacket, had a tape measure around his neck, and was in the act of showing a customer to the door.

'Ah, Inspector Hardcastle. Good to see you again, sir. Come in, come in. I presume you'd like to take up my offer. I can give you a very generous twenty-five per cent discount.' Partridge revolved his hands around each other in a washing motion, and ran a discerning eye over the DDI as if estimating his size. 'What can I show you?'

'Nothing at the moment, Mr Partridge, but if you can spare me five minutes of your time, I'd like a word with you. If you're not too busy.'

'Of course, of course, Inspector.' Partridge

glanced at a young man. 'Edgar, mind the shop while I speak to the inspector.'

'Yes, Mr Partridge.' Edgar picked up a tape measure and placed it around his neck, as though it were a badge of office.

'It might be better if you came into the back room,' said Partridge, and showed the detectives into the parlour-cum-office. 'This is my lady wife Gladys, Inspector. This is the policeman who came to see me on New Year's Eve when poor Reuben was murdered, Glad.'

'How d'you do, Mrs Partridge,' said Hardcastle. Partridge's wife, her grey hair woven into a neat bun, was seated at a desk poring over a large ledger. There was a pile of papers – accounts and invoices – close to her left hand.

'You'll have to excuse me for a tick, Inspector, while I finish running up this column of figures. Then I'll have done with last year's stocktaking.'

'Of course, Mrs Partridge,' said Hardcastle. 'We'll try not to disturb you.'

'Now, sir. Take a seat, take a seat.' Partridge pointed at a sofa on the far side of the room, and hovered in front of the DDI. 'What can I do to assist?'

'I understand from one of my officers that Reuben Gosling's wife died about ten years ago, Mr Partridge,' Hardcastle began.

'She might be dead now, but she wasn't then.' Gladys Partridge pushed a pencil into her hair and swung round to face the detectives. 'She ran off with a commercial traveller.'

'I don't think the inspector wants to know about that, Glad,' said Partridge hurriedly.

'Oh, but the inspector most definitely does,' said Hardcastle, his interest immediately aroused.

'His name was Joseph Morgan, and he was a bit younger than Sarah, so I heard.' Gladys Partridge's keenness to relate the tale indicated to Hardcastle that she was a woman who enjoyed a bit of scandal. 'He was a traveller in bracelets, necklaces and watches, that sort of thing. He used to visit Reuben about once a week. I don't know if he ever sold him anything, but he certainly took his wife off of him.'

'When was this, Mrs Partridge?' asked Marriott, already scribbling notes in his pocket-book.

'About nine years ago, I suppose. Yes, of course; it was 1907. I remember that because it was the day after William Whiteley was murdered. It was in all the papers.'

'Twenty-fourth of January,' murmured Hardcastle. He remembered the Whiteley case well. William Whiteley was the owner of a large department store in Westbourne Grove. Horace Rayner, a man of twenty-nine, laboured under the belief that Whiteley was his father and had made demands for money. When no money was forthcoming, he walked into Whiteley's office in his emporium and shot him dead. At the time,

Hardcastle had envied the detectives on the Marylebone Division, having been presented with such an open-and-shut case.

'Have you any idea where they went?' asked Marriott.

'No, no idea. Oh, just a minute though...' Gladys Partridge paused. 'I seem to remember some of the neighbours mentioning Brighton, but I don't know if there was any truth in it.'

'Were there any children of the marriage, Mrs Partridge?' asked Hardcastle.

'I did hear that they had a son, but I don't recall him ever coming near the place. I don't think him and his dad got on too well. Reuben and Sarah certainly never mentioned him, apart from Reuben saying that the boy was always going on about the need for a Jewish homeland. Whatever that meant. But he was quite passionate about it, so Reuben said.'

'Do you happen to know the son's name?' Marriott looked up expectantly.

'No, I'm sorry. Sidney and I took over this business twenty years ago...' Gladys Partridge paused again. 'It was twenty years ago, wasn't it, Sid?'

'Yes, that's about right,' agreed her husband.

'My, how time does fly. But I imagine their son was long gone by the time we moved in here, Mr Marriott.'

'Thank you both for your assistance,' said Hardcastle, as he and Marriott rose from the sofa. 'If you should think of anything else that might help me, perhaps you'd let me know, at Cannon Row police station.'

'We're getting nowhere with this damned enquiry, Marriott.' Hardcastle reached for his pipe and began to fill it with tobacco from a worn leather pouch. He dropped the pouch on to his desk. 'I had hoped that I might be given a new pouch for Christmas,' he complained in an aside.

'D'you think there's anything in this business of Sarah Gosling running off with Joseph Morgan, sir?' said Marriott, not greatly interested in his chief's disappointment about a tobacco pouch.

'Time will tell, Marriott. Time will tell.'

'Excuse me, sir.' Detective Sergeant Herbert Wood stood in the doorway of Hardcastle's office.

'What is it, Wood?'

'The results of my searches at Somerset House, sir.'

'Well, come in, man, and tell me what you've discovered,' said Hardcastle impatiently.

'I've got dates of birth here for Reuben and Sarah Gosling née Barak, sir. They were married at the Great Synagogue in Aldgate in 1879. They have a son named Isaac who was born in Vauxhall Bridge Road, Westminster, on the sixteenth of March 1883.' Wood looked up. 'That would be over the shop, sir.'

'Did you find anything about the Goslings

getting a divorce?'

'No, sir. I didn't know they'd divorced. It's a different registry, you see.'

'Yes, yes, I know that, Wood. So, have another look. And while you're about it, find out anything you can about a commercial traveller called Joseph Morgan. According to the Partridges, the Goslings' neighbours, Sarah Gosling ran away with Morgan in 1907. Morgan is said to be a year or two younger than Sarah Gosling.'

'Very good, sir.' Wood made a note in his pocketbook.

'Right, Wood. Give the details of what you've found so far to Sergeant Marriott, and then see if you can find out anything about Joseph Morgan. Go to Brighton if necessary, but wait until I tell you to go in case something else crops up.'

'Is any of that likely to help, d'you think, sir?' asked Marriott, once Wood had left.

'No idea,' said Hardcastle, 'but I'm interested in whether Morgan making off with Reuben's wife has got any bearing on the case.'

'I can't see any motive in that, sir, not now. There might've been an argument when it happened, but that was all nine years ago.'

'You never can tell, Marriott,' said Hardcastle mysteriously.

'Sir!' The door burst open and Catto stood on the threshold.

'Is there something wrong with your right hand, Catto?' barked Hardcastle.

'Er, no, sir.'

'Then bloody well knock before you come barging into my office. Now, what are you in all of a lather about? And it'd better be good.'

'I've just taken a telephone call for Sergeant Marriott, sir, from Mr Parfitt, the jeweller in Victoria Street.'

'Well, don't keep us in suspense, Catto.'

'A man's just gone into his shop trying to flog some of the tom that he thinks might've been nicked from Gosling's,' said Catto breathlessly.

'Well, why the hell didn't you say so?' growled Hardcastle. 'And is that man there now?'

'He was when Mr Parfitt telephoned, sir.'

'Come, Marriott.' Hardcastle leaped up from his chair and pausing only to seize his bowler hat and umbrella, made for the door.

Fortunately, a cab was turning in the forecourt of New Scotland Yard, having just set down a fare there.

'Parfitt's the jewellers in Vic Street,' yelled Hardcastle, as he and Marriott clambered into the cab, 'and be quick about it.'

Gilbert Parfitt was known throughout the trade, including Hatton Garden, as the owner of a high-class jewellery business, and a man who would never knowingly handle stolen property.

He looked up as Hardcastle and Marriott strode hurriedly into his shop.

'I'm afraid you're too late, Mr Hardcastle.'

'Dammit! What can you tell me, Mr Parfitt?'

'This man came into the shop just under half an hour ago and produced a diamond and sapphire dress ring, silver mounted, that he wanted to sell. I told him that I'd have to check with my catalogue before I could give him a price, but I could see at a glance that it was worth at least thirty pounds.'

'Can you describe this man, Mr Parfitt?' asked Marriott.

'In his late twenties, I'd've thought, or maybe early thirties, but not very well dressed.'

'A moustache or a beard?' Marriott glanced up from his pocketbook.

'No, he was clean-shaven, but he wore spectacles, metal-framed with small, pebble lenses.' Parfitt paused for a moment. 'Oh, and he had a bandage on his right hand.'

'Sounds like our man, sir,' said Marriott.

'Is that helpful?' enquired Parfitt.

'We're fairly certain that one of Gosling's murderers cut his hand when he broke into a showcase, Mr Parfitt,' said Hardcastle. 'So the ring could be proceeds from the robbery. But what happened next?'

'I had a feeling about that ring. It rang a bell, if you'll excuse the pun. It's the sort of thing you develop a nose for in the trade, if you know what I mean.'

'Indeed I do, Mr Parfitt,' said Hardcastle warmly. 'Please go on.'

'The first thing I did was to check the lists that you send round every day. Now here's the funny thing: it was on a list all right, but on the list dated the twenty-fourth of October last year. I always keep back copies of the lists, you see.'

'That was well before Gosling's murder, sir,' said Marriott.

'I know that,' said Hardcastle impatiently. 'And you're sure it was the same ring, Mr Parfitt.'

'Definitely. The one this chap produced was engraved with the initials JW next to the hallmark. And that information was in the list.'

'I'll have to check, sir,' said Marriott, 'but I've a feeling that someone was arrested and convicted for that burglary. It was one of the big houses in Grosvenor Place.'

'But when you went back to the man, Mr Parfitt, I presume he'd gone,' said Hardcastle.

'Yes. Having discovered that it was stolen, I telephoned the police station to speak to Sergeant Marriott, but the man must've heard me. When I returned to the front of the shop, he'd gone.' Parfitt placed the ring on a green baize cloth on his counter. 'But he went without this.'

'The trouble is,' said Hardcastle, 'we haven't found anyone who could tell us what was taken from Gosling's shop. Nevertheless, I'm grateful to you, Mr Parfitt. It's another piece in the jigsaw, so to speak.'

'Circulate that description, such as it is, to surrounding stations, Marriott,' said Hardcastle, once the two detectives were back at Cannon Row police station. 'And check on that Grosvenor Place burglary.'

'Already in hand, sir.' Marriott was always irritated when the DDI told him to do something that, as a first-class sergeant, he would have done automatically. But, as usual, he masked that irritation.

'I've put the information about that Grosvenor Place burglary on your desk, Sergeant,' said DC Watkins, when Marriott returned to his office.

Marriott spent a few moments examining the Criminal Records Office file before going back to the DDI.

'The ring that Parfitt handed over was the property of a Mrs Jane Weaver of Grosvenor Place, sir, and was reported stolen last October as Mr Parfitt said. Albert Harris was sent down for a five stretch at the Inner London Sessions just in time for Christmas. He's currently in Pentonville prison, sir.'

'Albert Harris, eh?' said Hardcastle thoughtfully. 'Yes, I remember that little toerag of old. We'll pay him a visit, Marriott, and wish him a Happy New Year.'

SIX

The cab delivered Hardcastle and Marriott at the gates of the fortress-like edifice of Wandsworth prison in Heathfield Road.

'Pay the cabbie, Marriott,' said Hardcastle, 'and don't forget to take the plate number.'

'Of course, sir,' said Marriott, trying to keep the annoyance out of his voice. The DDI said that every time they took a cab together.

Hardcastle yanked at the handle set to the left of the heavy wooden doors and heard a bell jangling somewhere inside.

'Yes?' A heavily bearded warder had opened the wicket gate a fraction.

'DDI Hardcastle, Metropolitan Police, and DS Marriott to see Albert Harris.' Hardcastle and Marriott produced their warrant cards.

'Ah, right you are, gents. We got a message to say you'd be coming.' The warder pulled open the wicket gate wide enough for the two detectives to enter.

Another warder appeared. 'Welcome to the best hotel in London, guv'nor,' he said. 'Follow me and I'll get hold of Harris for you.'

Hardcastle and Marriott were led along several labyrinthine passageways pervaded with the overpowering odour of urine, until eventually they were shown into a small, dank, stone-flagged room. The only light came from a barred window high in the wall.

'I'll enquire if Mr Harris is at home, guv'nor. If he is, I'll have him along here in two shakes of a lamb's tail,' said the warder, and laughed. 'I think he's receiving visitors today.'

'Cheerful sort of bloke, ain't he, Marriott?' Hardcastle took out his pipe and began to fill it.

Five minutes later the shambling figure of Albert Harris was escorted into the room. He was attired in the standard prison uniform of canvas jacket and trousers embellished with the broad arrows designed to aid apprehension in the event of an escape. Not that there was much chance of a prisoner escaping from this particular prison.

'I'll be outside when you've done with him, guv'nor,' said the cheerful warder.

'Hello, Mr 'Ardcastle. Fancy seeing you. You ain't been sent down an' all, 'ave yer?'

'Just keep your smart remarks to yourself, Harris, unless you fancy a transfer to Dartmoor. And I can fix it, just like that.' Hardcastle flicked his fingers in Harris's face. 'Now sit down.'

'No offence, Mr 'Ardcastle,' said the chastened Harris. 'Just a joke, that's all.'

'You got five years for screwing a drum in Grosvenor Place last October, Harris,' said Marriott.

'It's common knowledge, Mr Marriott.'

'And among the other stuff you nicked was this.' Marriott placed the ring on the table; his statement was made in such a way that brooked no denial.

Harris examined the ring. 'Yeah, maybe,' he said.

'Definitely,' said Marriott. 'Who did you fence it to?'

Hurriedly dropping the ring, Harris shot back in his chair. 'I ain't no grass, Mr Marriott,' he protested. 'You should know that.'

'You are now, Harris,' growled Hardcastle menacingly. 'Unless you want to be on the night train to Dartmoor. If they don't make you walk, that is.'

'Can we keep this to ourselves?' pleaded Harris. He cast a furtive glance around the small room, as though fearful of being overheard.

'I'm waiting,' said Hardcastle.

'It was Reuben Gosling.' Harris almost whispered the name. 'But for Gawd's sake don't let on I told you. He's got friends in here and I don't fancy getting a striping for grassing.'

'He hasn't got any friends, not any more,' said Marriott. 'Someone topped him on New Year's Eve. And his killers helped themselves to a load of tom, that included most likely,' he added, picking up the ring.

'Oh my oath! Who done for him, then?'

'That's what I'm trying to find out, Harris,' said Hardcastle.

'Well, don't look at me, Mr 'Ardcastle. I was celebrating the New Year in here.' Harris gave a nervous laugh.

Hardcastle laughed outright. 'That's the first time in your life you've ever had a watertight alibi, Harris.'

'So, Gosling was a fence, sir,' said Marriott, when he and the DDI were in a cab on their way back to Cannon Row.

'Comes as no surprise, Marriott,' said Hardcastle. 'But it makes our job that much harder.'

'It could be that the man who tried to fence the ring with Parfitt was the man who topped Gosling, sir.'

'Maybe,' said Hardcastle thoughtfully. 'A fence makes all sorts of enemies. On the other hand, he might've got the ring from whoever did the deed. But any way up he's got some questions to answer when we do find him. And we will.'

And of that, Marriott was in no doubt. 'But Mr Parfitt said that the man who tried it on with him had a bandaged hand, sir,' he said.

'I don't suppose he's the only man in London who's hurt himself, Marriott,' said Hardcastle, and for the remainder of the journey, he remained silent, sunk in deep contemplation.

Once back at the police station, Hardcastle swept through the front office and bounded up the stairs with an agility that was incompatible with his bulk.

Throwing open the door of the detectives' office, he glared round at his staff.

'Listen carefully. Sergeant Marriott and me have just had a word with Albert Harris in Wandsworth nick. He's doing a handful for screwing and he told me that Reuben Gosling was a fence, which I'd suspected all along. Yesterday a man tried to fence a ring to Gilbert Parfitt in Vic Street. Catto knows that already. Don't you, Catto?'

'Yes, sir.'

'But we know that Harris nicked it in the course of a burglary at Grosvenor Place last October, and finished up in chokey for his pains. Now, for once in your lives you lot are going to pretend to be real detectives and get out on the street. Speak to your informants, if you've got any,' said Hardcastle sarcastically, 'and find out who else has been fencing bent tom to Gosling. Got it?'

'Yes, sir,' chorused the detectives.

'Well, what are you waiting for,' said Hardcastle, and returned to his office.

Moments later, Marriott knocked and entered. 'I've just had a call from Sergeant Glover at the APM's office, sir.'

'Don't tell me, Marriott, they can't find Tindall.'

'On the contrary, sir. Glover said that the APM has urgent information for you, if you'd care to call in next time you're passing.'

'We'll be passing in about ten minutes' time,'

said Hardcastle, donning his Chesterfield overcoat and seizing his hat and umbrella. 'Come,
Marriott.'

'Second Lieutenant George Tindall of the
Royal Field Artillery has disappeared, Mr
Hardcastle,' said Lieutenant Colonel Ralph
Frobisher.

'Is he missing in action, sir?' asked Marriott.

'No, he's absent without leave. That's how we
were able to get an answer so quickly. Sergeant
Glover always looks at the list of absentees and
deserters whenever you make an enquiry,
Inspector.' Frobisher glanced at Hardcastle with
a half-smile on his face. 'I think he's formed the
view that anyone in whom you have an interest
is a criminal of some sort.'

'Your Sergeant Glover's obviously a shrewd
fellow; you might even make a policeman of
him one day,' said Hardcastle drily. 'What more
do you know, Colonel?'

'Apparently things were a bit quiet on Christmas Day in that theatre of the Front covered by
Colonel Powell's brigade of the RFA. In fact,
the brigade was in rest. They weren't playing
football with Fritz like they did in 1914, but
there was, by all accounts, a small celebration
among the officers; as much as there could be in
a theatre of operations. However, after a while
Colonel Powell noticed that Tindall wasn't
there. He made a few enquiries as to the officer's whereabouts, but he hadn't been seen

since midday on Christmas Eve.'

'Is it possible that he'd been wounded and evacuated, sir?' queried Marriott.

'Seems a bit of rum do, losing an officer,' commented Hardcastle quietly.

'It happens, Inspector,' said Frobisher. 'But to answer your question, Sergeant Marriott, Tindall had been seen alive and well after the last action in which the brigade had been involved and, indeed, after they'd been pulled back. Just to make sure, enquiries were made with the regimental aid post and the casualty clearing station. There was no trace of him anywhere. The matter was reported to Colonel Cunningham's office – Cunningham's the provost marshal of the BEF – and Tindall was officially reported as absent without leave.'

'Is there any chance he might've made it back to this country, Colonel?' asked Hardcastle.

'The brigade was down near Neuve Chapelle...' Frobisher stood up and crossed to a wall map. 'It's a good seventy miles from there to Boulogne,' he said, roughly tracing the route with a forefinger. 'Assuming he managed to get there and talk his way on to a troopship, it's a possibility. I doubt he'd've had much luck trying to get passage in a civilian craft. What few there are, are coastal fishing vessels.'

'So, he could still be in France, sir,' suggested Marriott.

Frobisher resumed his seat behind his desk. 'The short answer to that, Sergeant Marriott, is that he could be anywhere.'

'If we find him in London, Colonel,' said Hardcastle, 'we'll let you have him back. Provided he don't have an appointment with John Ellis.'

'Who?' asked Frobisher, mystified, as he so often was, by one of Hardcastle's enigmatic remarks.

'He's the official hangman,' said Hardcastle.

'D'you think that Tindall's our man, sir?' asked Marriott, when he and the DDI were back at the police station.

'I'm not so sure,' said Hardcastle pensively, a statement that surprised Marriott in view of what the DDI had said to Colonel Frobisher. 'But if Tindall is in this country, then young Villiers could be in danger.'

'There's not much we can do about that, sir.'

'Oh, but there is, Marriott. We'll have another word with Villiers.'

'Now, sir?'

'No. I think we'll call on him a bit later. Fetch Catto in here.'

'You wanted me, sir?' said Catto, displaying his usual measure of apprehension.

'You did an observation on Prince of Wales Drive on Monday, Catto, when you tracked down Captain Villiers.'

'Yes, sir.' Catto was certain that the DDI was about to find some fault with the way in which that observation had been conducted or that he was about to query the expenses that he and Watkins had incurred.

'Good. Well, you're about to do it again. I want to be certain that Captain Haydn Villiers is there before Sergeant Marriott and me go traipsing all the way out there to speak to him. Start about six this evening.'

'But how can I be sure he's there without knocking on the door, sir?' asked Catto, fearing that once again he was to be faced with an impossible task.

'Then, Catto, you knock on the bloody door. I'd've thought that was obvious. Use your common sense, but don't show out. You are supposed to be a detective, after all.'

'Yes, sir.' Catto was on surer ground now that he had a specific instruction, and turned to leave. But wondering how he could knock at the door and still not show out.

'Just a minute,' said Hardcastle. 'Have any of you learned anything from your informants about Gosling's fencing activities?'

'Not yet, sir.'

'Don't forget,' growled Hardcastle.

Henry Catto was far more confident when he was out of the DDI's presence. He rang the bell of Hannah Villiers's apartment and waited.

Having passed the hurdle of Mrs Villiers's maid, Catto was eventually shown into the drawing room.

'I'm a police officer, madam,' said Catto.

'Detective Constable Catto,' he added, producing his warrant card.

'Captain Villiers isn't here, if that's who you want,' said Mrs Villiers with a sigh. 'He's visiting his lady friend, and I've no idea where she lives.'

'I'm sorry, madam, but I don't know anything about a Captain ... who did you say?'

'There were two policemen here on Monday. Haven't you come about the same thing?'

'No, madam, I'm merely warning people in the area that there have been a number of thefts locally by a man pretending to be from the water board. He usually asks the householder to go upstairs and turn on the bathroom taps while he pretends to check the downstairs pipes for leaks. While she's doing that, he steals whatever he can lay his hands on and makes off.'

'Oh, I see. Thank you, officer. I'll be on my guard, and I'll inform my servants.'

'If any suspicious characters should call, madam, don't admit them, and call a constable.'

'Thank you,' said Hannah Villiers again, and rang for Elsie to show Catto out.

Just to guard against the possibility of Mrs Villiers mentioning his visit to her neighbours, Catto called at the apartments on either side of Mrs Villiers's and warned them against the fictitious water board official. That done, he made his way to nearby Battersea police station and sent a message to Sergeant Marriott.

* * *

111

'A message from Catto, sir. He called at Mrs Villiers's place and she told him that Haydn Villiers was visiting his lady friend, but that she didn't know where she lived. It looks as though Annabel Powell's forgiven him after all. If that's where he's gone.'

'I just hope Catto didn't blow the gaff,' said Hardcastle, as ever reluctant to give praise, even when it was due.

'He's a very reliable officer, sir.' Marriott was always finding himself in the position of defending Catto against what he saw as the DDI's unjustified criticism.

'So you say, Marriott, so you say.' Hardcastle put on his hat and coat, and took hold of his umbrella. Finally, he took his pipe from the ashtray and thrust it into his pocket. 'We'll pay another visit to Annabel Powell and have a word with young Villiers.'

'But he might have another lady friend who lives somewhere else, sir.'

'Judging by the cut of young Villiers, I wouldn't mind betting he's got a whole stable of fillies in London, Marriott,' said Hardcastle. 'But if that's the case, we'll know soon enough.'

Hardcastle beat a loud rat-a-tat on the lion's head knocker of Annabel Powell's Elm Park Gardens house. To his amazement, the door was opened by Haydn Villiers himself.

'What on earth are you doing here, Inspector?

It's not very convenient at the moment.'

'I don't suppose it is, Captain Villiers, but I have something of vital importance to tell you.'

'You'd better come in, then.' Reluctantly, Villiers showed the two CID officers into the drawing room.

'Who was that at the door, Haydn darling?' Annabel Powell, wearing the same silk kimono and slippers in which she had greeted the detectives on their last visit, swept into the drawing room. 'Oh, my good God!' she exclaimed, as she sighted Hardcastle and Marriott.

Villiers laughed. 'That's what comes of giving the maid sixpence to visit a picture house every evening, darling.'

'It's not funny,' said Annabel. 'Anyway, you know why I give her the evenings off.'

'Your secret's quite safe with me and Sergeant Marriott, Mrs Powell. I shan't tell the colonel,' said Hardcastle. 'Right now, we have bigger fish to fry.'

'Sounds serious,' said Villiers. 'You'd better sit down.'

'I have reason to believe that your life may be in danger, Captain Villiers,' said Hardcastle.

'It has been since the war started,' said Villiers, with a cheerful laugh behind which was an element of cynicism.

'I'm not talking about the war,' said Hardcastle, and went on to tell Villiers of the desertion of George Tindall. And he reminded him of the threat that Tindall had made against him.

'Crikey! I'll bet the colonel was in a temper when he found out about Tindall going adrift,' said Villiers.

'So long as that's all he finds out about,' said Annabel. Resigned to having been caught out, she had taken a seat in an armchair opposite Hardcastle and Marriott. Using both hands, she attempted to restore some order into her untidy hair.

'Do you really think he's got as far as Blighty, Inspector?' Villiers did not seem greatly disturbed by Hardcastle's information, and that made the DDI wonder.

'Your guess is as good as ours, Captain Villiers,' said Marriott. 'But the assistant provost marshal for London District doesn't know where he is, obviously, otherwise he'd've had him arrested.'

'Which is what I'll do if I find him,' said Hardcastle.

'I'm going back to France tomorrow,' said Villiers. 'Not that I'll be much safer over there.'

'D'you think that this man might come here, Inspector?' asked Annabel. Having heard of the threat that Tindall had made, she appeared more concerned than her paramour.

'I doubt it very much, Mrs Powell,' said Hardcastle, 'but be careful when you open the door. I saw that you had a chain on it; make sure you keep it fastened.'

'Do you happen to know the names of anyone Second Lieutenant Tindall owed money to,

114

Captain Villiers?' asked Marriott.

'No, I don't. But given that he was a gambler, I can only think that it's a bookmaker.'

'Watch your back over there, Captain Villiers,' said Hardcastle, as he and Marriott stood up to leave. 'As well as your front.'

'Oh, I shall, Inspector.'

'One other thing, Mrs Powell...' said Hardcastle. 'Did Captain Villiers in fact spend the night of New Year's Eve with you?'

Annabel Powell sighed. 'Of course he bloody well did, Inspector.'

Once in the street, Hardcastle paused. 'I'm going back to the office, Marriott. But I want you to call on Mrs Villiers and tell her about Tindall. It's possible that he might call there. And it would be as well if we posted a man there until Tindall is arrested.'

'Very good, sir.'

'And take a cab, Marriott.'

'Thank you, sir.' *And now he's going to tell me not to forget to take the plate number,* thought Marriott.

'And don't forget to take the plate number,' said Hardcastle.

SEVEN

It was almost half past eight by the time Marriott arrived at Prince of Wales Drive in Battersea.

'A police officer to see you, ma'am,' said Elsie, Hannah Villiers's maid, when she showed Marriott into the sitting room.

'Oh, not again! This is becoming a habit. You're the second policeman who's called here today. Is it about this bogus water board person? If it is, I was told all about it by a detective only an hour or two ago. I think he said that his name was Catto.' Hannah Villiers paused as she recognized Marriott. 'Ah, but I remember you now. You came here with that inspector on Monday.'

'That's correct, madam, and it's nothing to do with bogus water board officials,' said Marriott, making a mental note to give Catto a word of praise for his subterfuge. 'It concerns a man who has made a threat to kill your son, Captain Haydn Villiers.'

'There are thousands of men who've done that, Sergeant, and they're all Germans.' Hannah Villiers laughed, apparently declining to

116

take Marriott's warning any more seriously than her son had done.

'This one is closer to home, Mrs Villiers. He's an officer in your son's regiment. In fact, in your son's battery.' Marriott explained about the threat, and that Second Lieutenant Tindall had deserted from his brigade. 'It's possible that he's now in this country.'

'Good gracious! An officer deserting? But that's unheard of, surely?' Hannah Villiers put a hand to her mouth. 'Tindall you say? Oh, my God!' she exclaimed, suddenly remembering. 'He was here.'

'When was that, Mrs Villiers?'

'I think it was the day after Boxing Day. He called one evening and I'm sure he said his name was Tindall. He said that he was a friend of Haydn and that they were each on leave at the same time.'

'Did he say what he wanted?'

'He said something about having arranged to meet Haydn for a drink, as they were both in London. But I told him that I didn't know where Haydn was or when he'd be returning.'

'Did Tindall come back again?'

'No. He said that he'd catch up with Haydn at some other time. He didn't seem at all bothered that Haydn wasn't here, but now you say he's intent on murdering my son.'

'Did you mention Tindall's visit to your son, Mrs Villiers?'

Hannah Villiers gave a guilty laugh. 'No, I

must admit it slipped my mind. I didn't think it awfully important at the time. D'you really think it's a genuine threat, Sergeant?'

'Whether it is or not, madam, we're inclined to take such a matter seriously. My inspector and I have just spoken to your son—'

'How did you know where to find him? He didn't even tell me where he was going, other than to say he was visiting a lady friend.'

'He gave us the lady's address when we first spoke to him, Mrs Villiers.' That was untrue, of course, and Marriott did not mention the woman's name, thinking it unwise to tell Hannah Villiers that her son was bedding his colonel's wife. 'We know that Captain Villiers is returning to the Front tomorrow, but my inspector thought it might be a sensible precaution to post a police officer here, just in case Tindall should turn up looking for him.'

'D'you really think that's necessary, Sergeant?'

'Better to be safe than sorry, madam. But obviously it'll only be until your son leaves for France. Tindall will probably know that Captain Villiers's leave expires tomorrow.'

'Very well, but where will this man of yours be? In my apartment?' Hannah Villiers did not sound enamoured of the idea.

Marriott had not given that any serious thought, but immediately made a decision. 'In the entrance hall downstairs,' he said. 'In that way, he'll be in a good position to challenge anyone entering the building.'

'If you think that's best,' said Hannah Villiers, 'but Lord knows what my neighbours will think.'

'They'll not know why he's there, madam, and he'll be in plain clothes. Should your neighbours query it, you could always tell them it's in connection with this water board impersonator that the local police warned you about.' Marriott took his leave and descended to the ground floor.

'All correct, Sergeant.' Detective Constable Gordon Carter was waiting in the entrance hall to the apartments.

'What are you doing here, Carter?' asked a surprised Marriott.

'Mr Hardcastle sent me, Skip. He said that Mrs Villiers's apartment needed to have an eye kept on it in case this Tindall chap turned up.'

'But she's only just agreed to have someone posted here.'

'The DDI said he thought she would, Skip. But he said I was to keep watch here whether she agreed or not.'

'I presume you're posted here for the night, Carter. What arrangements has the guv'nor made for relieving you tomorrow morning?' Marriott, unlike the DDI, was always concerned about the welfare of junior officers.

'I don't know, but I hope someone will turn up.'

'Right, well you can stay here in the entrance

hall. Question anyone who looks suspicious, and if Tindall turns up, nick him. In the meantime, I'll make some arrangements for your relief.'

'Do we know if Captain Villiers is here, Skip?'

'No, he's not, but I doubt if it'll be long before he shows his face. He's due back from leave tomorrow, and I suppose he'll have to do some packing.'

Carter did not, however, have long to wait. Half an hour after Marriott had departed to make his way back to Cannon Row, an officer in the uniform of the Royal Artillery entered the lobby where Carter had stationed himself.

'Mr Tindall?' queried Carter, taking a chance that he was right.

'Yes.' The officer stopped and turned. 'Who are you?'

'I'm a police officer, Mr Tindall, and I'm arresting you for being a deserter from His Majesty's Land Forces.'

'I'm afraid you're making a serious mistake, Officer. I've come here to arrest Captain Villiers of the RFA, not the other way round.'

'Have you indeed? Well, he's not here. Now then,' continued Carter, taking a step closer to the officer, 'we don't want any trouble, so we'll take a cab and make our way to the police station.'

'Who's your superior? I demand to be taken

to him immediately.'

'Don't you worry about that, Mr Tindall. It's Divisional Detective Inspector Hardcastle of the Whitehall Division at Cannon Row police station, and you'll be seeing him very soon.' But Carter did not realize just how soon that would be.

It was past ten o'clock by the time Carter and his prisoner arrived at the police station. The DDI had already gone home, but Marriott was tussling with a report for the DPP when Carter entered the office.

'What are you doing back here, Carter?'

'I've got Second Lieutenant George Tindall in the charge room downstairs, Skip, and he's screaming blue murder about wanting to see the guv'nor.'

'Is he now? Well, he'll just have to wait until tomorrow morning, won't he? What were the circumstances? Did he just turn up at Battersea?'

'Yes, Skip, and what's more he said he was there to arrest Captain Villiers.'

Marriott laughed. 'A likely tale. Well, I'm not going to disturb Mr Hardcastle at this hour.' He shuffled together the papers on which he had been working and dropped them into a tray on his desk. 'I'll come down and have a word with this young shaver, and see what this cock-and-bull story of his is all about.' Buttoning up his waistcoat and donning his jacket, he followed

Carter downstairs.

The moment Marriott and Carter entered the charge room, Tindall leaped to his feet, only to be restrained by the uniformed constable who was guarding him.

'Are you Inspector Hardcastle?' said Tindall, shaking off the constable's hand.

'No, I'm Detective Sergeant Marriott.'

'I demand to see this inspector,' said Tindall.

'You're in no position to demand anything,' said Marriott. 'You've been arrested by Detective Constable Carter for being a deserter, and you'll appear before the Bow Street magistrate tomorrow morning. Unless, of course, you admit to being a deserter, in which case you'll be handed over to the military police.'

'Then I need to see the assistant provost marshal immediately, Sergeant. In the circumstances you leave me no alternative.'

'You told Detective Constable Carter that you'd gone to Prince of Wales Drive to arrest Captain Villiers. Is that correct?' Marriott posed the question with an amused expression on his face.

'Yes, that is correct.'

'I think you'd better explain yourself.' Marriott was highly suspicious of Tindall's statement, certain that it was a device to avoid being handed over to the military, either before or after a court appearance. He dismissed Tindall's request to see the APM as mere bluster.

Tindall emitted a deep sigh and for a moment

or two sunk into a mood of contemplation.

'I can see we've reached an impasse, Sergeant,' he said eventually. 'But you must understand that what I am about to tell you is in the strictest confidence. Much depends on the work I've been doing.' He withdrew a document from his breast pocket and handed it to Marriott. 'I am Captain Hugh Wetherby of the Royal Garrison Artillery, seconded to the Military Foot Police.'

Marriott studied the document closely before returning it. 'That seems to be genuine enough,' he said.

'Oh, it is, Sergeant, I can assure you. And now I need to see the APM as a matter of urgency. It's of vital importance to the security of the state.'

'That could be a problem, Captain Wetherby. We only ever talk to the APM at his office at Horse Guards. And he's only there during working hours. I've no idea how to contact him at this time of night.'

'There's a detachment of the Military Mounted Police at Great Scotland Yard,' said Wetherby. 'They should have a night duty NCO, and he'll know how to get in touch with the APM.' He took out a cigarette case and offered it to Marriott and Carter. 'And I must again emphasize the urgency.'

'I'll do what I can,' said Marriott, declining the offer of a cigarette. He turned to Carter. 'Get down to Great Scotland Yard as fast as you can, and tell the duty NCO that it's necessary for me to get in touch with Colonel Frobisher as quickly as possible. I've no idea where he lives, but if he can telephone me at the nick it might save a lot of time. But do *not* tell the military police NCO you speak to what it's about.' That done, he slid open the glass panel between the charge room and the front office. 'Send an urgent message to Kennington Road nick, Harry, and get an officer to call on the DDI. He's to tell Mr Hardcastle that Tindall has been arrested, but that there are complications that require his attendance here immediately.'

'Right you are, Charlie, but I doubt that that'll make you his favourite skipper,' said the station officer, and began writing on a message pad.

'Was I ever?' muttered Marriott.

'I don't believe it.' Hardcastle was in the act of checking the blackout curtains before going to bed when there was a knock at the door. A policeman was standing on the step. 'What the hell is it now, lad?'

'An urgent message from Cannon Row, sir,' said the young constable, proffering a message form. 'And it's bucketing down,' he added, risking a grin. The PC's helmet and cape were glistening with rain.

'I can see that,' muttered Hardcastle, as he quickly scanned the brief missive. 'God Almighty!' he exclaimed. 'Can't they deal with a simple knock-off of a deserter without sending

124

for me? All right, lad, find me a cab while I get my coat and hat.' He walked to the foot of the stairs. He knew that his wife would still be awake and reading one of the women's magazines to which she subscribed. 'I've got to go back to the station, Alice.'

'You take care, Ernie,' came Alice's voice from the bedroom.

Unbeknown to Marriott, Colonel Frobisher, the assistant provost marshal, had an apartment in Admiralty Arch at the other end of Whitehall, within walking distance of the police station. When a military police sergeant telephoned him, the NCO received a response similar to that made by Hardcastle when he had been called out.

Hardcastle and Frobisher arrived at the entrance to the police station at the same time.

'What are you doing here at this hour, Colonel?'

'I was about to ask you the same question, Inspector,' said Frobisher. 'According to the message I got from your Sergeant Marriott, it's something to do with Second Lieutenant Tindall. Apparently your chaps have arrested him.'

'So I understand,' muttered Hardcastle. 'You had better come up to my office, Colonel.' He opened the door to the front office. 'Tell Sergeant Marriott to bring Tindall up to my office, Skipper.'

'Yes, sir,' said the station officer, and walked

through to the charge room.

It was fast approaching midnight by the time that Frobisher, Marriott, Carter and the officer claiming to be Captain Wetherby, were crowded into the DDI's office.

'Get some more chairs in here, Carter,' said Hardcastle, 'and then we'll find out what all the fuss is about.'

Once the group was settled, Frobisher studied the artillery officer closely. 'I think you'd better explain why it's necessary for Inspector Hardcastle and me to be called out at this hour of the night, Tindall.'

'This is a very delicate matter, sir. I think it would be better if I spoke to you in private.'

Frobisher, who was no less pleased at being called out than was Hardcastle, was in no mood to be dictated to by a junior officer. 'Whatever you have to tell me, you can do so in front of Inspector Hardcastle. He's a senior police officer and I trust him implicitly.'

'I am Captain Hugh Wetherby of the Royal Garrison Artillery, attached to the Military Foot Police, Colonel.' After a pause during which he decided that he was not going to get his own way, Wetherby had eventually yielded.

'Are you indeed?' said Frobisher, as yet unconvinced by the officer's claim. 'In that case, you'll have a warrant signed by the provost marshal.'

'I have indeed, Colonel.' Wetherby produced the document he had previously shown Marriott. It bore the signature of Brigadier General Edward Fitzpatrick, Provost Marshal of the British Army, and testified to the holder being an officer of the Military Foot Police engaged on undefined 'special duties'.

'That seems to be in order,' said Frobisher, returning the warrant. 'Now perhaps you'll tell me what's so damned important that you require my presence here.'

Once again, Wetherby glanced around at the assembled officers.

'You can go, Carter,' said Hardcastle, sensing that Wetherby would be happier with less people in the office. 'Think yourself lucky you've got the night off. Make sure you're here at eight o'clock tomorrow morning.'

'Yes, sir, thank you, sir,' said Carter, thinking that to be back at the police station in less than eight hours' time was not as lucky as the DDI seemed to believe.

'D'you mind if I smoke, Colonel?' asked Wetherby.

'It's Mr Hardcastle's office, Captain Wetherby. Ask him, not me.' Frobisher was still irritated at being roused from his bed at the behest of a captain.

Hardcastle waved a hand of permission and lit his pipe.

'As a matter of interest, Captain Wetherby, how did you get back to this country?' asked Frobisher, still doubtful about the officer's story. 'You were posted as deserter from your brigade.' The APM, a non-smoker, waved away the smoke of both Hardcastle's pipe and Wetherby's cigarette.

'Quite easily, Colonel. Surprising though it may seem, I just walked away from the brigade early on the morning of Christmas Day. I identified myself to the first military policeman I came across, and arrangements were made for me to travel by train to Boulogne and cross to Blighty from there on a troopship.'

'When I interviewed Captain Villiers he said something about you being in debt all over the place, including gambling heavily,' said Hardcastle. 'And that you threatened him.'

Wetherby laughed. 'Villiers took a violent dislike to me the moment we met, Inspector. I wondered briefly whether he suspected I wasn't the George Tindall I claimed to be, which was a little disturbing. And I wondered if he had somehow discovered that I was a provost officer. But I can assure you that there was no conversation between us about any supposed debts, neither did I threaten him.'

'Can we get back to why you intended to arrest Captain Villiers, Wetherby?' Frobisher was becoming impatient.

'Some time ago, Colonel,' Wetherby began, 'field intelligence officers...' He paused and glanced at Hardcastle. 'As a matter of fact, they were Special Branch officers from the Metropolitan Police attached to army headquarters, Inspector.'

'Were they indeed?' Hardcastle had jousted with the political department of the Metropolitan Police on more than one occasion, and had not enjoyed the experience. Little did he know then, though, that he was about to become involved with Special Branch more closely than before.

'As I was saying,' continued Wetherby, 'field intelligence officers, aided by their French opposite numbers, intercepted Morse code signals being sent from a house about two miles behind our lines at Neuve Chapelle. The signal was tracked and proved to be coming from a house occupied by a French Jew named Pierre Benoit, a farmer. But he turned out to be more than just a farmer. When the house was raided it was found that Benoit was in possession of both Morse code equipment and information regarding the disposition and strength of various British Army units. And more than those in the immediate Neuve Chapelle area. Under interrogation, he revealed that he was spying on behalf of the Germans. Enquiries are now in hand to discover the other sources of his information, although I doubt we will identify them, now that Benoit is in custody.'

'But why?' asked Frobisher. 'What motive could a French Jew possibly have for giving this sort of information to the Germans?'

'After a little of what you might call gentle persuasion by his French interrogators,' continued Wetherby with a smile, 'Benoit admitted that the Germans wanted to pass it on to the Ottomans. They had apparently promised the Zionist movement a Jewish homeland in Palestine under a Turkish or German mandate after the war was over. But this could only be achieved if the British and French were defeated.'

'This here Benoit seems to know a lot for a farmer,' commented Hardcastle drily.

'But hasn't our government also promised a homeland to the Jews, under a British mandate?' queried Frobisher.

'So I believe, Colonel, but apparently the Zionists don't trust us. However, Benoit agreed to continue passing information to the enemy. But that information would in future be furnished by our people and would, of course, be misleading.'

'Do we know who was at the receiving end of these Morse code messages that Benoit was sending?'

'No, Colonel, although it's been suggested that it might be someone in London. I understand that MI5 is trying to identify the recipient.'

'Good luck,' said Hardcastle, who dismissed MI5 as a bunch of amateurs trying to be detectives.

'But what has any of this to do with Haydn Villiers, Captain Wetherby?' asked Frobisher, impatient to get to the nub of the matter.

'Ah yes, Captain Villiers. Our enquiries have revealed that Villiers is of Jewish extraction, and makes no secret of his passion about this business of a homeland.'

'But how did you know that Villiers was involved?' asked Frobisher. A tension had arisen in the office as the police officers, civil and military, waited to see what was coming next.

'After his arrest, Colonel, Benoit, under threat of the guillotine, admitted that this information had come from Villiers. Quite simply, Villiers called at the farm, usually about once a week, to obtain eggs, chickens and milk, and that's when he handed over the information. That tallied because much of the intelligence concerned the theatre of war in which Villiers was serving. However, we were not prepared to take a French farmer's word that a British officer was a traitor. In an attempt to obtain confirmation the provost marshal arranged for me to be posted to Villiers's brigade as Second Lieutenant George Tindall. Unfortunately, Villiers went off on leave before I could find out anything substantive.'

'But if he was a suspect, why was he allowed to return home on leave?' asked Marriott.

'Very simply,' said Wetherby, 'because his commanding officer knew nothing of Villiers's involvement or, for that matter, mine, and it was thought safer not to tell him. The fewer people who know about these operations, the better. Consequently, there was nothing that could be done to prevent Colonel Powell granting him furlough over the Christmas period.'

'If he knew what else Villiers was going to get up to when he got home, he might've had second thoughts about giving him leave at all,' commented Hardcastle quietly.

'What was he up to, Inspector?' asked Wetherby, a puzzled expression on his face.

'Every night since he got back here, he's been sleeping with Colonel Powell's wife, Captain Wetherby.'

'Good God!' exclaimed Wetherby. 'Is that true?'

'I thought you said that that was just a rumour, Inspector.' Frobisher was as surprised as Wetherby had been.

'I only said it was a rumour because I thought it would be seen as an offence by the army, but a not very serious one.'

'On the contrary, Inspector. That sort of behaviour is taken very seriously,' said Frobisher.

'But it doesn't really matter, does it, because I suppose you'll hang him now?' said Hardcastle. 'For spying, I mean, not for having a bit of jig-a-jig with Annabel Powell.'

'Agreed,' said Wetherby. 'If he's guilty of spying he'll undoubtedly be executed.'

'What d'you want to do about arresting Villiers, Captain Wetherby?' asked Frobisher.

'He's probably on his way to Southampton already, Colonel. The best idea is to alert the assistant provost marshal there and have Villiers detained when he attempts to board the troopship. I'll travel down and personally take him into custody.'

'If you come across to my office in Horse Guards Arch, we can arrange it from there.' Frobisher stood up. 'By the bye, why did it take you so long to track down Villiers, given that you must've arrived here on Boxing Day or the day after?'

'I didn't know where he was, Colonel. I called at the Battersea address, but his mother told me that she had no idea where he'd gone. But knowing that he was due back from furlough tomorrow, I guessed that he'd be there this evening to pack.'

'Well, he wasn't, Captain Wetherby. I'd already checked,' said Marriott. 'But as Mr Hardcastle and I had spoken to Villiers earlier this evening, and suggested that you had deserted and were intent on murdering him, it's possible that he took flight.'

'Whatever made you think I was going to murder him?' asked Wetherby, clearly amazed by this latest revelation.

'We didn't,' said Marriott. 'Villiers did.'

'It might've been better if we'd been told of your suspicions, Captain Wetherby,' said Hardcastle. 'We could've nicked him for you. However, if you do manage to knock him off at Southampton, where will he be taken?'

Wetherby glanced at Frobisher before replying. 'He'll be brought back to London, Inspector.'

Frobisher nodded his agreement before turning to Hardcastle. 'He'll probably be confined in the Tower of London. Do you have an interest in this officer, Inspector?' he asked.

'Yes, I do, Colonel. Although it's been confirmed that on the night Reuben Gosling was murdered, he was in Mrs Powell's bed, he might know more than he's telling about his father's car and its involvement in that murder.'

'If he was a party to that murder, it'll make no difference to the sentence,' said Frobisher.

'Only whether they'll hang him instead of shooting him, I suppose,' said Hardcastle drily.

'Oh, he'll be shot, Inspector,' said Frobisher. 'As an army officer, he's entitled to a firing squad.'

'I've no doubt he'll be delighted at being accorded that privilege,' said Hardcastle.

It was almost two o'clock on Friday morning before Hardcastle and Marriott got to bed. Nevertheless, they were back at the police station by eighty thirty the same morning.

But before then, the arrest of Captain Haydn Villiers had been effected, somewhat unceremoniously, on a cold quayside at Southampton docks.

EIGHT

At six o'clock on that same Friday morning, a line of army officers was waiting to pass through the military police checkpoint at Southampton prior to boarding the troopship that would take them to Boulogne.

Captain Haydn Villiers of the Royal Field Artillery handed his identity document, leave pass and movement order to a military police corporal.

The corporal briefly scanned the documents and returned them. Turning his head, he signalled to Lieutenant Colonel Lionel Chapman of the Manchester Regiment, the assistant provost marshal of Southampton Garrison.

As Villiers walked towards the gangway, the colonel tapped him on the shoulder. 'Captain Villiers?'

'Sir?' Villiers turned to face Chapman and saluted.

'Be so good as to come with me, please, Captain Villiers.'

'Is there a problem, Colonel?'

'You could say that, yes,' replied Chapman with a smile.

Villiers followed the APM, but failed to notice the two military police NCOs who fell in behind him. He wondered why he was being prevented from boarding, positive that he was not late in returning from leave.

But then other thoughts crowded into his mind. Had something happened to one of his parents? Perhaps his father had had an accident in that high-powered car of his, or his mother had been killed in an air raid. And surely to God, no one had found out about his brief affair with Annabel Powell. These and a dozen other questions flashed through his mind during the short walk to an office over which was a sign that said MILITARY POLICE.

'Come in and take a seat,' said Chapman affably. He ushered Villiers into the office, and glanced at the two NCOs. 'Carry on.'

Villiers entered the sparsely furnished, workmanlike office, and was astounded to see George Tindall seated in a chair near a glowing pot-bellied stove. Suddenly Villiers thought he understood why he was there, and felt a great sense of relief that he was not in trouble himself, or that bad news about a member of his family was about to be broken to him.

It all now became clear. The police officers who had interviewed him in London had passed on what he had told them about Tindall being in serious debt and they had informed the military.

Tindall was obviously under arrest and, as the officer's battery commander, Villiers would be required to make a statement about the officer's indebtedness. But at the same time he knew that he would have to think quickly if he were to maintain the entire fiction of Tindall being in debt and a gambler who had lost heavily. He did not like Tindall and wanted rid of him from his battery. In his view, Tindall was an overconfident Scotsman, and far from being a gentleman.

Villiers, beneficiary of a privileged upbringing and a public school education, could not tolerate an officer who was not a gentleman. The truth of the matter was that Tindall had unwittingly riled Villiers from the moment they had met; instinctively he had seen Tindall as a threat. There was something that was not quite right about the man. But Villiers was confident that anything he said about Tindall would be accepted without question by the assistant provost marshal, and later, a court martial.

There was something else, too. Villiers's commanding officer, Colonel Powell, would not have granted leave to two officers in the same battery at the same time. So, it was true what Hardcastle had said: Tindall was a deserter. That was even better; that would mean a firing squad. General Sir Douglas Haig, recently appointed commander in chief of the British Expeditionary Force, would have no qualms about confirming the death sentence on an officer who had abandoned his post in the face of the enemy.

But then Villiers's world fell apart.

'This gentleman,' said the APM, indicating the officer Villiers believed to be Second Lieutenant George Tindall, 'is Captain Hugh Wetherby of the Royal Garrison Artillery, attached to the Military Foot Police, and he has a warrant for your arrest on a charge of imparting information to the enemy. That warrant is signed by the Provost Marshal.'

The blood drained from Villiers's face, and had he not been seated would undoubtedly have fallen to the floor in a dead faint.

'This is preposterous,' he gasped eventually, gripping the arms of his chair. 'What makes you think I have done such a thing? There must be some mistake.'

Ignoring Villiers's protestations, Wetherby said, 'You will be taken to London, Captain Villiers, where you will be further questioned.'

Villiers turned to the APM. 'But this man is George Tindall, an officer in my battery, Colonel. He's a liar and a cheat, and a deserter as well.' It was a desperate statement, but Villiers knew that none of that was true, apart from Tindall being a deserter. And Villiers also knew that the allegations being made against himself were not without foundation.

Lieutenant Colonel Chapman just smiled.

By the time that Hardcastle and Marriott arrived at Cannon Row police station at eight thirty, Captain Haydn Villiers was already lodged in an officer's quarter in the Tower of London, guarded by a captain in the Grenadier Guards.

It was midday when Sergeant Glover, the APM's clerk, appeared in Hardcastle's office, just as the DDI was discussing the Gosling case, yet again, with Marriott.

'Colonel Frobisher has asked me to tell you that Captain Villiers is under arrest, Inspector. He thought it best to let you know in person, rather than by telephone.'

'Quite right, Sergeant Glover,' said the DDI. 'Whereabouts is he being held?'

'In the Tower of London, Inspector. Where else?' Glover permitted himself a brief smile. 'But the real reason I've called in is that Colonel Frobisher wished to know if you wanted to interview Captain Villiers about the murder you're investigating.'

'Thank the colonel for me, Sergeant Glover, but there wouldn't be any point in my talking to Villiers. I'm satisfied with the alibi that he gave for the time of the murder. And despite what I told Colonel Frobisher last night, I have since decided that Villiers had nothing to do with the murder.'

'I'll let him know straight away, Inspector.'

'I wonder if there's a connection even so, sir,' said Marriott, once Glover had departed.

'Connection? What sort of connection?'

'One of the things we learned from Captain Wetherby, sir, is that Villiers is of Jewish extraction; you probably noticed that his mother was wearing the Star of David as a necklet.'

'Of course I did, Marriott. I don't miss things like that.'

'Reuben Gosling was a Jew and a fence,' continued Marriott, 'and I wondered if there was a connection between the two, bearing in mind that the Frenchman Benoit was also a Jew.'

'What on earth are you talking about, Marriott?' asked Hardcastle, his face expressing amazement.

'It was just a thought, sir.' Marriott knew that if the DDI had floated such an idea, he would have expected it to be taken seriously. 'And Wetherby said that Haydn Villiers is just as passionate about a Jewish homeland as Benoit. I wondered if Reuben Gosling was the man who was receiving the Morse code messages that Wetherby mentioned.'

But any further discussion on the matter was interrupted by the arrival of a smartly dressed young man in the DDI's doorway.

'Mr Hardcastle, sir?'

'Yes. Who are you?'

'Detective Constable Sean Rafferty of Special Branch, sir.'

'Oh dear, Marriott!' exclaimed Hardcastle. 'Something tells me that the arrival of Detective Constable Rafferty does not bode well.'

'Mr Quinn sends his compliments, sir,' said Rafferty, 'and would be grateful if you would see him as soon as possible. He's in his office now.'

'Very well, Rafferty.' Hardcastle knew that when a superintendent wanted to see him 'as soon as possible', it meant immediately.

Superintendent Patrick Quinn, head of Special Branch for the past twelve years, was a tall, austere-looking man with a grey goatee beard, an aquiline nose and black, bushy eyebrows beneath which piercing blue eyes stared searchingly at the world.

'Divisional Detective Inspector Hardcastle of A Division, sir. I understand you wanted to see me.'

'That's correct.' For a moment or two, Quinn studied the inspector who now stood in front of his desk. 'I have a job for you.'

'But I'm heavily engaged investigating a murder at the moment, sir.' Hardcastle could well do without an additional task.

'I presume you're talking of the murder of Reuben Gosling, the pawnbroker and receiver of stolen goods, Inspector.' Quinn spoke with a soft Mayo accent; like many members of what had originally been the Special Irish Branch, he hailed from the Emerald Isle.

'Yes, sir.' Hardcastle was amazed that Quinn, so concerned with security matters, was aware of what was happening on A Division.

'You'd better hand the day-to-day running of that investigation over to Neville. He is one of your deputies, isn't he?'

Detective Inspector Alexander Neville was in

charge of the CID for the Rochester Row sub-division, but Hardcastle had no intention of handing him the investigation.

'Yes, sir, but the problem is—' he began.

'This is far more important, Mr Hardcastle,' said Quinn, interrupting sharply. 'I understand that you were recently involved in enquiries into the activities of Captain Haydn Villiers of the Royal Field Artillery who is being detained in the Tower of London.'

'That's correct, sir.'

'I know it's correct, Mr Hardcastle. I make it my business to know about such things. You'll be aware therefore, that Allied intelligence sources have discovered that a Frenchman named Pierre Benoit was using Morse code to transmit the information he got from Villiers. And it was, they believed, being sent to some-one in this country.'

'Yes, sir, that was mentioned.' Hardcastle was amazed at the depth of Quinn's knowledge about something that was occurring in France.

'Therefore, you probably know that MI5 were asked to assist in identifying the recipient of that information,' continued Quinn.

'Yes, sir, so I understand.' Hardcastle was beginning to wonder why he was being told all this.

'A man called Peter Stein was found shot to death early this morning in his lodgings at Bow Road on H Division.'

'I'm afraid that name doesn't mean anything

142

to me, sir.' Hardcastle was busy wracking his brains in case it had been mentioned by Wetherby or had come up in connection with the Gosling murder. He was finding some difficulty in following Quinn's mercurial account.

'It wouldn't,' said Quinn bluntly, 'but it will. MI5 has identified Stein as the man to whom they believed Benoit was sending his messages. And now he's dead. As you've been involved, up to a point, with this matter, I am directing you to discover who murdered him. And I suggest you start by speaking to the DDI on H Division who will doubtless be pleased to hand over the enquiry to you.'

Detective Sergeant Herbert Wood was waiting outside Hardcastle's office when the DDI returned.

'What d'you want, Wood?' Hardcastle beckoned Wood to follow him into his office.

'It's about the enquiries we were making to find out if anyone else was fencing stolen property to Reuben Gosling, sir.'

'I now know he's a fence, Wood.' Hardcastle waved a dismissive hand. 'You can forget all about that. Far more important things have since occurred that I have to deal with now.'

'Very good, sir.' Wood, fuming inwardly, returned to the detectives' office. He and his fellow officers had spent hours talking to informants, and in some cases buying them beer, only to be told by the DDI that the information they had gleaned was no longer of any consequence.

Two officers, each attired in an army uniform bearing the red gorget patches of the General Staff, were shown into the comfortably appointed room occupied by Captain Haydn Villiers at the Tower of London. One of the officers purported to be a colonel, the other a major. In fact, the two officers were from MI5 and the ranks they held were honorary. At that moment, they were unaware of the death of Peter Stein and its ramifications. Not that it mattered; they were here for a different reason.

'Perhaps you would leave us,' said the colonel, addressing the Grenadier Guards captain who was acting as Villiers's escort.

The Grenadier, aware of the visitors' true identity, just nodded and left the room to take up station outside.

The two MI5 officers settled themselves in the comfortable armchairs with which the room was furnished. The colonel opened a slim folder and rested it on his knee.

'Captain Villiers, you will shortly be charged with serious offences under the Official Secrets Act,' began the colonel.

'What in hell's name has that to do with the General Staff?' asked Villiers rudely. 'I suppose you're base wallahs from Intelligence who've never seen a shot fired in anger.'

'It won't help your case to adopt that sort of

churlish attitude, Villiers,' said the colonel mildly.

'Is anything likely to help my case?'

'That depends on you. If you are prepared to give us details of your contacts, other than Pierre Benoit whom we know about, it's possible that the authorities may take a more benevolent view of your treachery.'

'The hell they will!' scoffed Villiers. 'I don't think you really understand what this is all about.'

'We know that you and your supporters harbour some idealistic concept that the Jews will one day be given a homeland and a state of their own.'

'It's more than idealistic,' snapped Villiers. 'The Ottomans have promised it to us, whereas the British have merely paid lip service to some half-baked proposals that they have no intention of honouring.'

'You're hardly in a position to talk of honour, Captain Villiers,' observed the major quietly.

'Clearly we each have a different concept of honour, Major, and it depends on one's standpoint,' said Villiers. 'And in answer to your question, Colonel,' he said, turning to the other officer, 'I refuse to give you any information whatsoever.'

The colonel closed his folder and stood up. 'In that case you will almost certainly face a firing squad. Is that what you want, Captain Villiers?'

'I am not the only one prepared to die for our cause,' said Villiers. 'You may not live long enough to see it, Colonel, but one day there will be a sovereign state of Israel.'

'We'll leave you with your dreams, then, Captain Villiers,' said the colonel, as he and the major left the room.

Hardcastle and Marriott arrived at Bow Road police station at half past two. Having identified himself to the station officer, Hardcastle mounted the stairs to the DDI's office on the first floor.

Carl Sawyer was the divisional detective inspector of the H or Whitechapel Division, but was known invariably as 'Tom'. Fifty-two years of age, he was a rotund, jovial fellow with full sideburns, a flowing moustache and thinning auburn hair, and had spent all his service in the East End of London. An unashamed rough diamond, he was regarded by policemen and villains alike as a walking encyclopedia of local criminals, their methods and their families. He had even been known to give the occasional few shillings to the family of a villain he had been instrumental in having put away, knowing that the man's dependants were, as a result, in dire straits.

'Welcome to where the real police work's done, Ernie.' Sawyer laughed the moment that Hardcastle entered his office. 'You've caught a good one this time, and bloody glad I am to get shot of it,' he said, crossing the room with his hand outstretched.

'Oh, you don't know just how grateful I am to you, Tom. There's nothing I like more than having a good murder to get my teeth into,' said Hardcastle with heavy irony. 'This here is DS Marriott, my bag-carrier,' he added, indicating his sergeant.

'You have my deepest sympathy, Skipper.' Sawyer laughed again as he shook hands with Marriott, and then invited his guests to take a seat. Taking a bottle of whisky and three glasses from the bottom drawer of his desk, he poured liberal measures.

'To be honest, Tom, I don't see why I'm getting stuck with this topping,' said Hardcastle, taking a sip of whisky.

'Nor do I,' said Sawyer. 'Apparently Arthur Ward created merry hell about it. He reckoned that an East End topping ought to stay with East End coppers.' Ward, an ailing detective chief inspector, destined to die before the year was out, was the head of the CID and had his office at Scotland Yard. 'But Patrick Quinn outranks him, *and* he has the ear of Basil Thomson. So that was that.' Since the outbreak of war, Thomson, the assistant commissioner for crime, had taken a greater interest in the workings of Special Branch almost to the exclusion of ordinary crime. 'Your trouble, Ernie, is that you're too handy, being just across the road from the Yard. You ought to put in for a transfer to a working division.'

'Have you caught Jack the Ripper yet, Tom?' asked Hardcastle. 'His toppings were on your manor, weren't they?'

'You certainly know how to punch below the belt, Ernie,' said Sawyer with a laugh.

'Well, the message I got was that you couldn't cope and needed help from a real detective, Tom. And I'll thank you for a drop more of that Scotch of yours.' Hardcastle pushed his glass across the desk.

'Where's Stein's body now, sir?' asked Marriott, attempting to steer the conversation away from badinage and back to the reason for their being there.

'We were going to shift it to St Clement's hospital for a start, Skip,' said Sawyer. 'Just down the road, but that was until Dr Spilsbury turned up. He's doing the post-mortem and he ordered it to be moved to St Mary's in Paddington. And that's where it is now.'

'At least that's on the decent side of my toby,' said Hardcastle, finishing his whisky. 'Well, I suppose we'd better have a look at where Stein was topped.'

Sawyer grabbed his bowler hat and paused only to tell one of his detectives where he was going.

Peter Stein had lived in lodgings over a chandler's shop within walking distance of the police station. A constable was stationed outside.

Tom Sawyer pushed open the door of the shop and strode in, followed by Hardcastle and Marriott.

'Hello, Mr Sawyer.' The chandler wiped his hands on a dirty cloth, and nodded to H Division's DDI.

'This here is Percy Dyer, Ernie,' said Sawyer. 'Used to be a useful boxer in his time, but then he took to burgling. But a carpet in Pentonville nick soon sorted him out. Didn't it, Perce?'

'That it did, Mr Sawyer. But you know as well as me that I'm going straight now.'

'Maybe,' said Sawyer pensively. 'So how come someone in a room over your shop gets hisself topped, eh?'

'Oh, come on, Mr Sawyer, you know that weren't nothing to do with me.'

'Yes, I know, Perce,' said Sawyer. 'Topping ain't your style. Anyhow, we're going up there to take a gander.'

'How long's that copper going to be stuck outside my shop, Mr Sawyer?'

'As long as Mr Hardcastle here thinks he ought to stay. Why? Putting the mockers on your trade, is he?'

'I ain't no fence, Mr Sawyer, if that's what you're thinking,' exclaimed Dyer nervously.

'I know that, Perce. You wouldn't dare, being only a stride from the nick.'

'What d'you know about this murder, Mr Dyer?' asked Hardcastle.

'It was about half past six this morning, sir. I

was woken up by shouts coming from Stein's room and then I heard a shot. So I leaped out of bed just in time to hear someone racing down the back stairs. Then I heard a door slam. I s'pose it was the back door into the alley. So, I went into Stein's room and found him dead on the floor. So I got dressed a bit *jildi*, told the missus to stay where she was and legged it down to the nick.'

'I had one of my lads take a statement from Percy here, Ernie,' said Sawyer. 'It's down at the nick. Now then, Perce, let me and these gentlemen through the shop, save us going round the back alleyway.'

Passing through a door at the rear of the shop, the three detectives mounted a rickety staircase to the first floor.

'All correct, sir,' said a second constable stationed there.

'Anyone been nosing around since I was here last, son?' asked Sawyer.

'No, sir.'

'That's all right, then,' said Sawyer, and pushed open the door of the first room on the right, a room that was immediately over the shop and facing the road. 'This is where he was found, Ernie.'

Hardcastle glanced around the small room. A filthy rug covered part of the boarded floor. There was an iron-framed bed with a bare mattress, a couple of crumpled blankets and a ticking-covered pillow. In one corner was a washstand on which were a chipped bowl and a ewer.

'Where exactly, Tom?' asked Hardcastle.

'Right there on the carpet, if you can call it that. You can see the bloodstains. Stein was wearing a pair of dirty underpants and a vest when he was found, and must've leaped out of bed when his killer came in. He was lying on his back, and he'd been shot in the chest. I reckon he was a goner before he had time to draw a second breath. I was called out at about five minutes to seven and the divisional surgeon got here at around half past eight.'

'Any idea what the motive was, sir?' asked Marriott.

'Your guess is as good as mine, Skip, but I reckon you can rule out robbery. It doesn't look as though Stein had anything worth nicking. Mind you, there was a couple of blokes from Special Branch who turned up, straight after the murder was reported to the Yard.'

'There's a surprise,' said Hardcastle. 'What did they want?'

'Damned if I know, Ernie,' said Sawyer. 'You know what that lot's like; always play their cards close to their chest. But they did take some equipment and a writing pad away with them.'

'What sort of equipment?' Hardcastle took a sudden interest; Quinn had mentioned something about Morse code equipment.

'It was a sort of key thing and a set of earphones. I asked them why they wanted it, but they wouldn't tell me. Personally I thought Stein had nicked it.' Sawyer spent a few minutes filling his pipe and lighting it.

'How did Dr Spilsbury get involved, sir?' asked Marriott.

'The divisional surgeon reckoned that a murder was too much for him; he usually only deals with prisoners who have been injured prior to their arrest and that sort of thing. He sent for Spilsbury who arrived at about ten. There wasn't much he could do here, of course, other than to ask for the body to be sent to St Mary's hospital. We already knew the time of death from what Dyer had told us.'

'Bit of a dog's dinner,' commented Hardcastle.

'The next thing I know is Arthur Ward getting in touch and telling me that this job was down to you, Ernie, but I still don't know why. Anyway, good luck.'

Hardcastle thought it unreasonable that Sawyer should not have been told, and despite what Quinn had said about the need for secrecy, decided to tell the H Division DDI what he knew.

'Well I'm buggered,' said Sawyer, once Hardcastle had explained why he had become involved. 'So that's it. Are you saying that Stein was a bloody spy, Ernie?'

'Special Branch seems to think so, Tom.'

'In that case I've probably wasted my time

sending my men out to lean on their snouts.'

'You never know,' said Hardcastle, who set great store by the value of informants. 'Just because Special Branch reckon he was spying don't mean that some of the local villains don't know anything.'

'If I hear anything, Ernie, I'll let you know. I s'pose you've got one of those telephone instruments, being the Royal A Division?'

'Yes, we have,' said Hardcastle. 'Another flash in the pan. It won't last, Tom, you mark my words. We always managed to do the job without all this newfangled rubbish they're giving us.'

'I sometimes think I'm getting too old for this job, Ernie. It all seems to be passing me by. I'll be glad when I've got me time in and I can push off to some nice little cottage in the country with my Martha. Somewhere in Kent takes me fancy.'

Hardcastle laughed. 'You'd be bored out of your mind, Tom.'

'Not me, Ernie. A nice little garden with a few roses, and the grandchildren coming to see us. No, I can't wait.'

'You mentioned back stairs just now, sir, and a back alley,' said Marriott.

'Yes, there's an alley that leads off Harley Grove, Skipper. It gives access to the rear of these premises,' said Sawyer. 'I had a look at the door this morning and there aren't any locks. Anyone could've walked in and it looks as though someone did.'

'And made his escape the same way,' suggested Hardcastle.

'That's about the strength of it, Ernie.'

'Well, there's not much here to whet our appetite,' said Hardcastle, as he began wandering around the small room. Stein appeared to have owned very little in the way of personal property. A cupboard contained a few items of clothing and a pair of boots in need of repair.

'This coat's got a button missing, sir,' said Marriott, taking a worn, serge reefer jacket from the back of the only chair in the room. 'There should be six buttons, but there's only five. And I'd swear they match the one we found in Gosling's shop. There's what looks like bloodstains on it, too, sir.'

Hardcastle took hold of the jacket and examined it closely. 'I think you're right, Marriott. Bring it with you. And bring those boots with you, too. If they don't match the footprint we found in Gosling's shop, Kaiser Bill's my uncle.' He felt in the pockets of the reefer jacket. 'Well, well,' he said, taking out a silver necklace, a wristwatch and an albert watch chain. 'If these ain't proceeds from Gosling's shop, I don't deserve to be a DDI.'

'D'you think this topping's tied up with another job, then, Ernie?' asked Sawyer.

Hardcastle explained about the murder of Reuben Gosling.

'How lucky can you get?' said Sawyer, laughing once again. 'Two for the price of one.'

'Maybe,' said Hardcastle thoughtfully. 'When you examined Stein's body, Tom, did you happen to notice whether he'd got a cut on either of his hands?'

'Now you come to mention it, Ernie, he had a bandage on his right hand. I didn't look any further, but I dare say Dr Spilsbury will be able to give you chapter and verse.'

'What about fingerprints, Tom?' asked Hardcastle.

'Oh, I never bother with that, Ernie. I know where to find my villains, and I've got some good snouts on the manor.'

Hardcastle, who had himself only recently begun to appreciate the value of this comparatively new science, nodded. 'Yes, Tom, I think you're right; the Job is passing you by. I'll get Charlie Collins down here to give the place the once over. You never know, I might get lucky.'

'And luck is what you'll need, Ernie.'

'I've just had a thought, Marriott,' said Hardcastle.

'Really, sir?' Marriott tried to keep the sarcasm from his voice; he knew that the DDI's 'thoughts' often led the enquiry off on some wild goose chase.

'Have a look at the windows. It's just possible that the sash weight we found in Gosling's shop came from here.'

Marriott crossed to the only window in the room. The glass was filthy and it was almost

155

impossible to see out of it. He attempted to raise the lower window, but succeeded only after applying all his strength.

'You're right, sir. The wooden fillet has been removed and the left-hand weight is missing.'

'I'll put money on it being the one that Catto found under the cabinet in Gosling's shop, Marriott,' said Hardcastle, a satisfied smile on his face. 'Get Mr Collins to have another look at it with a view to comparing any prints on it with those of Stein's. He'll probably have to go to St Mary's to take Stein's dabs.'

NINE

It was half past six by the time that Hardcastle and Marriott got back to Cannon Row.

'I've compared the button we found in Reuben Gosling's shop with the remaining five on the coat we seized from Stein's room, sir,' said Marriott, 'and I'm as sure as can be that it matches.'

'What about the boots we found, Marriott? Any luck with those?'

'I compared them with the photograph of the footprint in Reuben Gosling's shop that Simpson's photographer took for us, and I'd swear that the right boot is identical, sir.'

'Now we're getting somewhere, Marriott,' said Hardcastle. 'Get on to Mr Collins, and ask him to meet us at Stein's room at Bow Road tomorrow to make a thorough examination for fingerprints. I'll be particularly interested to know if any of those he finds match any he found in Gosling's shop or in Sinclair Villiers's car.'

Marriott glanced at his wristwatch. 'I doubt that he'll still be in his office, sir.'

'Not in his office, Marriott?' Hardcastle

raised his eyebrows and stared at his sergeant. 'Mr Collins is a CID officer. Of course he'll still be in his office. See to it.'

'Yes, sir,' said Marriott, and left the police station to make his way across the courtyard to what was known to members of the Force as Commissioner's Office.

Hardcastle had just started to check the reports that were awaiting his attention when DC Rafferty of Special Branch appeared in his office.

'Oh, it's you again, Rafferty,' said Hardcastle, laying down his pen with a sigh of exasperation. 'What is it now?'

'Mr O'Rourke would like to see you as soon as possible, sir.'

'Who?'

'Detective Chief Inspector O'Rourke is acting as Mr Quinn's deputy, sir, while Mr Quinn and Mr McBrien are away. He's currently occupying Mr Quinn's office.'

'Where is Mr Quinn, then?'

'Mr Quinn is currently engaged on other duties, sir.'

'Really? And what sort of other duties might they be?'

'I'm afraid I'm not at liberty to say, sir.'

'You mean you don't know, Rafferty. Very well.' Although Hardcastle did not regard Special Branch officers as being real detectives, he acknowledged that they were very good at prevaricating. He deluded himself that his own detectives would know where he had gone at any given time. Seizing his hat and umbrella, he followed the SB officer across to the Central Building of New Scotland Yard. When he was halfway there, he met Marriott on his way back.

'Mr Collins will go down to Bow Road tomorrow morning as requested, sir. He said to tell you that he'll meet you at Stein's room at nine o'clock.'

'I told you he'd still be on duty, Marriott,' said Hardcastle. 'Send a telegraph to Mr Sawyer and let him know. In the meantime I've got to see Mr O'Rourke.

'Who's Mr O'Rourke, sir?'

'He's a senior Special Branch officer, Marriott. I'd've thought you'd've known that. Wait for me until I get back.'

'Very good, sir.'

Hardcastle tapped on the heavy oaken door of Superintendent Quinn's office and waited until bidden to enter.

'Be so good as to report on the progress of your enquiries into the Stein murder, Mr Hardcastle.' James O'Rourke, like Quinn an Irishman, was a man not accustomed to wasting words.

What Hardcastle did not know, however, was that although Quinn was supposedly engaged on 'other duties' he had in fact ceded the enquiry into Stein's murder to O'Rourke, who was an expert in Jewish extremist factions within the United Kingdom and Ireland.

'An interesting development has occurred, sir.'

'And what might that be?' O'Rourke frowned at Hardcastle, and stroked his beard.

Hardcastle explained about the button and the footprint that had been found at the scene of Gosling's murder, and that he was now fairly certain that there was a connection between Gosling's death and the killing of Peter Stein.

'That comes as no surprise, and it's interesting that they are both Jewish.' O'Rourke scribbled a few notes on a pad. 'I'll pass that on to Mr Quinn and to MI5. Anything else?'

'Captain Haydn Villiers is detained in the Tower, sir. I understand that he's likely to be charged with treason.'

'I know that, Mr Hardcastle, but I doubt that the charge will be one of treason. It's more likely to be under Section One of the Official Secrets Act. But we shall see.'

'It would seem that Villiers is also Jewish, sir. When I interviewed his mother, I noticed that she was wearing a Star of David around her neck.'

'On a chain, I presume,' said O'Rourke acidly, pausing and looking up from his note-taking.

'Yes, sir, on a chain.' Hardcastle felt as though he was being treated like a junior detective.

'I suspect that this whole business has something to do with the Zionists, Mr Hardcastle, and their desire for a Jewish homeland. We

160

already know that Villiers is to be charged with passing information to the French Jew Pierre Benoit, who in turn passed it to Stein ... or maybe Sinclair Villiers.' O'Rourke emitted a deep sigh. 'As if we had not got enough to do tracking down secret agents that the Germans have the audacity to send here, we now have to deal with the home-grown variety. Very well, keep me informed of any developments.'

'Very good, sir.' Hardcastle was surprised that Special Branch was now including Sinclair Villiers in the conspiracy.

'That's all,' said O'Rourke, waving a hand of dismissal.

When Hardcastle returned to his office, he had told Marriott to go home, telling him it was time that they had an early night. A quarter past eight was not exactly early in Marriott's book, but at least it was an improvement on the previous few evenings.

Leaving his bicycle outside, Marriott let himself into his police married quarters in Regency Street as quietly as possible. He knew that the two children, James and Doreen, five and three respectively, would both be in bed. *One day*, he thought, *I might even be home early enough to read them a bedtime story.* He took off his coat and hat and hung them on the hook in the tiny hall.

Lorna Marriott was in the kitchen preparing supper. She stopped what she was doing to give

161

her husband a kiss. 'Been let off the leash, love?' There was surprise in her voice.

'It's what the guv'nor calls an early night, pet.'

'Well, I suppose it's earlier than usual,' said Lorna, returning to the cooker.

'Mr Hardcastle sends you his regards,' said Marriott.

'I'd rather he sent you ... earlier than this.' Lorna looked pointedly at the kitchen clock before turning to face Marriott. 'What was it this time?'

'The murder we're dealing with has got a bit complicated, pet.' Hanging his jacket on the back of a chair, Marriott opened a bottle of brown ale and settled himself at the kitchen table. 'We're investigating another murder that took place on Bow Road's patch in White-chapel Division,' he said, admiring the trim figure of his twenty-eight-year-old wife as she darted back and forth across the small kitchen.

'Haven't they got any detectives down there, then, love?' asked Lorna sarcastically.

Marriott laughed. 'Yes, of course they have, but it seems that the job at Bow Road is some-how tied up with the murder of Reuben Gosling in Vauxhall Bridge Road.'

'I sometimes think you'd've been better off if you'd stayed in the Uniform Branch, Charlie,' said Lorna, as she put a plate of haddock, peas and mashed potatoes on the table in front of him. 'Meg Lewington's husband Sid works eight-hour shifts and has one day off a week. And I'll bet he'll be an inspector before you are.' Sidney Lewington, a station-sergeant at Gerald Road police station on B Division, lived with his wife Meg next door to the Marriotts.

'I'd be bored to tears, pet.' Marriott was unwilling to enter into a discussion about career prospects in the Metropolitan Police, even though he occasionally wondered if becoming a CID officer had been a wise move. 'What's for pudding?'

'Apple pie and custard,' said Lorna.

Alice Hardcastle's reaction to the arrival of her husband was different from Lorna Marriott's. But, as she often said, she had been 'married to the police force' for the past twenty-three years and had grown accustomed to the hours her husband was obliged to work.

'You're early tonight, Ernie,' she said, as Hardcastle appeared in the kitchen doorway.

'There wasn't much more I could do today, love. But tomorrow's going to be busy. I've been stuck with a murder on Bow Road's toby.'

Alice turned from the stove and flicked a stray lock of hair out of her eyes. 'Why's that? I thought you were dealing with that one in Vauxhall Bridge Road.'

'I am, but the two of them are connected.' Hardcastle poured a whisky for himself and an Amontillado for his wife. 'The bosses at the Yard thought it'd be a good idea if I handled both cases.'

'I sometimes think they take unfair advantage of you, Ernie. It's time you were promoted and given an easy job at the Yard.'

Hardcastle laughed. 'Fat chance of that,' he said. 'I don't kowtow to the right people.'

'That's a fact, Ernie, but perhaps you ought to try.'

'What, and change the habit of a lifetime? I don't think so, love.'

'No, I don't think so either,' said Alice. 'I've grown used to you the way you are. And I've no doubt the Metropolitan Police has as well. And you know what they say about teaching old dogs new tricks.'

At nine o'clock on Saturday morning, Hardcastle and Marriott arrived at the room in Bow Road where Peter Stein had been murdered. DI Collins and DDI Sawyer were already waiting.

'I left the PC on duty here, Ernie,' said Sawyer.

'Thanks, Tom,' said Hardcastle, 'but once we're done today you can let the chandler downstairs have the room back.'

'I'll make my way back to the nick, then, Ernie. Let me know if there's anything else I can do.'

'Thanks, Tom. By the way, how's your boy getting on?'

'He's in Gallipoli,' said Sawyer.

'In Gallipoli? What's he doing out there? I

thought he was in France.'

'He's with the Highland Light Infantry, and they got sent.'

'How did he finish up in a Scottish regiment, Tom? You're not a Scotsman, are you?'

'Bethnal Green, born and bred, so's the lad, but that's got nothing to do with it. They put 'em in any regiment that's short of men, whether they like it or not. But that's the army for you.'

'Bit like the Job, Tom.' Hardcastle spoke with feeling; unpalatable postings had happened to him over the years. 'I hope he keeps his head down.'

'So do I, but I have heard they're pulling our lads out of there in the next few days. General Monro took over from Hamilton last October, and straightaway began talking about evacuating our boys and the Anzacs.'

'Bloody good job, too. It was a daft idea of Churchill's, thinking we could sort out the Turks on their own patch.'

'Couldn't agree more, Ernie,' said Sawyer, 'but Squiffy has a lot to answer for in that regard.' The prime minister, Herbert Asquith, was invariably known as Squiffy because of his fondness for alcohol. 'Anyway, I'll leave you to it. Anything you need, just let me know.'

'I'll get to work, then, Ernie,' said Collins, once Sawyer had departed.

'Right you are, Charlie. In the meantime, I'll have another word with the shopkeeper downstairs. What was his name again, Marriott?'

'Percy Dyer, sir.'

'Yes, that's the fellow.'

The two detectives entered Dyer's shop from the rear door and found the chandler dealing with a crowd of customers.

'Won't keep you a moment, sir,' said Dyer, over his shoulder. 'There's always a rush on of a Saturday morning.'

'Take your time, Mr Dyer.' Hardcastle gazed around the shop, and realized that Dyer was more than just a chandler. Candles, brooms and brushes and mops, boxes of black lead and furniture polish and bars of soap vied with each other for space on the groaning shelves. On the floor on the customers' side of the counter were several oil heaters and a *Star* vacuum cleaner. An overpowering odour of vinegar pervaded the entire shop and, Hardcastle had noticed earlier, it was a stench that permeated even the floor above.

Dyer filled a can with methylated spirit from a drum at the end of the counter, and handed it to a small boy in exchange for a few pennies.

'Now, sir,' he said, wiping his hands on his apron, and turning to face the DDI as the last customer left the shop, 'how can I help you?'

'How long had Peter Stein been occupying the room upstairs, Mr Dyer?'

The chandler turned to a calendar on the wall behind him. 'He moved in a few days before Christmas, sir. Monday the twentieth, to be precise.' He paused and rather shamefacedly added, 'It wasn't really meant for living in. I used it as a storeroom, but Stein was desperate for somewhere to live, so I took him in. But he said he wouldn't be here for long.'

'He wasn't,' observed Hardcastle.

'Where were you on New Year's Eve, Mr Dyer?' asked Marriott, cutting into the chandler's conversation with Hardcastle.

'Upstairs with Queenie, sir. That's the missus. We toasted the New Year at midnight and then went to bed.'

'D'you happen to know if Stein was in at that time?'

'No, he wasn't, sir. He went out ... now let me see. Yes, about nine o'clock or thereabouts. It was just as I was closing up and he asked if he could go out the front way in time to catch the next tram. Well, I hadn't locked up, so I let him out through the shop.'

'Did he say where he was going on this here tram?' asked Hardcastle.

'No, he never said, but I s'pose he was going up the West End somewhere. Trafalgar Square's quite the place to see the New Year in. Not that it's ever taken my fancy. Too many people, if you know what I mean.'

'I do indeed,' said Hardcastle, but for a different reason. There were always crimes to investigate arising out of the Trafalgar Square festivities which seemed to act like a magnet to pickpockets.

'How was Stein dressed, Mr Dyer?' asked Marriott.

'He had on that reefer jacket what he always wore. I don't think he owned an overcoat. Leastways, I never saw him in one.'

'Was he wearing a scarf?'

'Come to think of it, he was, sir,' said Dyer.

Marriott produced the scarf found in Sinclair Villiers's precious Haxe-Doulton, and showed it to the chandler. 'This one?'

Dyer took hold of the scarf and examined it closely. 'I couldn't say for sure, sir, but I must say it looks very like the one he had on at the time.'

A young ragamuffin entered the shop and touched his cap. 'Please, Mr Dyer, ma says can she have two candles.'

'You must be burning 'em all night, young Willy,' said Dyer, taking the candles from a shelf and wrapping them in newspaper. 'A ha'penny to you, my boy, and give your ma my regards.'

'Thank you, sir,' said the lad, and ran from the shop.

'Should've charged him a penny, sir,' said Dyer, 'but his pa's doing time for burglary and the family's a bit short of the readies.'

'Very charitable of you, Mr Dyer,' said Hardcastle. 'Did Stein have any visitors that you know of?'

'None that I ever saw, sir. Mind you, if there was any, they'd likely have come in from the alley off of Harley Grove and in the back door. Of course, he had a visitor on the day he was killed.'

'Yes, I gathered that,' said Hardcastle drily, 'but you don't know of any other callers at any other time.'

'I did hear a bit of a barney going on on Christmas Eve,' said Dyer, 'so I s'pose he must 'ave 'ad a visitor then. I thought it was high jinks on account of it being the festive season, but then I heard raised voices like they was having a bit of a bull and cow. It only lasted a couple of minutes, and then I heard the back door slam and it was all quiet after that.'

'Marriott, take a statement from Mr Dyer,' said Hardcastle, 'and I'll go back upstairs and see how Mr Collins is getting on.'

'I've already made a statement to Mr Sawyer,' said Dyer.

'Well, now you'll be making another one,' said Hardcastle.

'I'm just about finished, Ernie,' said Collins, when Hardcastle joined him in the room once occupied by Stein. 'Got a few dabs and on a quick examination I reckon one or two of them match those found at Gosling's shop and in Villiers's car. But I can't be absolutely certain until I get back to the Yard.'

'D'you mean you can remember what they look like, Charlie?' Hardcastle, to whom the comparatively new science of fingerprints was still largely a mystery, was surprised and at once sceptical about Collins's claim.

'I get to know prints like you get to remember faces, Ernie, but like I said, I'll have to make sure.'

'I hope you're right, Charlie, because if you are, it might've solved who did for Reuben Gosling.'

'I thought you said there were two of them,' said Collins, and laughed.

'Yes, I did. Trust you to ruin my day.'

'I don't think I have, Ernie. I found two distinct sets, so one of them could belong to Stein's accomplice. Your problem is finding the bugger. But I should be able to let you know before the day's out.' Collins packed up his equipment and made his way back downstairs.

It had only taken Marriott twenty minutes or so to take another statement from Percy Dyer regarding Stein's tenancy and movements, and by twelve thirty he and Hardcastle were being set down from a cab in the courtyard of New Scotland Yard.

'Time for a wet, Marriott,' said Hardcastle, and led the way to the downstairs bar of the Red Lion on the corner of Whitehall.

'Morning, Mr Hardcastle. The usual?' Albert, landlord of the Red Lion, knew all the Cannon Row detectives as well as those at Scotland Yard.

'Yes, and a couple of fourpenny cannons, Albert.'

'You must be busy with this Gosling murder, Mr Hardcastle. You too, Mr Marriott.' Albert placed two pints of best bitter on the bar together with two hot steak and kidney pies.

'Enough to keep us burning the midnight oil, Albert,' said Hardcastle, taking the head off his beer. 'But nothing I can't cope with.' He drained the last of his beer and glanced at his watch. 'Still, I think we can make time for one more pint, please, Albert.'

After each had downed a further glass of beer, the two detectives made their way back to the street. 'Time we were getting up to St Mary's, Marriott,' said the DDI, and they walked the short distance into Whitehall.

Dr Bernard Spilsbury was at work on another cadaver when Hardcastle and Marriott arrived at the mortuary attached to the hospital in Paddington.

'I won't keep you a moment, Hardcastle, my dear fellow. I'm just dealing with a prostitute who clearly offended someone in Praed Street late last night.' Spilsbury carefully removed the liver from the body and placed it in a bowl alongside a heart. 'Judging by the state of her liver, I would say that this young whore consumed far too much alcohol,' he said. 'Not that she'll have to worry about that any more.'

Tossing his bloodstained rubber gloves into a medical waste bin, the pathologist removed his rubber apron and placed it on a bench.

'I've recovered the round that did for your poor fellow, Hardcastle.' Dr Spilsbury picked up a pair of forceps and used them to point at a solitary bullet resting in a kidney-shaped enamel bowl. 'Straight into the heart. The killer was either an excellent shot or a damned lucky one. Whichever way it was, it took only a single round to send your man Stein off to wherever the dead go.' He laughed cheerfully. 'I'll let you have my statement by first thing tomorrow.'

'I'm much obliged to you, Doctor,' said Hardcastle.

At a quarter past four, when Hardcastle was in the process of metaphorically tearing one of Catto's reports to pieces, Detective Inspector Charles Collins almost bounced into the DDI's office.

'They tally, Ernie,' he said, sitting down in one of Hardcastle's chairs and opening a folder.

'What tally, Charlie?' Hardcastle put the cap on his fountain pen.

'The prints I found at Bow Road are a match for the prints I found in Villiers's Haxe-Doulton down at Wandsworth,' said Collins. 'An unknown set were on the steering wheel, and Peter Stein's were on the dashboard. And I found Stein's in Gosling's shop,' he added triumphantly.

'All I need to do now, Charlie, is to find the man whose prints you couldn't identify.'

'Yes,' said Collins gloomily. 'There's nothing

in my records that's a match. Looks as though he's kept his nose clean up to now. If there's anything else I can help you with, Ernie, you know where to find me.'

'There's one thing that's vexing me in all this business, Marriott.' Following DI Collins's departure, Hardcastle leaned back in his chair and began to fill his pipe.

'What's that, sir?' There was, in fact, more than one thing puzzling Marriott about the murders of Reuben Gosling and Peter Stein.

'Why was Sinclair Villiers's car used in the robbery and murder at Gosling's shop?'

'A coincidence, sir?'

'Coincidence my arse,' exclaimed Hardcastle vehemently. 'Haydn Villiers is up for a court martial for selling out to the bloody Germans. And it looks as though the information he passed to Benoit, the Jewish farmer in France, was sent on to Stein. And Stein finished up dead. Where's the coincidence in that, Marriott?'

'D'you think that Sinclair Villiers lent his car to the killers, sir?'

'Either that or he's the owner of the fingerprints that Mr Collins can't identify.'

'There's not much we can do about that, sir. Anyway, we know that Villiers was at home for all of New Year's Eve. In fact, he said that Henwood the butler woke him at just after seven o'clock the next morning.'

'But do we know that for sure, Marriott?'

'Villiers's butler said that his master was at

home all night, sir. And he claimed to have noticed that the car had disappeared at about the time he took Villiers his tea the next morning.'

'Of course he did,' said Hardcastle. 'If Henwood didn't back up his master, Villiers would likely give him the sack. And that'd mean that Henwood would be in the trenches before you could say Jack the Ripper.'

'So what do we do now, sir?'

'We get Henwood on his own and scare the living daylights out of him, Marriott, that's what we do,' said Hardcastle.

'But won't Sinclair Villiers kick up a fuss, sir? He's got plenty of money and could probably afford to brief an expensive lawyer, even to defend his butler.'

Hardcastle laughed. 'D'you see anything wrong in requiring Henwood to come to the nick to make a statement about the loss of Sinclair Villiers's motor car, Marriott?' He paused. 'But Monday morning will do for that. Go home and take tomorrow off.'

TEN

Although Hardcastle had his newspaper delivered on weekdays, he preferred to walk down to Horace Boxall's corner shop on a Sunday morning to buy the *News of the World*.

Unbidden, Boxall placed a copy of the newspaper on the counter. 'There's some good news in there today, Mr Hardcastle,' he said, pointing at an article on the front page.

'That makes a change, Horace. What's happened?'

'They've brought all our lads off the Gallipoli peninsula, together with the Aussies and the New Zealanders. According to this, they spirited 'em away under Johnny Turk's nose and he never even noticed. At least, not until the booby traps that our lads had set started to go off.'

'Good news indeed,' commented Hardcastle, thinking that Tom Sawyer, the DDI at Bow Road, would be pleased. Provided, of course, that Sawyer's son was one of those who had been evacuated safely.

'But at what a cost, Mr Hardcastle. Two hundred and fifty thousand casualties since the campaign started last April.'

'It was a hare-brained idea to start with, and all for nothing,' complained Hardcastle. 'I'll have an ounce of St Bruno and a box of Swan Vestas, as well, Horace, if you please.'

Boxall placed the tobacco and the matches on top of the newspaper. 'I see the House of Commons voted overwhelmingly in favour of conscription last Thursday. According to the *Daily Herald*, Sir John Simon, the Home Secretary, resigned over it.'

'You don't read that Labour Party rag, Horace, surely?'

'No, but I sell it. Not that the *Herald*'s a daily any more; only comes out once a week. I can't see it lasting out the war. Mind you, I've still got a few customers who buy it.'

'It's about time some of the scrimshankers were rounded up, Horace,' said Hardcastle. 'A chap who lived a few doors up from me was killed last week in Ypres. Left a wife and six children. God knows how they'll manage because the pension she'll get won't feed and house 'em. But all these young single men are still loafing about. It's time they were getting in amongst the muck and bullets.'

'It's a wicked old world, Mr H,' said Boxall, handing Hardcastle his change.

For the remainder of Sunday, Hardcastle, tiring of the more depressing news in the Sunday paper, absent-mindedly mooned about the house. Frequently admonished by Alice for getting in her way, he was fretting about the

Gosling and Stein murders, and would rather have been at his office. But he realized that there was little he could do, even if he were there.

Hardcastle arrived at the police station at eight o'clock on Monday morning, tired rather than refreshed by an idle and frustrating weekend. All that he had done was to replace a washer on the kitchen tap, and that only after repeated nagging by his wife; but Alice had been complaining for weeks about it dripping and leaving a brown stain in the sink.

He spent several minutes sitting at the station officer's desk, perusing the occurrence book. One entry caused him to chuckle. A man had been beaten up by a group of prostitutes in Great Peter Street after he had assaulted one of their number in a dispute over payment. Three of the women had then sat on him while one of the others called the police. When the assailant was eventually taken into custody by a constable, he was found to be a deserter from the Connaught Rangers.

'That'll teach him to mix it with Westminster whores, Skipper. He'll probably be shot at dawn, and all because he argued about the price of a tumble with a tart.' Hardcastle closed the occurrence book and mounted the stairs to his office, shouting for Marriott as he passed the door to the detectives' room.

'What's happened about getting Henwood,

Villiers's butler, in here, Marriott?'

'I've sent Bert Wood to bring him in, sir. He can be very persuasive when the mood takes him.'

Hardcastle nodded his approval; he knew that Detective Sergeant Wood was a tenacious officer. 'I'm sure he won't be put off by Sinclair Villiers or his hoity-toity manservant, Marriott. When did he go?'

'About ten minutes ago, sir. I told him to take a cab.'

'Yes?' Henwood scathingly appraised the man standing on the doorstep of Villiers's Flood Street house, and deduced from his appearance that he was probably an ex-serviceman down on his luck. 'You should've gone down the area steps and knocked on the servants' door,' he said.

'Is your name Henwood, mate?' Detective Sergeant Wood knew exactly how to deal with butlers who had ideas above their station.

'Yes, it is, if it's any of your business.'

'I'm a police officer and I need you to come to Cannon Row police station with me.'

'Whatever for?' demanded Henwood, maintaining his lofty attitude.

'To make a statement regarding the theft of your employer's car.'

'My dear man,' said Henwood, waving a hand as if to dismiss the sergeant, 'I can't just leave my post simply to comply with some whim of

178

the police. It'll have to be at some other time. I'll telephone your station to make an appointment if you think it's absolutely necessary.'

'Oh, you will, will you, Henwood? I'd remind you that we are dealing with a brutal murder and, like it or not, the demands of your employer will have to take second place.'

'Well, I'm afraid it's not possible to abandon my duties at a moment's notice.'

'In that case, I suggest you tell Mr Villiers that your presence is required forthwith. I'm sure that as a law-abiding citizen, Mr Villiers would be only too glad to know that one of his servants was assisting the police.'

'I'm afraid I can't do that,' said Henwood, with an expression bordering on a smirk. 'Mr Villiers is not at home.'

'Oh? Where's he gone, then?' Wood immediately suspected that Sinclair Villiers had disappeared for a reason, and he was certain that the DDI would be interested to know where he had gone.

'I have no idea,' responded Henwood with a lofty disdain. 'Mr Villiers only said that he would be away for a few days. He does not vouchsafe his arrangements to me, and it's not my place to ask.'

'Are there no other servants here, then?' asked Wood.

'Of course there are. There's a footman, a housekeeper, a cook, a house parlourmaid and a kitchen maid.'

'Then I suggest you tell them where you've gone. I'm quite sure they're capable of looking after the house for an hour or so in your absence. Particularly as Mr Villiers isn't here.' Wood paused. 'Unless you fancy having me arrest you for obstructing a police officer in the execution of his duty.'

'*Arrest me!*' Henwood's voice rose, a mixture of outrage and disbelief. And a frisson of fear.

'Don't think I won't, Mister.'

The expression of determination on Wood's face convinced Henwood that he was serious. The superior attitude vanished and the butler caved in. 'I'll just get my hat and coat.' Moments later, the butler reappeared on the doorstep attired in a melton cloth overcoat and a bowler hat.

'Henwood is downstairs in the interview room, sir,' said Wood, standing in the doorway of the DDI's office.

'Any trouble, Wood?' asked Hardcastle.

'No, sir. He kicked up a bit of a fuss, but after a short discussion I persuaded him that it'd be in his best interests to come with me.'

'I'm sure you can be very persuasive when the occasion demands it, Wood,' said Hardcastle, with something approaching a smile.

'There's something else, sir. Sinclair Villiers isn't at home. Henwood said he'd gone away for a few days, but claimed that he didn't know where.'

'That's very interesting, Wood,' said Hardcastle. 'Right, carry on.' Once Wood had returned to the detectives' office, the DDI considered the implications of Villiers's disappearance. 'That damned man Villiers has something to hide, Marriott,' he said thoughtfully, 'but I reckon he's so bloody confident that he decided it was safe for him to take a holiday.'

'It might be quite innocent, sir,' said Marriott, who had yet to be convinced of any culpability on Villiers's part.

'Innocent my foot,' muttered Hardcastle, and picked up his pipe from the ashtray. 'We'll go down and see what his retainer has to say for himself.'

'It's very cold in here,' said Henwood, when Hardcastle and Marriott entered the interview room. The butler was still wearing his overcoat.

'Seems all right to me,' said Hardcastle, as he took a seat. 'I understand from my sergeant that you were reluctant to come here, Henwood.'

'Only my master calls me Henwood,' said the butler. 'Below stairs I'm called *Mister* Henwood.' The implication was that Hardcastle sprung from a class more likely to be found in the servants' hall than in the drawing room.

'Well, you're not below stairs now,' snapped Hardcastle. 'You're in a police station. My police station. Why were you so anxious to avoid seeing me?'

'I have my duties and responsibilities,' said Henwood, maintaining his usual arrogance.

'Even when your boss is away?' Hardcastle examined the butler with an amused expression.

'The household still has to be run and the staff supervised, whether my master is in residence or not.'

'When did he go?'

'Last Thursday,' said Henwood, after a pause.

'And where did he go?' Hardcastle was immediately aware that Thursday was the day before Peter Stein's murder, but made no comment.

'He doesn't tell me such things. As I told your man.'

'I'm going to put some questions to you, Henwood, and I advise you to think very carefully before you answer. Because if you lie to me, and your master's committed a crime, you'll go down with him for conspiracy. And they rather fancy hoity-toity butlers in His Majesty's prisons. And Mr Sinclair bloody Villiers won't help you once you're in there, neither.'

For the first time since his encounter with Sinclair Villiers's butler, Hardcastle was pleased to see that the man was extremely discomfited by that remark. And his next comment confirmed his disquiet.

'I dunno know what you mean, guv'nor.' Suddenly Henwood's assumed refined accent vanished along with his superior attitude. 'I ain't done anything wrong.'

'Where d'you come from, Henwood?' asked

Hardcastle, intrigued by the butler's sudden reversion to type.

'Hoxton,' said Henwood.

'I thought so. I walked a beat there years ago,' said Hardcastle, pausing to light his pipe. 'Now perhaps we can get down to brass tacks.'

But before the DDI could begin, DS Wood appeared in the doorway of the interview room.

'What is it, Wood?' asked Hardcastle sharply. He disliked being interrupted during an interrogation, and his detectives knew it. It must be something important for Wood to have broken that rule.

'I thought you'd like to have a look at this before you go any further, sir.' Wood handed the DDI a file. 'I did a search in records and this is what I found.'

Hardcastle opened the slim folder and spent a few moments reading its contents.

'Well done, Wood.'

'Thank you, sir.' It was not often that the DDI paid Wood a compliment or, for that matter, anyone else. Not that Wood was impressed by the blandishments of a senior officer; he realized that a good reputation only lasted until the next mistake. 'Will that be all, sir?'

'Yes, carry on, Wood.'

During this exchange, Henwood's apprehension increased. He was now white in the face and his hands were clasped tightly together on the interview room table. He sensed what was coming next.

'So, Wilfred Henwood, you're a thief.' Hardcastle closed the file and stared at the butler.

'I can explain, sir,' said Henwood, now thoroughly cowed by Hardcastle's statement.

'That'd be a start,' said Hardcastle. 'According to this file from the Criminal Records Office, you were convicted of stealing from your employer on the seventh of June 1912, and sentenced to three months at Rochester Row police court.'

'It was all a terrible mistake, sir.'

'Oh, it undoubtedly was, Henwood. On your part for getting caught. You stole money while in trusted employment as a butler and you call that a terrible mistake?'

'It was the horses, sir.'

'Ah!' Hardcastle leaned back in his chair and spent a few moments relighting his pipe. 'Did you hear that, Marriott?' he enquired sarcastically. 'It was the horses. Isn't it strange that when it comes down to an excuse, there's always a horse or two at the end of it?'

'Indeed, sir,' said Marriott. 'Very strange.'

'I had a run of bad luck, and I owed the bookies a fair sum,' said Henwood desperately. 'It was the only way I could get out of trouble. Bookies can turn very nasty when you owe them.'

'And you presumably got no character from the employer you stole from, Henwood?'

'No, sir,' said Henwood miserably.

'So how did you obtain your present post?'

Henwood remained silent, and looked down at the table.

'So there we have it, Marriott. Our Wilfred Henwood has undoubtedly committed the offence of furnishing Mr Villiers with a false character reference.' Hardcastle turned his attention to the butler. 'And that, Henwood, is an offence under the Servants' Characters Act of 1792. Very handy, these old statutes, don't you think, Marriott?' he added with a chuckle.

'It was the only way I could get another post, sir,' whined Henwood. 'And I suppose you'll tell Mr Villiers now.'

'Setting that aside for a moment, Henwood, let's talk about New Year's Eve, and we'll see if we can't come to an arrangement, so to speak. But for a start, let's see if your memory's returned. Where has Villiers gone?'

'I honestly don't know, sir. He comes and goes in that motor car of his, and never tells anyone what he's up to.' Even then, Henwood was only telling half the truth.

'When I called at Flood Street on New Year's Day, Henwood, you told me that you hadn't left the house since the day before, and neither had your master. D'you want to think about that again?'

'I could get the sack for this, Inspector.'

'You probably will anyway,' said Hardcastle mildly, 'especially if your master finds out about your false reference.' It was a veiled threat that did little to boost Henwood's flagging morale.

'He went out at about eight o'clock on New Year's Eve.'

'And when did he return?'

'I don't know. The master has his own key, and I went to bed at about half-past midnight. After the cook and I had drunk a toast to the New Year.'

'No doubt with a bottle from the master's wine cellar,' observed Hardcastle drily. 'Have you any idea where Villiers went?'

'No, sir, but he was back home the next day. As I said before, he never tells me anything. It makes it very difficult for the staff, not knowing whether he'll be in for meals or not.'

'When did you take him his tea, Henwood? I know what Villiers said, but I want the truth.'

'I didn't take him tea. I'd had a lie-in on account of it being New Year's Day and the master not being there. I didn't think he'd be coming back so soon, and I didn't know he was in until he rang for me about midday to tell me that the car had gone.' Henwood looked downright miserable at having to reveal details of his master's habits and movements.

'And you've really no idea where he went?' asked Marriott, leaning forward.

'No, sir.' Henwood paused, as if undecided whether to reveal another confidence. 'But I think he might have a fancy woman somewhere. You see, he and his wife have parted. I don't think they're divorced, but that wouldn't make any difference to the master.' And then the butler opened up. 'Actually, Sinclair Villiers is a bloody awful man to work for. He's always finding fault in what we do, and coming down to the kitchen interfering with cook.'

'What d'you mean, interfering with the cook?' asked Marriott.

'Oh, not in that way, sir, but he's always telling her how to do her job, and me and the rest of the staff. It was the same when his wife was there. He was forever ordering Mrs Villiers about and complaining about her going out to meet her friends. It's no wonder she left him. I've been with him since I came out of Pentonville and Mrs Jarvis is the third cook we've had in my time. They just won't put up with it, you see. I'd've left him too, but I'd have difficulty getting another place because I'm certain the master wouldn't give me a character.'

'D'you think he knows about your past, then, Henwood?' asked Hardcastle.

The butler shrugged. 'I don't know, sir, but Mr Villiers seems to know everything that's going on.'

'Did the staff know that you were coming to the police station this morning?'

'No, sir. I only talked to your man on the doorstep, and I told Frederick the footman that I had to go out for an hour. I often do and Frederick knows better than to ask where I'm going.'

Hardcastle spent a few minutes scraping the

ash from his pipe and emptying it into the tin lid that did service as an ashtray. He opened the CRO file again.

'You're thirty-eight and a single man, Henwood.'

'Yes, sir.'

'Eligible for conscription, then, if this new Act of Parliament comes into force.'

'I suppose so, but I'm not a well man.'

Hardcastle laughed. 'Save it for the medical board when you get called, Henwood. But I've a proposition to put to you. From now on, I want to know everything Sinclair Villiers does. And see if you can find out who this woman is that he's seeing.'

'I couldn't do that, sir,' said Henwood, clearly appalled by the DDI's suggestion. 'It would be a breach of trust.'

'An ex-convict who got his present post with a false reference is in no position to talk about trust,' said Hardcastle sharply. 'The option is that I tell Villiers about your past, and exactly how you worked your way into his employment with a false reference. That'd mean you getting the sack a bit *jildi*, and you'd be in the trenches before you could say Jack the Ripper.'

'You've got me in a right fix, sir, and no mistake.'

'From time to time, Sergeant Wood – he's the officer who brought you here – will call at Flood Street to have a word with you. And if anyone asks, you tell them he's a friend of yours. You are not to tell anyone that he's a policeman. Understood?'

'Yes, sir,' said Henwood miserably.

'Is there a telephone at Flood Street?'

'Yes, sir. It's in the kitchen and I transfer any calls for Mr Villiers to the extension in the drawing room.'

'Good. The moment Villiers gets back, telephone this police station and leave a message for *Mister* Marriott, not *Sergeant* Marriott mind, and just say "The order's been cancelled". Got that?'

'Yes, sir.'

'Now then, repeat what you have to say?'

'I'm to ask for *Mister* Marriott and say the order's been cancelled, sir.'

'Right, you can go,' said Hardcastle, 'and if you mention our arrangement to Villiers, I'll be having a serious chat with him myself.'

Henwood, clearly grasping the implication of Hardcastle's last remark, stood up, a vastly different man from when he had entered the interview room forty minutes earlier.

'See him off the premises just to make sure he don't nick anything, Marriott,' said Hardcastle jocularly, 'and then come up to my office.'

Marriott returned a few minutes later. 'He's gone, sir, but he's not a very happy man,' he said.

'We had a bit of luck there, Marriott. It was as well that Wood decided to do a search of records.' Hardcastle paused. 'Mind you, I'd've got around to it myself eventually.'

'D'you think there's anything in Villiers disappearing on New Year's Eve and on the day before Stein was topped, sir?'

'It looks promising, Marriott, but at the moment I'm not sure why. And despite putting the squeeze on Henwood, I'm not sure he'll deliver the goods. After all, he's just a two-faced con man when it comes down to it.'

'But supposing Villiers *was* seeing a woman, sir?'

'That'll put him in the clear, I suppose,' said Hardcastle reluctantly. 'But we'll make sure. Who's on duty?'

'Lipton and Keeler, sir,' said Marriott promptly.

'Well, I suppose they'll have to do, Marriott.' Hardcastle had no high opinion of any of his detective constables. 'Fetch 'em in.'

'Now, you two,' said Hardcastle, when the two detective constables appeared in his office, 'I've got a job for you. Sinclair Villiers, who lives in Flood Street, has got a fancy woman somewhere. I want to know who she is and where she lives, and I don't want Villiers knowing that you're tailing him. Got that, Lipton?'

'Yes, sir,' said Lipton, unhappy that he had been selected, yet again, for a following job. 'When do we start, sir?'

'As soon as Sergeant Marriott tips you the wink. Villiers is adrift at the moment, but I've arranged to be told when he gets back home.'

ELEVEN

It was at five past three the same afternoon that a young PC appeared in the detectives' office.

'Yes, what is it?' asked Marriott.

'I'm relieving on the switchboard, Sergeant, and I've just received a strange telephone call. The caller never gave his name, but said...' The PC glanced at the message form in his hand. 'He said to tell Mister Marriott that the order's been cancelled and that the man's going out later this evening about seven. Would that have been meant for you, Sergeant?'

'How long ago did you get this call?' asked Marriott.

'About two or three minutes ago, Sergeant. It seemed a bit of an odd thing to say, so I asked him what he meant, but he just hung up.'

'Take a word of advice, young man,' said Marriott. 'Now that telephones are becoming increasingly common, you'll often get strange calls for detectives, and they're frequently anonymous. You don't ask questions, either of the caller or of the detective, because the call could be from an informant who doesn't want anyone to know who he is. People of that sort are often criminals giving information to the police about other villains. They're playing a dangerous game and could well be putting their lives in danger by grassing.'

'Sorry, Sergeant, I didn't think.'

'What's your name?'

'Henry Paget, Sergeant.'

'You've got your name down to come out on winter patrol, haven't you, Paget?' Winter patrols comprised young uniformed police officers selected to patrol the streets in plain clothes between October and March. It was regarded as the first step towards becoming a full-blown detective.

'Yes, Sergeant.'

'Well, if you want to be a CID officer, Paget, learn to keep your eyes open and your mouth shut. And *never* query what other detectives are doing or who they're meeting, ever. If you eventually become a detective, you'll doubtless acquire informants of your own, and then you'll know exactly what I mean. Got that?'

'Sorry, Sergeant,' said Paget again.

'What service have you got, lad?'

'Two years last month, Sergeant.'

'Right, I'll bear you in mind. And before you go, I'll take that message form and you're to forget you ever got that call.' Marriott took the form and put it in his pocket.

Paget left the office wondering whether he had just ruined his chances of joining the CID or if, in fact, he had enhanced them. Being 'borne in mind' by the first-class sergeant was somewhat enigmatic.

Marriott glanced around the office. 'Lipton, Keeler?'

'Yes, Skip?' said Lipton.

'You're on for your following job. Sinclair Villiers is back at Flood Street. And the DDI wants to know if he's seeing some good-time girl. But if he's not, he wants to know what he is up to.'

'When should we start, Skip?' asked Keeler.

'Today, but the information is that he's going out at about seven this evening,' said Marriott. But then he paused. 'Can either of you drive?'

'I can, Skip.' Lipton's girlfriend's father was a chauffeur. Using his employer's car, he had spent one weekend teaching Lipton the rudiments of driving.

'Wait here.' Marriott put on his jacket and crossed the corridor to the DDI's office.

'Sinclair Villiers is back at home, sir. I've just had the telephone call from his butler, and I've got Lipton and Keeler standing by. According to Henwood, Villiers is going out later on.'

'Why aren't they out on the street finding out what Villiers is up to, then, Marriott?' asked Hardcastle impatiently. He put the cap on his fountain pen and laid it carefully on his desk.

'According to Henwood, Villiers isn't going out until seven o'clock, sir, but it won't be that easy. If he goes anywhere, he's almost bound to go in that car of his. And that means that Lipton and Keeler will be at a disadvantage, particularly if there's no cab in the offing at the time he takes off. And there's never a cab when you want one, particularly these days with half London's cabbies in the army.'

'Can either of them drive, Marriott?'

'Yes, sir. Lipton assures me he can.'

'Good. Get on to the transport department and tell them that I want use of that taxicab they keep for observations and the like, and I want it now.'

'Very good, sir.'

'And then tell Lipton to go and collect it from wherever they keep the thing.' Hardcastle shook his head. 'I really don't know what the world's coming to, Marriott. Everything we touch seems to involve a motor car. There are times when I think I ought to retire.'

'Are you sure you know how to drive this vehicle, lad?' asked a suspicious sergeant at the transport depot.

'Yes, Skip.'

'Right, drive it round the yard for me and let me see how you get on.'

Lipton drove a few circuits and pulled up in front of the sergeant.

'Yes, well it looks as though you've got a rough idea. D'you know how to light the acetylene lamps?'

'Yes, Skip.'

'Good, because you'll need 'em. It's dark

194

enough already. Now then, here's a white coat and a cap so's you'll look the part, and put this on,' the sergeant said, handing Lipton a metal licence tag. 'Don't want you getting stopped by the police for not wearing it, do you?' he added with a cackle, followed by a distressing cough. 'And make sure you keep the taximeter flag down or you'll have the gentry writing to the Commissioner complaining that you've refused to pick up a fare. And you'll need a passenger, otherwise it'll look suspicious.'

'That's him,' said Lipton, pointing to DC Keeler.

'And don't break anything or you'll get assessed for it.'

'Thanks, Skip,' said Lipton. Keeler got into the cab and Lipton was about to mount the driving seat when the sergeant spoke again.

'Hold on, my lad, you've got to sign for it all first.' The sergeant produced a form and spent a few minutes completing it. 'Can't do anything without bits of paper in this Job, lad. It's the coming thing.'

It was half past six exactly when Lipton drove the cab into Flood Street. Sinclair Villiers's Haxe-Doulton was parked outside his house.

'What are we going to do, Gordon?' asked Basil Keeler, sliding open the glass screen between him and Lipton. 'We can't stop outside his house.'

'We'll keep driving round, Baz,' said Lipton.

'One cab looks much like another, so we won't look too obvious. Anyway it's dark.'

'Unless someone makes a note of the number,' said Keeler, ever the pessimist.

'And who the hell's going to stand about in midwinter collecting cab numbers?' Lipton was always impatient with people who made silly statements or asked stupid questions.

For the next twenty minutes, Lipton piloted the cab around the tight circuit of Flood Street, Alpha Place, Flood Walk, Chelsea Manor Street and back to Flood Street. By now it was pitch dark with a threat of fog and, thanks to wartime restrictions, the few street lights that were illuminated had been dimmed. The chances of anyone realizing that the same cab was circling the block were minimal.

On the fourth circuit, Lipton turned into Flood Street in time to see a man come out of Sinclair Villiers's house. He was attired in a Harris Tweed motor coat and a cap upon which was a pair of goggles.

'Here we go,' yelled Lipton above the noise of the engine.

'How do we know it's Villiers?' shouted Keeler.

'Can't be anyone else,' responded Lipton. 'His son's in the Tower and I don't suppose he'd let his butler drive that bloody thing.'

The man went to the front of the vehicle, a starting handle at the ready.

'Time for another quick turn round the block,'

shouted Lipton, and accelerated.

As the police cab turned into Flood Street for the fifth time, the driver of the Haxe-Doulton was moving off. He quickly accelerated so that Lipton was hard pressed to keep up with him.

'I reckon he's doing more than twenty miles an hour,' shouted Keeler from the passenger compartment.

'I think you're right,' shouted Lipton in response. 'There's no way of telling for sure, but if you think I'm going to stop him and report him for exceeding the speed limit, you can forget it. The DDI would have a blue fit if we showed out for the sake of a paltry summons.'

Fortunately, heavy traffic and a collision between an omnibus and a car forced Villiers to slow down when he turned north off Victoria Embankment and entered the City of London. But when he reached Cannon Street, he stopped.

'Why on earth is he stopping here, Gordon?' asked Keeler.

'I don't know, do I?' replied Lipton testily. 'Anyhow, he's getting out.'

Villiers walked round the vehicle to the front offside and then, hands on hips and an exasperated expression on his face, he stared up and down the road.

'This looks like a bit of luck, Baz. He's got a flat tyre. I reckon this is our chance. If I bring him back to the cab, you're to agree with anything I say. All right?' Without waiting for an answer, Lipton leaped out of the cab, and strode across to Villiers. 'Are you all right, sir? I thought you might've had an accident.'

'No, I've got a puncture, dammit! I suppose you've got a fare?'

'Yes, I have, sir.'

'Blast! I'm already late and you can't get a cab for love or money these days. It's this damned war, you know; half the cabbies in London seem to have disappeared.'

'Where were you making for, sir?' asked Lipton.

'Mile End. Hannibal Street, as a matter of fact.'

'I might be able to help you there, sir. I'm taking my fare to Mile End Road. I'll see if he's willing to share the cab with you.'

'I'd be most grateful, cabbie,' said Villiers warmly, and followed Lipton to the cab.

Lipton opened the door of the passenger compartment, and addressing Keeler, said, 'This gentleman's in a bit of a fix, sir. He's going to Mile End, same as you. Would you be willing to share with him? It'd be doing him a favour.'

'Of course, cabbie,' agreed Keeler readily, adopting what he believed to be a polished accent.

'There we are, sir,' said Lipton, turning to Villiers. 'In you get.' Pausing, he added, 'What about your car, sir?'

'I'll telephone the Royal Automobile Club when I arrive, cabbie. They'll deal with it, and no one can drive it away with a flat tyre.'

'That's handy, sir, being a member of a club that helps you out like that.' Lipton did not know much about the Royal Automobile Club.

'It has its advantages, including a good restaurant,' said Villiers, getting into the cab as Keeler moved across to make room on the seat.

It was fortunate that Lipton had served in the East End of London before being posted to Cannon Row police station; had he not been able to find Mile End Road it would have looked suspicious. London cab drivers were expected to know London thoroughly, but Lipton had not done 'the knowledge', as the taxi drivers' comprehensive examination of routes was known.

Lipton stopped the cab in Hannibal Street, and Villiers alighted, having thanked Keeler effusively for his assistance.

'Now, cabbie, what's the fare?'

Lipton glanced at the taximeter. 'Well, sir, we started off in Lambeth, and the meter's showing thirty shillings. But, as we picked you up on Cannon Street, I suppose it'll only be—'

'Nonsense,' exclaimed Villiers. 'You and your passenger did me a great service.' Taking out his wallet, he extracted a five-pound note. 'I insist on paying this gentleman's fare as well as my own. The rest is a tip for you for being so helpful.' He stared at the licence tag that Lipton was wearing. 'What's more, I shall write to the Commissioner of Police, telling him what a helpful chap you are.'

'There's no need for that, sir,' said Lipton, touching his cap with a forefinger as he pocketed the white five-pound note with his other hand. In fact, he hoped that Villiers would not write any letters to the Yard; he could do without the complication of having to pen an explanatory report. And he would have to surrender the five pounds he had just been given.

Villiers crossed the pavement and entered a house. Lipton got back into the cab and drove around the corner and stopped.

'Did Villiers say anything useful, Baz?' asked Lipton, leaning back to talk to Keeler through the open partition.

'No, apart from thanking me several times. He just talked about the weather and then went on about Chelsea football club; apparently he's a supporter. How much did he give you, Gordon?'

'A flim,' said Lipton, flourishing the five-pound note. 'That's two pounds and ten shillings each.'

'Blimey!' exclaimed Keeler. 'More than a week's pay. Are we going to tell the guv'nor?'

'Try not to be stupid all your life, Baz. If we did that, it'd finish up in his pocket, not ours.'

Lipton returned the cab to the transport depot at seven o'clock the following morning.

The sergeant walked all round the vehicle, inspecting it closely. Occasionally, he rubbed his hand on a mark, but eventually satisfied himself that there was no damage that could be attributed to Lipton.

'That seems to be all right, lad,' the sergeant said, somewhat reluctantly. Lipton got the impression that he would have been delighted to find some imperfection. 'Successful observation was it?' he asked.

'I don't know, Skip,' said Lipton, 'you'll have to ask my guv'nor. It didn't mean anything to me.' He had no intention of divulging the reasons for having followed Villiers.

'Cagey lot, you CID blokes,' said the sergeant.

Lipton and Keeler were waiting outside the DDI's office at a quarter to eight later that morning.

Minutes later, Hardcastle appeared. 'Well?' he barked, as the two detectives followed him into his office.

Lipton gave a detailed account of all that had happened during the course of their observation, including the part when they had taken Villiers the last part of his journey, but omitting mention of the five pounds that he had given them for their trouble.

'Are you sure about that, Lipton?' Hardcastle frowned. He was always suspicious when one of his detectives claimed to have had a stroke of luck, and wondered whether they had engineered the situation to avoid a wearisome duty. And

Lipton had a reputation for being blessed with 'strokes of luck'.

'That's exactly what happened, sir.' Lipton sounded indignant. 'I thought how lucky we'd been that Villiers got a flat tyre.'

'What sort of place was this in Hannibal Street, Lipton?' Hardcastle decided not to question the matter of Lipton's luck any further.

'Just an ordinary house, sir. Villiers knocked on the door and was admitted straightaway. But we didn't hang about.'

'Quite right,' said Hardcastle. 'Off you go and get about your duties, and ask Sergeant Marriott to come in.'

'An interesting development, sir,' said Marriott, who had already been apprised of the result of the two detectives' evening's work.

'We'll need to find out about this place, Marriott,' said Hardcastle.

'It's on Mr Sawyer's patch, sir. Perhaps he can shed some light on it.'

'Get on that telephone thing and ask him what he knows, Marriott.'

'Yes, sir.' Marriott paused at the door. 'You ought to have an instrument installed in your office, sir.'

For a moment or two, Hardcastle stared at his sergeant. 'Don't be ridiculous, Marriott,' he said. 'The bloody thing might go off. Anyway, I don't want any Tom, Dick and Harry ringing me up.'

It took Marriott ten minutes to be connected

to Bow Road police station and a further five before he was able to speak to Divisional Detective Inspector Sawyer. But finally he was able to go back to Hardcastle with some interesting information.

'It seems that the occupant of the house in Hannibal Street is a Levi Rosner and he's a rabbi, sir.'

Hardcastle picked up his pipe and spent a few moments scraping out the bowl. 'That could've been a purely religious visit, Marriott, or it might be something more in view of all this business about a Jewish homeland. I think I'd better have a word with Special Branch. They might know more about this place.' He stood up and took his bowler hat and umbrella from the hatstand. 'Not that they're likely to tell me, even if they do know anything.'

'Well now, Mr Hardcastle?' said O'Rourke. 'What have you to report?'

Hardcastle told O'Rourke of the progress of his enquiries into the murder of Peter Stein at Bow, and explained what Lipton and Keeler had discovered. 'I wondered if Special Branch were aware of this place and whether it meant anything to you, sir.'

'It has been established that Sinclair Villiers is of the Jewish faith, Inspector,' said O'Rourke. 'The fact that he visited a rabbi in the East End of London does not seem to me to be at all pertinent to the discovery of the men who murdered Reuben Gosling or Peter Stein. One imagines that he also visits a synagogue from time to time.'

'Perhaps so, sir, but I thought I should inform you.'

'Well, now you've done so, Mr Hardcastle, so I'll not detain you any longer.'

'Very well, sir,' said Hardcastle, only just managing to contain his fury at the near snub he had received at the hands of the Irish chief inspector.

But when Hardcastle had departed, O'Rourke sent for Detective Inspector Lionel Frith.

'I have a job for you, Mr Frith.'

'Yes, sir?'

'I've just received some interesting information from the DDI of A,' began O'Rourke, and recounted what he had been told by Hardcastle. 'It may be entirely innocent, of course, but on the other hand there may be some connection between Captain Haydn Villiers, his father and this rabbi. I think we should take an interest in Rabbi Levi Rosner, Mr Frith.'

'A discreet observation, sir?' asked Frith.

'Not yet. A thorough search of records and contact with informants. We'll see what that produces and then decide on our next course of action.'

But, unbeknown to O'Rourke, Hardcastle had no intention of leaving it there, and determined to conduct his own enquiries.

TWELVE

'Have we done anything about tracing this man Morgan, Marriott?'

'Morgan, sir?'

'Joseph Morgan, the commercial traveller who was supposed to have run off with Sarah Gosling. According to Mrs Partridge, the wife of the gents' outfitter, Sarah Gosling left her husband for Morgan and went to live with him in Brighton.'

'But d'you think he might know anything that would help us, sir?' As was often the case, Marriott was having difficulty following Hardcastle's mercurial changes of direction in the enquiry.

'We won't know until we ask, Marriott. I seem to remember saying that Wood should go, but not until I told him to. I think he should go now.'

'I'll send him straight away, sir, although it remains to be seen whether there'll be any trace of Morgan or Mrs Gosling there. If I remember correctly, Mrs Partridge wasn't altogether sure that that's where the couple had gone. As a matter of fact, I think she was only guessing.'

'We can't rely on guesswork,' said Hardcastle, a comment that surprised Marriott. He had long since convinced himself that the DDI frequently relied on intuition. And often obtained a satisfactory outcome as a result. 'We need hard facts. Once you've sent Wood off, I think we'll have a chat with the rabbi that Villiers visited, and then we'll talk to Villiers himself.'

'Is that wise, sir? We've no evidence to indicate that Sinclair Villiers had anything to do with Reuben Gosling's murder.'

'Haven't we, Marriott?' Hardcastle leaned forward, hands linked on his desk and an earnest expression on his face. 'Wilfred Henwood, Villiers's butler, has told us that Villiers wasn't at home on the night of Gosling's murder. And that begs the question as to where exactly he was.'

The house where Rabbi Levi Rosner lived in Hannibal Street, Bow, was a modest dwelling in a row of equally modest dwellings. But it was well cared for, the paint was new and the windows sparklingly clean. The doorstep appeared to have been whitened that day. But it was probably whitened every day.

Hardcastle raised his hat as the rabbi answered the door, an enquiring expression on his face.

'Rabbi Rosner?'

'That is me, my friend.' Rosner had a full beard, wore rimless glasses, and was soberly dressed in a dark suit and the traditional yarmulke. Hardcastle guessed he was at least sixty.

'I'm a police officer, Rabbi. Divisional Detective Inspector Hardcastle of the Whitehall Division, and this is Detective Sergeant Marriott.'

'Come in, gentlemen, come in,' said Rosner warmly. 'It's too cold a day to stand talking on the doorstep. The cold gets right into your bones, especially when you reach my age.' He led the two detectives into a comfortable sitting room furnished with armchairs and several occasional tables. On one of the tables there was a chess set, the ivory pieces positioned as if a game was already in progress. There were pictures on the walls and over the mantelshelf a framed Hebrew scripture. A fire glowed in the grate. 'Please, tell me how I may help you, Inspector.'

'I'm wondering if you can be of assistance to me in a matter I'm investigating, Rabbi,' said Hardcastle, as he and Marriott accepted Rosner's invitation to take a seat.

'If I possibly can.' Rosner relaxed in a chair opposite the DDI, and selected a curved Meerschaum from a pipe rack on a side table. 'One of my sins is an addiction to tobacco, Inspector. I hope it doesn't offend you.'

'Not at all,' said Hardcastle, taking out his own pipe. 'I am too.'

'Excellent,' said Rosner, and offered the DDI a jar of tobacco. Once the DDI had taken his fill, the rabbi offered the jar to Marriott.

'He smokes cigarettes,' said Hardcastle. 'I keep telling him they'll do him no good.'

The rabbi laughed. 'If that's his only sin, he'll not come to much harm, Mr Hardcastle.'

When both men had their pipes alight, Hardcastle resumed the conversation. 'I'm investigating the murder of a man called Peter Stein who lived over Percy Dyer's chandler's shop in Bow Road, not far from the police station. The murder occurred early in the morning on Friday last. Inspector Sawyer suggested that you might've known the man.' Sawyer had said no such thing when Marriott had telephoned him, but Hardcastle had no intention of telling Rosner that Sinclair Villiers had unwittingly led them to the rabbi's door.

'Is Mr Sawyer not dealing with that case, then?' queried Rosner.

'No. But only because it would appear to be connected with another murder I'm dealing with.'

'A sad business, Inspector,' said Rosner, shaking his head, 'but the world is full of wickedness these days. It seems that this wretched war has given people a licence to kill their fellow man. I sometimes wonder when it will all end. But, mark my words, the world will be no better for it, once it's all over.'

'Did you know Stein, Rabbi?' asked Hardcastle, declining to be drawn into a discussion about the effects of the war.

'Alas no, although I knew of him. He was of the Jewish faith, but he was never to be seen in the synagogue.' Rosner stroked his beard thoughtfully. 'Regrettably, there is nothing I can tell you of this man.'

'As I said just now, we believe that his murder was connected to another murder I'm investigating, the murder of Reuben Gosling.'

'I don't know that name, Inspector. Was he a local man?'

'No, he was the owner of a jewellery and pawnbroking business in the Vauxhall Bridge Road in Westminster and was murdered on New Year's Eve.' Hardcastle, not usually circumspect, realized that he had to be so on this occasion. 'The murderers stole a car from Chelsea belonging to a man called—' He broke off and flicked his fingers. 'What was the man's name, Marriott?'

'Sinclair Villiers, sir,' said Marriott, playing along with Hardcastle's little pretence of forgetfulness.

'Ah yes, that's the fellow.'

'Sinclair Villiers, you say?' said Rosner, expressing genuine surprise and leaning forward in his chair. 'But I know Sinclair. Is there some suggestion that he was involved in these terrible events?'

'Good heavens no,' said Hardcastle, waving a deprecating hand. 'It was merely that his car was stolen from outside his house and used in the robbery, but what a strange coincidence that you should know him. I take it he's a friend of yours.'

'Yes, indeed. An old friend. He visits me often to play chess.' Rosner waved a casual hand towards the chessboard. 'I have to say that he's very good at it, too. Only rarely do I manage to beat him. As a matter of fact, he was here yesterday evening, but he didn't mention anything about this murder. But he beat me twice with a fool's mate.' The rabbi paused to rekindle his pipe. 'Sinclair is a Jew, of course, but then,' he added with a wry smile, 'so are most of my best friends.'

'I think he said that he spent New Year's Eve with you, Rabbi.' Hardcastle took a chance on that being the case. 'Another game of chess, was it?'

Rosner thought about that. 'Not your New Year, Inspector. The Jewish New Year is in September. The thirty-first of December doesn't mean a great deal to orthodox Jews, although some members of my faith take advantage of celebrating two new years.' The rabbi laughed. 'But that's Jews for you,' he added, mocking his own religion.

'Oh well, I suppose he must've been celebrating somewhere else.'

'Probably,' said Rosner. 'In fact, yesterday was the first time I'd seen Sinclair since just after Yom Kippur, and that was last September. I don't know where he'd been over your New Year; away for a holiday perhaps.'

'Well, thank you for your help, Rabbi,' said Hardcastle, as he and Marriott stood up. 'And thank you for the tobacco.'

'If I hear of anything about Peter Stein is there any way I can get in touch with you, Inspector?' Rosner stood up too, and shook hands with the two detectives.

'My sergeant will give you the telephone number of the station at Cannon Row, Rabbi. I'd be grateful to hear of anything you learn.'

It was quite a change for Detective Sergeant Herbert Wood to be assigned to an 'out-of-town' job, and he wasted no time in catching a train to Brighton on the south coast. There was a chill wind blowing when he arrived at just after midday. His only regret was that the assignment would have been more pleasant had it been midsummer and he could have taken a stroll along the beach.

The first surprise to greet Wood when he walked out of Brighton railway station into Queens Road was the sight of a line of German soldiers. Attired in grey uniforms and round hats encircled with red bands, they were chained together and were being marched along the street.

'What's that all about?' asked Wood of a policeman standing nearby.

'Prisoners of war, mate. They're on their way to the POW camp at Shoreham.'

'Are they going to march there?'

'It's only about six miles. It'll do 'em good.'
The policeman laughed. 'You didn't think we
were going to give 'em a ride in a charabanc,
did you?'

'No, I suppose not,' said Wood, and joined in
the Brighton policeman's laughter. 'Can you
direct me to the nick?'

'It's about three-quarters of a mile that way,'
said the policeman, pointing. 'It's in a street
called Bartholomews, next to the town hall. Is
there anything I can do to save you the walk?'

'No, I'm in the Job, Metropolitan. I've got an
enquiry to make of the CID.'

'Good luck, mate. You might find 'em awake.
If they're not in the local boozer, that is.'

Wood eventually found the police station that
was immediately beneath the headquarters of
the Brighton constabulary.

'Yes, sir? Can I help you?' asked the bearded
desk sergeant.

'I'm Detective Sergeant Wood, Metropolitan.
I've come down to make some enquiries into a
couple who are of interest to us in connection
with a murder.'

'Oh yes. And who might they be?'

'A Joseph Morgan and a Sarah Gosling,
although she might be calling herself Sarah
Morgan now. It's a bit of a long shot because
they were supposed to have moved here about
nine years ago.'

'Morgan, Morgan,' said the Brighton sergeant, savouring the name. 'Rings a vague bell,

mate. A murder, you say?'

'Yes, we're looking into the murder of a Reuben Gosling who was Sarah's husband until she ran away with this bloke Morgan.'

The sergeant chuckled. 'Well, they're bound to be here somewhere. Brighton's always the place that people choose for a bit of jig-a-jig on the sly, if that's what it was all about. I'll have a look through our books.' He lifted the flap in the counter. 'Come on through and take the weight off your feet.'

Wood sat down on a hard-backed chair while the sergeant began a search of the station's numerous record books.

'Got it,' said the sergeant triumphantly. 'I knew the name meant something. Here we are.' Running his finger down a page of the daily record, he came across the entry. 'On Wednesday the eighth of September last year, we received a message from F Division of the Metropolitan Police asking us to inform Mrs Sarah Morgan that Joseph Morgan had been killed in a Zeppelin raid. He was staying in a lodging house in Earls Court Road, London S.W., when it was hit by a bomb.'

'That sounds like the couple I'm looking for,' said Wood. 'What was Mrs Morgan's address at the time?'

'Grove Street, mate. I'll jot it down for you.' The sergeant scribbled the details on a sheet of paper and handed it over. 'Anything else I can help you with?'

'You can tell me how to get there.'

'Sure.' The sergeant took a street atlas from his desk drawer and pointed out the quickest way from the police station to Grove Street.

'Thanks for your help,' said Wood. 'I'll go round there and see what I can find.'

'Hope you catch your killer. D'you think it was this Morgan chap?'

'Couldn't've been,' said Wood. 'It happened after Morgan was killed. Apart from telling Mrs Morgan that her first husband's been murdered, I don't really know what my guv'nor hopes me to find out by talking to the woman. But once he gets his teeth into a job like this one, he doesn't let go until he's got his man dancing on the hangman's trap.'

The sergeant laughed. 'I've got a guv'nor like that,' he said.

The two-storied houses in Grove Street were terraced with only a narrow pavement separating them from the roadway. Eight or nine children were playing outside, most of whom, despite the cold weather, were inadequately clothed; some were even barefooted. An urchin with a bowling hoop flew past Wood, shouting some obscenity in the belief that he had right of way. But then some innate sense recognized Wood as a police officer. With a shout of 'coppers', the boy and his cohorts disappeared.

Wood ascended the three steps to the front door of the house said by the Brighton sergeant to be Sarah Gosling's last known address.

From what the police had discovered so far, Sarah Gosling would now be in her mid-fifties, but the woman who answered the door appeared much older. Her grey hair was unkempt and hung around her shoulders in untidy rat's tails. She wore a cheap and fading black bombazine dress; it was a material that, thanks to Queen Victoria's prolonged period of mourning, remained unpopular even fifteen years after her death. But Wood presumed that Sarah Gosling was unable to afford anything else.

'Mrs Gosling?' asked Wood, raising his bowler hat.

The woman emitted a scornful laugh. 'I haven't been known by that name for nigh on ten years. I'm known in these parts as Mrs Morgan, Sarah Morgan. Anyway, who are you and what d'you want?'

'I'm a police officer from London, madam. Detective Sergeant Wood of the Whitehall Division.'

'And what might the police be wanting with me?'

'I think it would be better if I came in, Mrs Morgan.'

'Suit yourself,' said Sarah churlishly, and turned away, leaving Wood to close the door and follow her.

The parlour, a small, cold room on the front of the house was sparsely furnished. The empty fire grate had been filled with a fan of folded newspaper; it was evident that coal was a luxury Mrs Morgan could not afford. Wood decided against removing his overcoat.

'I understand that you were once married to Reuben Gosling, Mrs Morgan.'

'I still am, as far as I know,' said Sarah. 'Anyway, what's it to you?'

'I'm sorry to have to tell you that he was murdered on New Year's Eve.'

That momentous news received no immediate reaction other than a cold stare. 'Have you come all this way just to tell me that?' asked Sarah eventually.

'Not exactly,' said Wood. 'I wondered if you knew of any reason why anyone should've wanted to kill him.'

'Quite a few people, I should think,' was Sarah's surprising reply. 'He was a bully and a skinflint, and he sailed a bit close to the wind,' she continued.

'What d'you mean by that, Mrs Morgan?' asked Wood.

'If you ask me, some of the stuff he had in the shop hadn't been honest come by, if you know what I mean. Any road, I couldn't stand it no more and that's why I left him. My Joe, God rest his soul, was the complete opposite. Always cheerful and always generous. And always ready to give me a good time when he was in funds. Mind you, things got a bit tight once the war started. People haven't got the money for the sort of stuff Joe was selling. He'd even begun going up London again to see how he'd fare up there. But he was killed in an air raid and left me flat broke.'

'I understand you had a son,' said Wood.

'Isaac,' said Sarah listlessly, and stared at the empty fireplace. 'Haven't seen him in years. For all I know he could be dead and buried in France.' She pulled her shawl more closely around her shoulders. 'Not that Isaac was the volunteering sort. Walked out his father's shadow did Isaac. Just as mean and just as spiteful. He might even be in prison, for all I know. And that'd come as no surprise.'

'So, you've no idea where Isaac might be now, Mrs Morgan.'

'No. Anyway, why d'you want to know all this?'

'Because we're trying to find out who killed your husband,' said Wood.

'Are you suggesting that it was Isaac what killed his father?' Sarah's expression was one of disbelief.

'Not at all,' said Wood, 'but he might be able to suggest someone who did.'

'Well, it wasn't me,' snapped Sarah, 'even though I was tempted and had good reasons.'

'What sort of man was your son, Mrs Morgan?'

Sarah Morgan appeared to give that question some thought before answering. 'Political,' she said eventually.

'In what way?' asked Wood.

'He was always banging on about a homeland for the Jews. I've no idea why. Perhaps he was going to live in Palestine.' Sarah emitted a throaty chuckle. 'Perhaps you ought to go there and see if you can find him.'

'Thank you, Mrs Morgan,' said Wood, rising to his feet. 'I'll see myself out.' As he had anticipated, his journey to Brighton had been largely wasted.

It was lunchtime when Hardcastle and Marriott returned to Westminster, and Hardcastle led the way directly to the downstairs bar of the Red Lion.

'Two pints of best, Albert, and a couple of fourpenny cannons.'

'Still keeping you busy, Mr Hardcastle?' asked Albert, placing two glass tankards of best bitter on the counter.

'Never a dull moment, Albert,' said the DDI, drinking a good half of his beer, and wiping his moustache with the back of his free hand.

'We're still no nearer finding out where Sinclair Villiers was on New Year's Eve, or on the night that Peter Stein was topped, sir,' said Marriott, once Albert had moved away to serve another customer.

'I'm beginning to have serious doubts about our Mr Villiers, Marriott. His butler tells us he was out both those nights, and Rabbi Rosner said he wasn't with him. So where was he?'

'Murdering Reuben Gosling, sir?' suggested

Marriott.

'We're a long way from proving that,' said Hardcastle, 'but Villiers has some serious questions to answer. The trouble is that I want Henwood the butler to keep his position in Villiers's household. If we let on that he told us that Villiers was out that night, Henwood will get the sack a bit tout de suite, I reckon. And that won't help us at all.'

'Well, Wood, what have you to tell me?' Hardcastle and Marriott emerged from the Red Lion just as DS Wood alighted from a bus that had brought him from Victoria railway station.

'Largely a waste of time, sir,' said Wood, and went on to recount the result of his visit to Sarah Morgan in Brighton. 'She wasn't the most helpful of witnesses.'

'And she'd no idea where Isaac Gosling is?'

'No, sir. She claims not to have seen him in years. She did suggest he'd gone to Palestine, on account of him being interested in a Jewish settlement. But I think that was all pie in the sky.'

'Not necessarily, Wood,' said Hardcastle thoughtfully. 'However, I've another job for you.'

'Yes, sir?'

'Find him.'

'Yes, sir,' said Wood, wondering how on earth he was to trace the missing son of Reuben and Sarah Gosling.

THIRTEEN

On Wednesday morning, Hardcastle arrived at the police station as usual at eight o'clock. As he passed the door of the detectives' office, he shouted for Marriott. Seating himself behind his desk, he began the morning ritual of filling his pipe.

'Good morning, sir,' said Marriott.

'I've been thinking, Marriott.' Hardcastle, rarely one to return a greeting, dropped his tobacco pouch on the desk, reached for his box of matches and leaned back in his chair.

'Sir?' Marriott was never very happy when the DDI announced that he was 'thinking'.

'Haydn Villiers is locked up in the Tower of London waiting for a court martial.'

'Yes, sir.' Marriott was wondering what was coming next.

'I can't believe that Sinclair Villiers didn't have something to do with his son's espionage.'

'But we've no evidence of that, sir.'

'Exactly, Marriott. So, we'll have to go out and find some. But that would mean treading on the toes of Special Branch and they don't like that. However, Villiers senior was adrift the night that Reuben Gosling was killed and at the time Peter Stein was topped. And I think that that justifies a search warrant.' Hardcastle paused thoughtfully. 'Nevertheless, I think I'll have a word with Mr O'Rourke first.'

'D'you want me to come with you, sir?'

'Certainly not, Marriott. I'm quite capable of dealing with Special Branch on my own.' The truth of the matter was that Hardcastle did not want a junior officer to witness him being made to appear a fool. It was something at which the senior officers of Special Branch seemed more than willing to do when dealing with those they disparagingly referred to as the *ordinary* CID.

Hardcastle eventually found DCI O'Rourke in his own office.

'Mr Hardcastle?' As usual, O'Rourke stared at the DDI with an expression of both surprise and impatience.

'I thought I should inform you that I intend to apply for a search warrant for Sinclair Villiers's house in Flood Street, sir.'

'Why should that be of interest to me or my Branch, Mr Hardcastle?'

'Sinclair Villiers is the father of Haydn Villiers, now held in the Tower on espionage charges, sir.'

'That seems to me to be an irrelevancy,' said O'Rourke. 'But why d'you want to search this man's house?'

'I have reason to believe he might've been

involved in the death of the pawnbroker Reuben Gosling, sir.'

'As I said just now, that's of no interest to me, Mr Hardcastle, but keep me informed of the outcome.'

'Yes, sir.' Hardcastle was puzzled as to why O'Rourke should wish to be kept informed about a matter that he had said was of no interest to him or his Branch. But Hardcastle would never understand the machinations of the political branch of the Metropolitan Police. Neither did he wish to understand it; as far as he was concerned Special Branch officers were not real detectives.

What was more, although he was going to apply for a search warrant, he had no intention of executing it unless it became absolutely necessary. He had other plans for acquiring the information he wanted. Plans that would not arouse suspicion.

The moment he returned to his office, Hardcastle sent for Detective Sergeant Herbert Wood.

'Wood, I want you to pay a visit to your "friend" Henwood the butler at Flood Street. Find out if Villiers is there. If he is, find out when he's next going away. If Henwood knows, that is.'

'Very good, sir,' said Wood, turning to go.

'I haven't finished yet, Wood,' growled Hardcastle. 'If he ain't there, find out when he's likely to be back and telephone Sergeant Marriott a bit *jildi*. You can use Villiers's telephone. Sergeant Marriott will tell you what to do next. And take a cab.'

'Very good, sir,' said Wood, amazed that the DDI had authorized the use of a taxi. He was usually as parsimonious with the Commissioner's money as he was with his own.

Wood descended the area steps of Sinclair Villiers's Flood Street house, knocked loudly and waited.

Eventually, a young girl peered round the half open door, a frightened expression on her face. 'Yes, what is it?'

'Is Mr Henwood about? I'm Bert Wood, a friend of his.'

'You'd better come in. He's in the servants' hall.'

Removing his cloth cap, Wood stepped over the threshold just as the butler came to the door.

Henwood turned to the young girl who had admitted Wood. 'Don't stand there gawping, Violet,' he said, 'get about your duties.'

'Yes, Mr Henwood,' said Violet, and fled back to the kitchen.

'That kitchen maid's all ears,' said Henwood. 'You'd better come into the pantry,' he added, clearly in a hurry to get Wood away from the inquisitive eyes of the other servants.

'Thanks, Wilf,' said Wood. If the foreshortening of the butler's name displeased him, he was at pains to disguise it.

Once in the butler's pantry, Henwood closed the door firmly. 'What d'you want?' he asked, his voice almost a whisper. 'It's not a good idea, you coming here.'

'Is Villiers at home?' asked Wood.

'No, he's gone to Worthing,' said Henwood. 'Went last night. Makes a change for him to tell me where he was going.'

'When's he coming back?'

'He'll be there until Monday morning. At least, that's what he said.'

'What's he doing there?'

Henwood smirked. 'Giving that fancy woman of his a seeing-to most likely.'

'How d'you know that's where he's gone?'

'Butlers know everything, Mr Wood.'

'If you know everything, you'll know who she is and where she lives.' Wood was always ready to acquire any information that came to hand, even though it might appear to have no bearing on the current case.

'Well, I did happen to come across the address when I was in the master's room packing for him.'

Wood laughed derisively. 'Yes, I'll bet you did, just by accident, eh? Doesn't he have a valet, then?'

Henwood scoffed. 'Not him. I'm surprised he's got any staff at all. He's a skinflint, and a bastard to work for.'

'You'd better give me a note of the name and

address, Wilf.' Wood handed over his pocket-book and Henwood scribbled down the address. 'And I need to use your telephone.'

'It's there,' said Henwood, pointing to the polished wooden box on the wall near the door. 'Take the receiver off the hook and wind the handle.'

'I do know how to use a telephone.' A few moments later Wood was receiving instructions from Marriott at Cannon Row police station.

'Get through all right?' asked Henwood.

'Yes thanks. Now then, Wilf, I've got news for you. You had a burglary here last night.'

'No we didn't.'

'Well, I'm telling you that you did. I want you to give me a couple of small bits of your master's jewellery: something like cufflinks, an albert and a tiepin will do. And don't let any of the staff see you. And you never told the staff about the burglary because you didn't want to worry 'em. That phone call I just made was you telephoning Cannon Row police station to report the burglary. Have you got all that?'

'But shouldn't I have informed Chelsea police station?' asked Henwood, totally bemused by this turn of events. 'That's the one that covers this area.'

'Probably, but let's pretend that you didn't know that. You just called the police station that you first thought of, and that was because officers from that station called here the other day in connection with the theft of your master's motor car.'

'But what's the point of all this?' asked Henwood, who was only just managing to keep up with Wood's instructions.

'The point, Wilf, old son, is that officers will attend here very shortly to investigate this burglary and miraculously find the jewellery in the garden.'

'Why?' asked Henwood. 'I don't understand what this is all about.'

Wood chuckled. 'You don't need to understand it.'

'I don't know as how I can go along with all this,' complained the butler. 'What if Mr Villiers finds out? I've got my position to think of, you know.'

'You'll go along with it all right, Wilf, unless you want to finish up in Pentonville nick again. Right now, your "position", as you call it, is hanging by a thread.'

The moment that Hardcastle had learned that Villiers was away from home until Monday, he sent Marriott across to the Yard to explain to DI Collins what he wanted of him. Collins assigned Detective Sergeant Locke, 'one of the best skippers in Fingerprint Bureau', to accompany Hardcastle to Flood Street.

Thirty minutes later, Hardcastle, Marriott and Locke alighted from a taxi outside Sinclair Villiers's house.

In accordance with Wood's suggestion, the

three officers descended the basement area.

Henwood, a worried expression on his face, answered the door.

'I don't like this at all, Inspector.'

'You're not meant to, Henwood.' Hardcastle glanced at Wood. 'All right, Wood, hand over the tom and then bugger off. I don't want you compromising your position. Not that I think we'll need to worry about that for much longer.'

Wood handed the DDI the few items of Villiers's possessions that had been given him by Henwood less than an hour ago, and promptly made his way back to Cannon Row.

'Now, Henwood, I've come to investigate this burglary of yours.'

'I don't like this at all, sir,' said the butler again.

'Just be quiet, Henwood, and show us to your master's bedroom. We'll do the rest.' Hardcastle handed over the items of jewellery that he had received from Wood moments earlier. 'We found these in the garden,' he said with a laugh. 'You can put 'em back where you took 'em from.'

'But what's the point of this, sir?' Henwood was now a very worried man caught, as he was, between the threats of Hardcastle and the fury of his employer.

Hardcastle sighed, realizing that he would have to tell the butler of his plans. 'I have reason to believe that your master may have committed a serious offence, Henwood, and I

need to get his fingerprints without him knowing. If they're not his, then he's in the clear.
Now show me up to his bedroom and his dressing room.'

The three officers followed Henwood up the
back stairs and into Villiers's bedroom.

'Right, Locke, get cracking.' Hardcastle stood
in the centre of the room, hands in pockets, and
waited for the fingerprint officer to start work.
'All right, Henwood, you can go.'

Half an hour later, Locke announced that he
had found a number of useful fingerprints. As
far as he could make out, he said, there were
only two differing sets, but he would have to
wait until he got back to the Yard to make sure.

'Shall I take the butler's fingerprints, sir, for
elimination purposes?'

'No need to worry about that, Locke,' said
Hardcastle. 'His are already in Mr Collins's
collection. He did a carpet for thieving back in
1912.'

It was an impatient Hardcastle who sat in his
office fretting. He picked up his pipe from the
ashtray, looked at it, and put it down again. He
toyed with reports and claims for expenses, but
could not really settle to doing anything important until the results came across from the
Fingerprint Bureau.

At one o'clock, he and Marriott went across
to the Red Lion for their customary liquid
lunch.

228

'I don't know what's taking so long, Marriott. I'd've thought that comparing fingerprints was a simple enough matter.' It was a comment that demonstrated how little the DDI knew of the finer points of the science.

At half past two, Detective Inspector Collins came into Hardcastle's office.

'Have you got something for me, Charlie?' asked Hardcastle.

Collins sat down and opened a file. 'I think you're in luck, Ernie,' he said calmly. 'The prints that Locke found at Flood Street were those of Henwood the butler, and one other set. I'm assuming that they belong to Villiers.'

'Well, I guessed that, Charlie,' said Hardcastle.

'And they match the prints taken from Villiers's motor car.'

'Comes as no surprise,' muttered Hardcastle. 'He drives the damned thing.'

'But they don't match those found on the showcase in Gosling's shop at Vauxhall Bridge Road, or on the sash weight that you found there.'

'Damnation!' exclaimed Hardcastle. 'And I thought he was up for it.'

'It's not all bad news, Ernie,' said Collins, 'because they do match prints found in Stein's room at Bow Road.'

'Aha! Got the bastard. Will it stand up in court, Charlie?'

Collins looked at Hardcastle with a pained

expression on his face. 'If I say they're a match, Ernie, they're a match. So, what are you going to do now?'

'What I'm going to do now, Charlie, is to go down to this address in Worthing and nick Mr Sinclair Villiers for the murder of Peter Stein. That'll make his eyes water.'

'I'll let you have my statement and Locke's statement in due course, Ernie,' said Collins. 'I just hope your bird hasn't flown.'

'He won't have done,' said Hardcastle. 'He's far too cocky to think that he'd get caught.'

'I'll leave you to it, then. Enjoy your day at the seaside, Ernie,' said Collins, as he gathered his papers together and made his way back to the Yard.

'What was that name and address in Worthing that Wood got from Henwood, Marriott?'

'The woman is Mrs Victoria Wheeler and she lives on West Parade, Worthing, sir.'

'Good. Tomorrow morning we'll go to this love nest in Worthing and ruin their weekend for them, Marriott.'

The train journey from Victoria to West Worthing took just over an hour. There was quite a strong wind blowing off the seafront when the detectives' cab turned into West Parade. The sea was rough, and white-capped waves hurled themselves at the beach, only to recede feebly until their next onslaught.

'We should've come in the summer, Marriott,' commented Hardcastle pointlessly.

Victoria Wheeler's house was an ornate double-fronted property, and clearly worth a substantial amount of money.

The first disturbing indication that the bird might indeed have flown was the absence of Villiers's Haxe-Doulton tourer from the drive of Mrs Wheeler's house.

'I've a nasty feeling that Villiers might have buggered off already, Marriott,' said Hardcastle.

'Good morning, sir,' said the housemaid who opened the door in response to Hardcastle's knock.

'Is Mrs Wheeler at home, lass?'

'Who shall I say it is, sir?'

'We're police officers.'

'Oh!' exclaimed the girl, apparently disconcerted by this announcement. 'If you care to step inside, sir, I'll enquire if the mistress is at home.' She returned a few moments later. 'This way, sir.'

A vivacious woman in her thirties greeted the two London detectives. She was a tall and slender blonde, and, even to Hardcastle's unpractised eye, the fine-wool navy blue costume that she wore had cost a deal more than Alice Hardcastle would have been able to afford. The jacket, popular for the period, had numerous buttons down the front and a simulated belt, undoubtedly influenced by the military uniforms that seemed to be everywhere since the war started. And the skirt, although long, neverthe-less revealed the woman's ankles and a pair of black, glacé-kid shoes. As she drew closer, Hardcastle detected the whiff of a delicate per-fume.

'Sarah tells me you are from the police.' The statement, almost an accusation, was delivered in cultured tones, and displayed no sign of apprehension.

'That's correct, madam. I'm Divisional De-tective Inspector Hardcastle of Scotland Yard.' Hardcastle often claimed to be from Commis-sioner's Office when out of London; he imagin-ed it lent him an extra authority that he did not really need. 'And this is Detective Sergeant Marriott.'

'I see. And why, pray, should two officers from Scotland Yard be paying me a visit?' As an apparent afterthought, Mrs Wheeler added, 'You'd better sit down and tell me what this is all about.'

'It's not you I wanted to see, madam,' said Hardcastle. 'I was hoping to find Mr Sinclair Villiers here.'

'Were you really?' The woman spoke in haughty tones, as though Hardcastle had accus-ed her outright of adultery. 'Well, I'm afraid you've had a wasted journey. He's not here.'

'I was given to understand that he was going to be here for the weekend, Mrs Wheeler.'

'That was the original intention, but late last night he received a telephone call from his butler who said something about his house having been burgled. As a result he rushed straight back to London. It was just as well because my husband was recalled yesterday as well.' As if to emphasize the point, she waved at a studio portrait of a man in the full dress uniform of a major in the Scots Guards holding a bearskin in the crook of his arm. 'Sinclair is a family friend, of course.'

'Of course,' murmured Hardcastle. 'I'm sorry to have bothered you, madam,' he said, as he and Marriott stood up.

'Are you going back to London?' asked Mrs Wheeler.

'Yes, I'll call on Mr Villiers at his Flood Street address.'

'You've met him before, I take it.'

'Indeed I have, madam.'

'It would have saved you a wasted journey if you'd telephoned me. I could have told you that he wasn't here.'

'I suppose so,' said Hardcastle, thinking that that would not have made the slightest difference.

'I'll have Sarah show you out, Inspector.'

'Thank you, madam,' said Hardcastle tersely.

The moment that Hardcastle had left the house, Mrs Wheeler went into a back room that she used as a study and made a telephone call.

The two detectives walked out on to West Parade and were immediately buffeted by the

233

strong wind. Hardcastle was in a foul mood, not helped by the fact that they had to walk some considerable distance before sighting a cab.

They were on the train, and in a compartment to themselves, before the DDI gave vent to his feelings.

'That bloody man Henwood tipped him off, Marriott.'

'Certainly looks like it, sir. So, a call at Flood Street?'

'If Villiers is there, Kaiser Bill's my bloody uncle, Marriott,' exclaimed Hardcastle crossly. 'He knows we're on to him, and he's run. The question is where.'

'D'you believe this story about Mrs Wheeler's husband being recalled, sir?'

'Not on your life! I doubt he even exists.'

'But there was a photograph of him, sir, in the uniform of the Scots Guards.'

'How do we know it's her husband, Marriott? Just because that's what Mrs Wheeler said don't mean it's true. It could've been anyone: her brother for instance, or even another paramour. No, Marriott, Villiers was down there for a bit of jig-a-jig, and the only thing that pleases me at all is that we've buggered up his passionate few days by the seaside.' Hardcastle lapsed into silence for a moment or two. 'We'll have a word with Colonel Frobisher about this so-called Major Wheeler of the...' He paused. 'Scots Guards, you say?'

'Yes, sir.'

'Well, we'll see if the colonel can tell us if the major exists and if he was recalled yesterday.'

'But what will that prove, sir?'

'Nothing, Marriott, except to give me some satisfaction, and to counter any story that Villiers might come up with when we eventually find him.'

Hardcastle was in no better mood when he reached Cannon Row. After a thoughtful five minutes, he made a decision.

'I think we'll go to Flood Street anyway, Marriott. I'm keen to know what Henwood will have to say for himself.'

'Unless he's disappeared too, sir.'

'One way of finding out,' growled Hardcastle. 'But we'll see the APM on the way.' He put on his overcoat and took his hat and umbrella from the hatstand.

'Inspector Hardcastle.' Colonel Frobisher skirted his desk and shook hands. 'And what trouble are you bringing me today?'

'A fairly simple enquiry, Colonel,' said Hardcastle, as he and Marriott accepted Frobisher's invitation to take a seat. 'In connection with certain enquiries I'm making, a Major Wheeler of the Scots Guards has come to my attention; he's apparently the husband of Mrs Victoria Wheeler. My information is that he was recalled from his Worthing home yesterday.'

'Are you absolutely sure about that, Inspector?' Frobisher appeared to have been taken aback by Hardcastle's statement.

'Most certainly, Colonel. I spoke to his wife only this morning.'

'There's something very wrong with this.' Frobisher stood up and wandered back and forth behind his desk. 'I happen to have known Jimmy Wheeler. He and I were at the Royal Military College at Sandhurst together, but he was killed at Givenchy on the eighteenth of December 1914. It was me who had to tell Victoria. Half Jimmy's battalion was wiped out during the course of a rather badly planned attack.' The APM paused; clearly there was something troubling him. 'You say you visited Victoria at Worthing, Inspector.'

'Yes, I did. At West Parade, Worthing.'

'I have to say that this is all very strange. I was best man at the Wheelers' wedding in 1906, and after their marriage he and Victoria set up home in the family seat, a rather splendid house in Esher that had belonged to Jimmy's late father. Perhaps Victoria moved to Worthing after Jimmy's death. Was there by any chance another man there, Inspector?'

'No, Colonel. There had been, but he left the previous evening. She described him as a family friend.'

Frobisher laughed. 'I'm not at all surprised,' he said. 'Victoria Wheeler always had a reputation for being a flighty young girl. Still, there's no reason why she shouldn't have a man friend now that she's a widow, and a damned attractive one at that.'

'How well d'you know her, Colonel?' asked Hardcastle.

'Very well indeed.' Frobisher emitted a rueful laugh. 'As a matter of fact, Jimmy just pipped me to the post. If I'd been quicker off the mark, I would have married her myself, but I suppose a Guards officer beats a humble Sherwood Forester every time. But none of this rings true, Inspector.'

'Can you describe Mrs Wheeler, Colonel?' asked Marriott.

'I can do better than that, Sergeant. I think I've a photograph of the wedding here somewhere that I'd like you to take a look at.' Frobisher returned to his seat and began rummaging through the drawers of his desk. 'Yes, here we are,' he said, eventually finding the print and handing it to Hardcastle.

For a moment or two, the DDI studied the photograph. It showed the newly-weds emerging from the church through an archway of raised swords held, presumably, by James Wheeler's brother officers. In the background was Ralph Frobisher in the full dress uniform of the Sherwood Foresters.

'That's not the Victoria Wheeler I saw.' Hardcastle handed the print to Marriott. 'What d'you think?'

Marriott needed only a cursory glance. 'That's definitely not her, sir. The woman we saw was a blonde, and the girl in this photograph has dark hair. And that is not the officer in the photograph that was on the mantel, sir. As far as I can tell.'

'Do you know who this male visitor was?' asked Frobisher, now becoming even more concerned as the tale unfolded.

'Sinclair Villiers, Colonel.'

'Oh my God!' That information shocked Frobisher even further. 'D'you mean Captain Haydn Villiers's father?'

'Yes, that's the man,' said Hardcastle.

'Far be it for me to suggest how you should do your job, Inspector, but the implications of all this could be very serious. In view of what we know of Haydn Villiers, this woman could somehow be tied up in passing information to the enemy.'

'I'd just come to that conclusion myself, Colonel.' Hardcastle stood up. 'Thank you for your assistance. I think it's time that I started making a few arrests.' He paused in the doorway. 'D'you happen to know the address in Esher where the Wheelers were living, Colonel?'

'I'll write it down for you,' said Frobisher, and scribbled the details on a slip of paper.

FOURTEEN

Instead of going to Flood Street to confront Villiers's butler, Hardcastle returned to his office.

'There's something funny going on here, Marriott,' said the DDI, and sat down behind his desk.

'So it would appear, sir,' said Marriott diplomatically. To him it was patently obvious that there was something sinister in a woman claiming to be the wife of a dead Scots Guards major. Especially as she had displayed a photograph of someone who was *not* James Wheeler in her sitting room, and had claimed that he had been recalled on the previous day.

'Before we do anything hasty, we'll make sure that what Colonel Frobisher told us is the truth.'

'But how do we do that, sir?' Marriott could not understand why the DDI should doubt the APM's word. He thought that Frobisher's personal knowledge of the Wheelers, together with the photograph of their wedding was sufficient proof.

'We go to Esher and find out, Marriott. I

should've thought you'd have worked that out for yourself.'

Marriott had worked it out, but he also knew that if he had suggested it, Hardcastle would have dismissed it as a waste of time. That said, he knew that the DDI would always check what others had told him. And then check it again.

The train journey from Waterloo railway station to Esher in Surrey took half an hour. Fortunately, there were several cabs waiting on the station forecourt.

The Wheeler house was a large white double-fronted mansion set in its own spacious grounds. 'This is some place, Marriott,' said Hardcastle, as the cab stopped at the end of a long winding drive. 'I reckon the Wheelers weren't short of a bob or two.'

'Good afternoon, gentleman.' The butler, immaculately attired, spoke with the deference of his profession combined with an air of superiority.

'I'm a police officer,' said Hardcastle, 'and I'd like a word with Mrs Wheeler.'

'Certainly, sir. I'll enquire if the mistress is receiving visitors today.' The butler paused. 'I trust there's no trouble, sir,' he said, with a slight lift of his eyebrows.

'No, not at all. It's just an enquiry that Mrs Wheeler may be able to assist me with.'

'Very good, sir. Perhaps you'd step inside.'

Hardcastle and Marriott entered a large

temple-tiled hall. There was a large round table in the centre upon which, neatly arranged, were copies of *The Times*, the *Morning Post* and the *Daily Mail*. Several portraits adorned the walls, most of which depicted soldiers in Guards uniform.

'It looks as though the army is a Wheeler family tradition, Marriott,' commented Hardcastle, looking around. 'And I wouldn't like to have to clean that, either,' he added, glancing up at the crystal chandelier that dominated the hall.

'This way, gentlemen,' said the butler, returning a few moments later. 'The mistress is in the drawing room.'

The woman who greeted Hardcastle and Marriott was, by any reckoning, a beauty who had yet to reach her thirtieth birthday. Her upswept brown hair was immaculately coiffed, and her red silk dress rustled as she crossed the room with her hand held out.

'I'm Victoria Wheeler, gentlemen,' she said, as she shook hands with each of them. 'How may I help you? Do please sit down,' she added with a smile, and indicated one of two leather chesterfield sofas that faced each other at right angles to a roaring log fire. She sat down opposite the detectives, leaned forward and opened a pewter box. Taking out a cigarette, she fitted it into a long holder. 'Please help yourselves if either of you smoke.' She pushed the cigarette box across the small table that separated them.

'I'm a pipe smoker, madam,' said Hardcastle,

who was still unaccustomed to the sight of a woman smoking, even in her own home. 'If you've no objection, that is.'

'None at all. Please go ahead. My late husband was a pipe smoker, and I grew to like the aroma of it.'

'I'm Divisional Detective Inspector Hardcastle of the Whitehall Division, madam, and this is Detective Sergeant Marriott. And I'm investigating two murders.' He took out his pipe and began to fill it.

'Good heavens!' exclaimed Victoria Wheeler, holding her cigarette holder aloft as her face expressed concern. 'Not here in sleepy old Esher, surely?'

'No, madam, in London.' Hardcastle directed a plume of smoke towards the ceiling.

'Oh, what a disappointment. Nothing like that ever happens here. Actually, the only exciting thing to have happened in the last couple of years was when our curate ran off with the wife of one of his parishioners.' Victoria Wheeler giggled and fingered a gold neck chain that caught the glimmer of the fire's flames, enhancing the marble-whiteness of her skin. 'How can you possibly think that I can help you, then?'

'I don't want to weary you with the details, Mrs Wheeler,' said Hardcastle, realizing that he had to be somewhat circumspect in his questioning, 'but the name of Sinclair Villiers came up in the course of our enquiries. His butler, a very unreliable fellow in my view, suggested that Mr Villiers was a friend of yours, and sometimes visited you.'

'How intriguing.' Victoria Wheeler looked Hardcastle straight in the eye. 'I do have one or two gentlemen admirers, Inspector, but your Mr Villiers doesn't feature among them. What sort of age is this man?'

'He's about fifty or so, I'm led to believe.'

'Much too old,' said Victoria, dismissing the prospect with a gay laugh. But then she stopped abruptly. 'Oh, I didn't mean to imply that being someone of that age is old, Inspector, but that he would be too old to interest me. In fact, my father is about the same age.'

'This butler fellow also claimed that you and your late husband – Major James Wheeler, I believe – were family friends of Mr Villiers.' Hardcastle had decided to put all the blame for his story on Henwood, rather than complicating the conversation by mentioning the other Mrs Wheeler.

'James was certainly my husband, but he was killed at Givenchy at the beginning of the war, so that would be impossible. I'm sorry, Inspector, but Mr Villiers's butler must be confusing me with someone else.'

'So it would seem, Mrs Wheeler, and I apologize for having troubled you,' said Hardcastle, as he and Marriott stood up. 'But these matters have to be followed up, especially in so serious a case as a double murder.'

'I quite understand, Inspector.' Mrs Wheeler

rose and once again shook hands. She crossed to a bell pull and summoned the butler. 'These officers are leaving now, Cross.'

'Very good, madam. This way, if you please, gentlemen.' When they reached the front door, the butler asked, 'May I call you a cab, sir?'

'No thank you, Cross,' said Hardcastle. 'I asked my cab to wait.' Firmly believing that his interview with Mrs Wheeler would not take long, he had had the foresight not to dismiss the taxi.

'Very wise, sir,' commented the butler.

Less than hour after arriving, he and Marriott were back on a train bound for London.

'I think I'm going to have to tread carefully, Marriott, because this whole business seems to be developing into a matter that Special Branch ought to be dealing with.' Hardcastle would have been quite content to pursue his enquiries on his own, but he had tangled with the political branch before, and it was not a pleasant experience. And it was particularly inadvisable to make an enemy of Superintendent Patrick Quinn. He took out his hunter. 'Half past six. I suppose Mr Quinn might still be there.'

Marriott was surprised at the DDI's decision. He knew from past experience that Hardcastle was loath to have dealings with Special Branch.

'What can I do for you, Mr Hardcastle?' Superintendent Quinn was standing by the hatstand in his office. Already clad in a raincoat, and holding his top hat and umbrella, he was on the point of leaving.

'I'm sorry to bother you so late, sir, but a matter has arisen that I think is urgent and may be of interest to Special Branch.'

'I see. Well, make it as quick as you can. I have another appointment.'

As succinctly as he was able, Hardcastle explained the curious matter of the bogus Victoria Wheeler in Worthing and her association with Sinclair Villiers. He mentioned also the sudden disappearance of Villiers and, finally, he reported the outcome of his interview with the real Mrs Wheeler in Esher.

'You'd better sit down, Mr Hardcastle.' Quinn placed his top hat on a bookcase, and took off his raincoat, his appointment forgotten.

Hardcastle went on to remind Quinn of the murder of Peter Stein in Bow and that he was aware that a Morse code transmitter had been removed by Special Branch detectives.

'How did you know that?' demanded Quinn, his bushy eyebrows lifting in surprise.

'The DDI at Bow Road told me, sir.'

'Did he indeed,' responded Quinn crossly, but the impression was one of irritation with his own men for making that information known to the Bow Road police.

'I presume that the equipment was examined for fingerprints, sir, and I was wondering whether Sinclair Villiers's were found anywhere on the machine.'

'We don't happen to have Villiers's finger-prints,' Quinn reluctantly admitted.

'I do, sir, or at least, Mr Collins has them.' Hardcastle explained the subterfuge he had employed in order to obtain those prints.

'I'm beginning to think that you're quite a resourceful officer, Mr Hardcastle,' said Quinn, affording the DDI a rare smile. 'In that case, I shall arrange to have the equipment examined forthwith. In the meantime, I shall inform MI5 of what you have discovered. In fact, I think you might have uncovered more of the espion-age network that we were already familiar with. But we will have to move quickly if we are to arrest this Mrs Wheeler. The Mrs Wheeler in Worthing, of course, not the one in Esher.' He paused. 'Although I fear we may be too late.'

'Will you require my assistance, sir?'

'I most certainly will, Mr Hardcastle, given that you know what she looks like,' said Quinn. 'You weren't thinking of going home, were you?'

'No, sir.' Hardcastle had been intending to do just that, but deemed it politic to make himself available for further duty. 'I have my sergeant standing by, as well, sir.'

'Good,' said Quinn. He pressed a bell-push on his desk and seconds later an officer appeared. 'Ah, Mr Strange, this is DDI Hardcastle of A.'

'Detective Inspector John Strange, sir,' said the officer as he shook hands.

'Mr Strange, get hold of Mr O'Rourke, wherever he happens to be,' said Quinn, 'and Sergeants Shaughnessy and Colter and Detective Constable Lacey. I want to see them here immediately.'

'Yes, sir.'

'And bring me a form for an OSA written order.'

'Yes, sir.'

'I propose to go to Worthing immediately, Mr Hardcastle, and search this house,' said Quinn, once Strange had departed, 'and I want you and your sergeant to accompany me and my officers.'

'But won't you need a search warrant, sir?' asked Hardcastle, somewhat bewildered by the speed at which Quinn was moving things along.

'I shall sign a superintendent's written order to search under the Official Secrets Act of 1911, Mr Hardcastle. That was the form I just asked Strange to bring me.'

Within minutes of Quinn's summons, his office seemed to be full of officers.

'I'll get Mr Hardcastle here to explain what he's discovered,' said Quinn, 'and then I'll tell you what I propose to do about it.'

Hardcastle repeated the details of his discovery and was pleased to see that the assembled Special Branch officers were taking a keen interest.

'We shall now go to Worthing and conduct a search of this woman's house,' said Quinn. 'But

247

first, I must give Mr Collins instructions.' He picked up the receiver of his telephone, tapped the rest sharply and asked to be connected to the officer in charge of the Fingerprint Bureau. Having told Collins to make an urgent comparison of Sinclair Villiers's prints with any on the Morse code equipment, he stood up. 'You ought to get a telephone in your office, Mr Hardcastle,' he suggested. 'A very useful piece of equipment.'

'Yes, sir,' said Hardcastle, deeming it unwise to say that he regarded the telephone as an infernal instrument that would not last.

Strange returned with the form that Quinn had requested. Scribbling his signature on the document, he handed it to O'Rourke.

'One more thing, Mr Strange. Arrange for a message to be sent to all ports regarding Sinclair Villiers. He is to be detained if he attempts to leave the country.'

'Very good, sir,' said Strange.

'Although God knows where he'd go in time of war,' added Quinn.

As the result of a telephone call to Basil Thomson, the Assistant Commissioner for Crime, Superintendent Quinn had been afforded the immediate use of two high-powered motor cars. Consequently, Hardcastle, Marriott and the group of SB officers arrived at West Parade, Worthing at nine o'clock that evening. By that time it was pitch dark and pouring with rain.

248

Having sent Shaughnessy and Lacey to the back of the house to guard against any possible escape by its occupants, Quinn, accompanied by Hardcastle, O'Rourke, Strange, Marriott and Colter, marched up to the front door and hammered loudly. There was no reply.

'Break in, Mr Strange,' said Quinn.

'Yes, sir.' Strange took his detective's stave from his pocket and smashed the glass panel in the front door. Putting his hand through the gap, he undid the Yale rim lock and opened the door.

Quinn led the other officers into the house. They were greeted by a loud scream, and were confronted by a young girl cowering at the back of the hall.

'Calm yourself, miss,' said Quinn. 'We're police officers. Who are you?'

'I'm Sarah, the maid, sir,' said the girl who, understandably, had been terrified by the sound of breaking glass and the fearsome sight of the bearded, top-hatted Quinn leading other officers into the house from the darkness.

'Why didn't you answer the door, colleen?' asked Quinn gently.

'The mistress told me not to answer the door to anyone, sir.'

'And where is your mistress? I presume you're talking about Mrs Victoria Wheeler.'

'Yes, sir, but she's gone.'

'Gone where?'

'I don't know, sir.' Sarah suddenly recognized Hardcastle and pointed an accusing finger at him. 'It was just after that gentleman had left this morning that she went, sir.'

'That comes as no surprise,' murmured Hardcastle.

'Did she take anything with her, Sarah?' asked Quinn.

'She threw a few clothes into a suitcase, sir, and asked me to call a cab for her.'

'Did you know where this cab was taking her?'

'No, sir, she never said.'

Addressing Shaughnessy, who had now joined the group of police officers, Quinn said, 'Get on to the cab company and find out where they took Mrs Wheeler.' He turned to the maid. 'Tell this sergeant which cab company you called, young lady, and show him where he can find the telephone.'

Minutes later, Shaughnessy returned. 'The cab driver took Mrs Wheeler to West Worthing railway station, sir. But he didn't know where she was going from there.'

'Get down to the station, Shaughnessy, and see if you can find out where Mrs Wheeler went,' said Quinn. 'Mr Hardcastle will give you a description. In the meantime,' he added, addressing O'Rourke, 'I want this house thoroughly searched.'

The maid looked extremely worried at this turn of events. 'What shall I tell the mistress when she returns, sir?'

'I think it's safe to assume that she won't be

returning, lass,' said Hardcastle.

'Where d'you live, Sarah?' asked Quinn.

'Why, here, sir. I live in.'

'Yes, but where are your folks?'

'Oh, I see. At Lancing, sir.'

'The best thing you can do is to take your belongings and go home. And use the telephone to call a cab for yourself.' Quinn gave the girl half a crown. 'That should cover the fare,' he said.

'Oh, thank you ever so much, sir,' said Sarah, and bobbed a curtsy.

Hardcastle was amazed by this brief insight into Quinn's character. In his previous dealings with the Special Branch chief, he had always seen him as an austere and rather unforgiving individual.

'But what about the house, sir?' asked Sarah.

'There's no need for you to worry about that, lass.'

'Are you sure it'll be all right, sir?'

'Don't fret yourself now, Sarah,' said Quinn. 'We'll make sure it's secure once we've finished here. One more thing, before you depart. Did your mistress ever go anywhere on a regular basis?'

'Yes, sir. She went to Shoreham harbour about once a month, sir. I always had to call a cab for her.'

'D'you know why she went there?'

Sarah looked embarrassed at the question. 'I think she might've had a gentleman friend there, sir.'

'Did she say as much?' asked Quinn.

Sarah looked down at the floor, a guilty expression on her face, and twisted her hands together. 'No, sir, I just assumed she must've been seeing an admirer.'

'What about Mr Villiers? Was he one of Mrs Wheeler's admirers?'

'I think so, sir. Mr Villiers was often here. He used to come and stay the weekend, but only when the major was away.'

'And was the major here last weekend, Sarah?' asked Hardcastle.

'No, sir. In fact I've never seen him. The mistress said he was in the army and couldn't get leave.'

'Off you go, then, Sarah,' said Quinn, 'and don't tell anyone what we're doing here, even your family. It's secret government work.'

'Of course not, sir,' said Sarah, seemingly much impressed by this latest instruction.

'I'll leave you to oversee the search, Mr O'Rourke,' said Quinn, once Sarah had disappeared to start packing. 'Mr Hardcastle and I will be in the drawing room.'

'Perhaps my Sergeant Marriott could assist your officers, sir,' said Hardcastle. 'I still have two murders to solve and he might come across something of use to me in my investigation.'

'Yes, of course. In my line of work, Mr Hardcastle, one tends to overlook mundane things like murders.' Quinn walked through to the drawing room and seated himself in a leather armchair.

It was eleven o'clock that evening by the time that Chief Inspector O'Rourke's team of searchers had finished.

'We found this, sir.' O'Rourke entered the drawing room holding a talcum powder tin, a pen and half a dozen sheets of paper. 'The talcum powder tin was in the bathroom, and the sheets of paper were secreted behind several pictures on the upstairs landing.'

'Sounds a bit amateurish,' commented Quinn, 'if it's what I think it is.'

'It is, sir, yes,' said O'Rourke.

'It's a talcum powder tin converted to take invisible ink, Mr Hardcastle,' said Quinn, seeing the DDI's bemused expression. 'And, if we're lucky, there'll be evidence of spying when we have the sheets of paper developed.'

'I thought that was storybook stuff, sir,' said Hardcastle.

'The simplest methods are often the best,' commented Quinn. 'Truth is often stranger than fiction,' he added.

'I'll arrange to have these sheets of paper examined immediately, sir,' said O'Rourke. 'There might be something useful on them.'

'We can but hope,' said Quinn. 'Let me know the result as soon as you have it.'

'I'll put it in hand the moment we get back to the Yard, sir.'

Quinn stood up. 'I think we've done all we

can do here,' he said, and walked out to the hall where the remainder of his team were gathered. 'Colter, you and Shaughnessy, when he returns from the railway station, will stay here in Worthing and follow up what the maid told us about Mrs Wheeler's monthly visits to Shoreham harbour. Tell Shaughnessy to telephone me the moment he has any information about where Mrs Wheeler went after the cab delivered her to the station. I shall return to London with everyone else.'

'Anything of interest to us, Marriott?' asked Hardcastle.

'No, sir, nothing to indicate any connection with the murders of Gosling and Stein.'

'I shouldn't be too sure about that, Sergeant,' said Quinn.

Superintendent Quinn and his team arrived back at Scotland Yard at gone midnight.

The moment Quinn entered his office, the duty inspector appeared. 'Shaughnessy telephoned about half an hour ago, sir. He said that a woman matching Mrs Wheeler's description booked a first-class ticket to Godalming in Surrey.'

'Interesting,' said Quinn. 'Contact the police there and ask them to check with local cab companies. They might be able to tell us where Mrs Wheeler went from there, although I hold out little hope.'

'Very good, sir,' said the duty inspector.

'I'll see you here at half past eight tomorrow morning, Mr Hardcastle. I'll speak to the assistant commissioner and ask for you to be temporarily attached to Special Branch. Good night to you.'

FIFTEEN

'I believe that you've previously interviewed Sinclair Villiers's butler, Mr Hardcastle,' said Quinn, when the DDI reported to him on Friday morning.

'Yes, sir, I've had several dealings with Henwood. He's an unsavoury character, and he has a previous conviction for larceny. He stole from his then employer in June 1912 and was sent down for three months.'

'How then did he obtain his present post as butler?' Quinn raised a querying eyebrow.

'By means of a false character reference, sir,' said Hardcastle.

'Excellent,' said Quinn, rubbing his hands together. 'Then I suggest you arrest him for that offence. And in the unlikely event that Sinclair Villiers is there, you can arrest him too.'

'What charge do you suggest for Villiers, sir?'

'Oh, something under the Defence of the Realm Act, I should think,' said Quinn airily. 'That covers most things, and it'll do until we find something substantive that we are able to charge him with.'

* * *

It was half past nine exactly that morning when Hardcastle and Marriott arrived at Sinclair Villiers's house in Flood Street, Chelsea.

They mounted the steps to the front door and Hardcastle hammered loudly on the knocker.

Wilfred Henwood, immaculate in tailcoat and striped trousers, answered the door.

'Oh, it's you, Inspector!' His face paled dramatically when he recognized the visitors. He knew instinctively that the DDI's arrival did not bode well.

'Yes, it's me, Henwood,' said Hardcastle, 'and I want a word with you.' The DDI took a step closer to the butler so that their faces were only inches apart. 'Where has your master gone?' he asked, as Henwood retreated into the hall.

'He's gone to Mrs Wheeler's house for the weekend, sir,' stuttered Henwood, severely shaken by Hardcastle's aggressive approach.

'He might've done, but you know damn' well that he's not there now because yesterday you tipped him off that I was after him.' Hardcastle was furious with the butler and it showed.

'I do have a duty to my master, sir,' said the whining Henwood plaintively. He had backed up against the large table in the centre of the hall and could not retreat any further.

'Yes, and you'll have a duty to the prison governor by the time I've finished with you, my lad. That's if you don't have an appointment with the hangman. I've got a couple of murders to solve and you're coming dangerously close to the top of my list of suspects.'

The last threat struck terror into Henwood and he began to shake violently. It was as well that the table was supporting him or he might have dropped to the floor in a state of collapse. 'What's Mr Villiers supposed to have done, sir?' he asked, only managing to get the words out in a sort of strangulated whisper.

'You'll find out soon enough,' said Hardcastle. 'In the meantime, I have a search warrant for this property and Sergeant Marriott and I are going to execute it right now. And we'll start with Villiers's study.'

'I don't think the master would like that, sir, not being here.' Henwood, still white-faced and shaking, was in the unenviable position of being petrified at the prospect of his master's reaction to a search of his house, and the certainty that Hardcastle would arrest him if he attempted to impede that search.

'I don't suppose he would, but I'm not expecting him to like it. So lead on.'

The study was a comfortable room with several armchairs and an oak desk.

'See what you can find that might tell us where Villiers has gone, Marriott.'

After ten minutes of searching both the study and the bedroom, Marriott found a leather-bound address book in one of the drawers in a bedside cabinet and handed it to the DDI.

'I suppose it might be useful,' said Hardcastle,

thumbing through the book, 'although I some-how doubt it. Take it with you, Marriott.'

The search revealed nothing else of value to the investigation. But Hardcastle had concluded from his previous dealings with Villiers that the man was far too shrewd to leave damning evi-dence for the police to find.

Returning to the hall on the ground floor, Hardcastle confronted the butler. 'Where's the footman, Henwood?'

'Downstairs in the servants' hall, sir.'

'Fetch him up here.'

'But why d'you want Frederick, sir?'

'Just fetch him, Henwood,' snapped Hard-castle irritably, 'and don't argue the toss.'

Henwood opened the door that led to the downstairs part of the house and shouted for Frederick.

When the footman appeared, Hardcastle said jocularly, 'I've decided to appoint you the butler of this household, Frederick.'

'But I'm the butler here, Inspector.' Henwood did not like the way in which this little scenario was being played out. It was a lame and formal protest, mildly made, but one that Henwood felt he should make. Especially in the presence of the footman.

'Not any more you're not, Henwood, because I'm arresting you for obstructing police in the execution of their duty. That'll do for a start, but other charges will undoubtedly follow.' Hard-castle turned back to the footman. 'And if you want to stay out of trouble, Frederick my lad, you'll call the police the moment Villiers gets back here.' Not that he thought that there was much chance of Villiers returning in the foreseeable future. 'And do it discreetly, because if Villiers finds out you've told us and he scarpers again, I'll nick you an' all. Got it?'

'Yes, sir,' said Frederick, now as cowed as Henwood by this inspector's bullying attitude.

Leaving the running of Villiers's household in the care of the bemused footman, Hardcastle and Marriott escorted Henwood into a cab.

'Scotland Yard, driver,' said Hardcastle, and turning to Henwood, said, 'Tell 'em Cannon Row, Henwood, and half the time you'll end up in Cannon Street in the City of London.'

Henwood did not seem to find the comment informative, but Marriott sighed inwardly; he had heard the DDI's little homily all too often.

It was half past twelve when Hardcastle and Marriott arrived at the police station with their prisoner.

'You can lock this man up, Skipper,' said Hardcastle. 'We'll let him sweat for a bit, and I'll have a word with him after I've had a bite to eat.'

'Very good, sir.' The station officer dipped his pen into the inkwell and began the laborious task of recording Henwood's details in the large occurrence book.

'All this police work's given me a thirst, Marriott. I think I deserve a pint,' said Hardcastle, and led the way to the Red Lion.

It was gone two o'clock by the time that Hardcastle and Marriott returned from imbibing their lunchtime refreshment.

'Bring Henwood up to the interview room, Skipper,' said Hardcastle. It was a different station officer from the one who had been on duty when Henwood had been brought in; the changeover of reliefs always took place at two o'clock.

Henwood carved a sorry figure as he shuffled into the interview room. Although still wearing his morning coat, he was holding up his striped trousers. The station officer had wisely deprived him of his collar and tie, bootlaces and braces. If a prisoner hanged himself while in police custody, it would be the station officer who faced an enquiry and possibly disciplinary action, if not a criminal charge. Exoneration only followed proof that all reasonable precautions had been taken.

Hardcastle spent the next few minutes in silence, filling his pipe and studying the butler. It did little to alleviate Henwood's fear of what was likely to happen to him.

'Well, my lad,' began Hardcastle, 'you're in Queer Street and no mistake.'

'I haven't done anything wrong, guv'nor,' protested Henwood. His hands, fingers intertwined, rested on the scarred wooden tabletop, continuously clenching and unclenching.

Hardcastle scoffed. 'Did you hear that, Marriott? Our Mr Henwood's done nothing wrong.' He shot forward in his chair. 'Furnishing a false reference in order to obtain your present post, for a start. Secondly, obstructing me in the execution of my duty by telling Villiers that I was keen to have a chat with him, as a result of which he ran away.' He leaned back again and lit his pipe. 'But that's only minor stuff, you see,' he said, waving his match to extinguish the flame, and emitting a plume of smoke towards the ceiling. 'If I take it into my head to charge your master with a serious criminal offence, you'll likely finish up next to him gripping the dock rail at the Old Bailey charged with conspiracy.'

'What conspiracy?' asked Henwood desperately, clearly shocked by this latest threat.

'That rather depends on which particular criminal offence I decide to charge Villiers with, don't it?' said Hardcastle airily. He glanced at the small window behind Henwood as though giving the matter his immediate and weighty consideration. 'But I haven't quite made up my mind yet.' In truth, he had no idea whether Sinclair Villiers had committed an offence at all, but his gut instinct told him that the châtelaine of Flood Street had been up to no good. 'However, Henwood, I might be able to make your problems all disappear if you're straight with me.'

'What d'you want from me, guv'nor?' pleaded the anguished butler, at last sensing a vestige of hope that he may escape punishment. His three months in Pentonville prison had terrified him, and he had no desire to repeat the experience.

'Your master went away quite often, didn't he?'

'Yes, he did.'

'What for?'

'I don't know, sir, and that's the God's honest truth.'

'He never let on where he was going?' asked Hardcastle.

'Never, sir.'

'Or when he'd return?'

'No, sir.'

'Seems a damned funny way to treat his staff, don't you think, Marriott?'

'Indeed, sir. Not like the well-regulated houses we've been accustomed to calling on.'

'That's true. Sergeant Marriott and me have been to some of the finest houses in the country, Henwood. Homes of peers of the realm, knights of the shires, proper gentry, and none of 'em would ever clear off without telling their butler where they was going or when they'd be back. It's only common courtesy, you see. I never go out without telling my staff where I'm off to. Ain't that the case, Marriott?'

'Yes, sir, definitely.' Marriott decided that now would not be a good time to argue with a chief who never revealed his plans to anyone but his sergeant. And not always then.

'Now, what about this here Mrs Wheeler who lives in Worthing? Go there often, did he?'

'I think so, sir.'

'So he did tell you where he was going.' Hardcastle stared at Henwood accusingly. 'Don't lie to me, lad.'

'Not directly, sir. He did say he was going to Worthing on one occasion and had to get the car filled up with petrol. I did a bit of nosing around while he was away and found Mrs Wheeler's address in his little book. So, I thought to myself, she's his lady friend.'

'I see. You did a bit of nosing around when your master was away, did you? Looking for some spare cash, was you? Like you did when you got nicked the last time, I suppose.'

'No, it wasn't like that, sir. I just wondered where he'd gone in case I needed to get in touch with him.'

'Very commendable,' said Hardcastle sarcastically. 'And that's how you managed to get in touch with him this time, I suppose.'

'What does Mr Villiers do for a living, Henwood?' asked Marriott.

'A living, sir?' Henwood was disconcerted by the sudden change of both question and questioner.

'It's a simple enough query,' said Marriott.

'He doesn't do anything, sir. Mr Villiers is a gentleman of independent means.'

'I'm not too sure about the "gentleman" bit,' murmured Hardcastle.

'And where do these independent means come from?' asked Marriott.

'I've no idea, sir. I think he must invest in stocks and shares, and that sort of thing. I've heard him on the telephone once or twice, discussing stock options and the like.'

'Did you find any evidence of this when you was doing your nosing about?' asked Hardcastle.

'Not really, sir. It was just sort of an assumption on my part.'

'How often did Mr Villiers go away on these jaunts of his, Henwood?' asked Marriott, taking up the questioning again.

'About once a month, and usually at the weekends. Mind you, he's been away midweek, once or twice, as well.'

'Are you sure of that, Henwood?'

'Yes, sir. You see, I keep a journal. All butlers do.'

'Ah, now we're getting to the truth of the matter. You never told me you kept a journal.'

'Most butlers do, sir.'

'Is that a fact? So, where is this journal?'

'At Flood Street, sir, in my pantry.'

Hardcastle spent a few moments lighting his pipe again. 'Send someone round to Flood Street a bit tout de suite, Marriott, and tell him to pick up this journal of Henwood's. Frederick, the new butler, will show him where to find it.

While he's there, he can ask the footman if he knows where Villiers has gone; see if he's more forthcoming now that our Mr Henwood ain't there. And tell the officer to take a cab.'

Marriott returned five minutes later. 'I've sent Wood, sir.'

'Good. Now, Henwood, this here journal of yours will show every time that Villiers pushed off on one of his little journeys, will it?'

'Oh, yes, sir. I keep accurate records.'

'And you've no idea where Villiers is at this moment?'

'No, sir. I thought he'd gone to Worthing again, but you said he wasn't there.'

'Of course he wasn't there. And you know he wasn't because you'd warned him off,' snapped Hardcastle. 'Now then, what d'you know about this Mrs Wheeler?'

'Nothing, sir. I've never met the lady.'

'And she never came to Flood Street?'

'Not to my knowledge, sir.'

'Not to your knowledge? But I thought you knew everything that went on in the household you supervise.'

'Not everything, sir,' said the anguished Henwood.

'Put him down, Marriott, and we'll have another chat with him when Wood gets back with this precious journal.'

'How long are you going to keep me here?' asked Henwood.

'As long as it takes to get this matter sorted

out,' said Hardcastle. 'Or until I've decided what to charge you with. In which case you'll be up in front of the beak the following morning.'

Detective Sergeant Herbert Wood returned to the police station at three o'clock. He made straight for the DDI's office and handed over the journal.

'Did Frederick have anything useful to say, Wood?'

'No, sir. I asked him where Villiers had gone, but he claimed that he didn't know.'

'Either he doesn't know, or like Henwood is too scared to say. Anyway, ask Sergeant Marriott to step in.'

'Is Henwood's journal likely to be of any use, sir?' asked Marriott, as he came through the door of Hardcastle's office.

'Remains to be seen, Marriott.' Hardcastle flipped through a few pages of Henwood's neatly written book. 'I think I'll have a word with Mr Quinn about this. If Villiers's days away at Worthing tie up with the bogus Mrs Wheeler's trips to Shoreham harbour, we might be getting somewhere.'

'But d'you think that that will get us any nearer finding out who murdered Gosling and Stein, sir?' Once again, Marriott was concerned that the DDI had lost sight of why A Division detectives had become involved in a Special Branch enquiry in the first place. And were spending more time on it than on the Gosling murder.

'Of course I do, Marriott. I've every reason to think that the two murders we're dealing with are linked to Villiers and the woman at Worthing.'

Marriott failed to see the connection, but he did not have the DDI's experience. 'By the way, sir, there was one telephone number in Villiers's address book that might be of interest.'

'Address book? What address book, Marriott?'

'The one we found at his house, sir.'

'Oh, that one. Yes, well, what about it?'

'I'm awaiting details from the post office, sir. To discover the name and address of the subscriber.'

'We'll have a word with whoever it is when we have a moment, Marriott. Remind me.'

'Might I ask what we hope to learn from them, sir?'

'They might be able to tell us something about Sinclair Villiers. Something we don't know already.'

For ten minutes Superintendent Quinn made a careful study of Henwood's journal. He then drew a Manila folder across his desk, and spent a further five minutes comparing its contents with the entries in the butler's day book.

'Interesting, Mr Hardcastle.' Quinn leaned back with a satisfied smile on his face. 'My detectives have made a number of discoveries that I'm prepared to share with you.' He paused. 'In the strictest confidence, of course.'

'Of course, sir,' murmured Hardcastle.

'For some time now we've been interested in a Spanish freighter that comes into Shoreham harbour about once a month. Looking at Henwood's journal, it would seem that Villiers travelled to Worthing, presumably to the woman's house, also once a month. It's an interesting coincidence, Mr Hardcastle, and if Henwood is to be believed, Villiers turns up at Worthing a day or two before the Spaniard docks at Shoreham.'

'The maid Sarah said she called a cab for her mistress once a month to go to Shoreham, sir.'

'Too much of a coincidence for my liking,' said Quinn. 'I think I'll speak to the Admiralty. It's time we had the Royal Navy keeping an eye on this Spaniard.'

Hardcastle was amazed that Quinn talked so blithely of summoning the assistance of the Royal Navy in much the same way as he would have sent for a constable.

Quinn looked up in time to see Hardcastle's expression of astonishment. 'When the security of the state is at risk, Mr Hardcastle, anything I need is at my disposal.'

SIXTEEN

It was at nine o'clock on Thursday the twentieth of January, almost a week after their last meeting, that Superintendent Quinn sent for Hardcastle again.

'I have received a signal from the captain of His Majesty's Ship *Derwent*, Mr Hardcastle, a destroyer patrolling the English Channel. A boarding party stopped and searched the Swedish freighter SS *Carlson* in the Strait of Dover just off the South Foreland at four thirty a.m. today. It was a routine search to check whether the vessel – the Swedes being a neutral nation – was carrying any weapons of war. The skipper of the *Carlson* informed the officer in charge of the boarding party that they were carrying only timber and this was verified. The *Carlson*'s captain also said that he was docking at Shoreham at approximately two thirty p.m. today.'

'Does this tally with the entries in Henwood's journal, sir?'

'It does indeed. On each occasion during the last six months when the *Carlson* docked at Shoreham, Villiers went to Worthing the pre-

270

vious day and, it seems, the bogus Mrs Wheeler booked a taxi to take her to Shoreham on the day of the ship's arrival.'

'Not a coincidence, then, sir,' said Hardcastle.

'If it is, Mr Hardcastle, it's the sort of coincidence I like,' said Quinn with a wry smile.

'Are you going down there, sir?'

'Yes, I am. And I suggest that you and your officers accompany me and my men. If Villiers appears there today, as I suspect he may, you'll have a chance to interrogate him with regard to the murders you're investigating.' Quinn paused to stroke his beard. 'On the other hand, if Villiers is a participant in some act of espionage, any such charges will take precedence over murder.'

'Of course, sir.' Hardcastle was not unduly concerned about the legal niceties of the matter; if Villiers was found guilty of either spying or murder, he would finish up on the scaffold.

Quinn took out his watch and studied it. 'I suggest we meet here again in one hour's time. I have a number of motor vehicles at my disposal, and they should get us to Shoreham in good time to set up an observation.' He paused. 'DI Strange and DS Shaughnessy have been at Shoreham harbour for some days now, and I shall have several of my other officers with me.'

That Quinn had arranged to keep Shoreham harbour under observation for some days surprised Hardcastle, and he reluctantly concluded that Special Branch officers were better detectives than he had originally given them credit for.

Hardcastle had decided that it would be sufficient for Detective Sergeants Marriott and Wood to accompany him to Shoreham harbour, and at ten o'clock the three of them assembled in Superintendent Quinn's office.

The journey, due south from London, took a little under two hours. By midday the detectives were in a position in the harbour to have a good sight of where the SS *Carlson* would dock, but sufficiently well concealed to ensure that they were not spotted by either Villiers or the woman using the name of Mrs Wheeler. Always assuming, of course, that they arrived when the *Carlson* did.

The Swedish freighter docked on time and the stevedores began the onerous task of unloading her. Of Villiers and the woman there was no sign.

But at four o'clock, once the unloading had been completed, the patience of the waiting police was rewarded. A taxi drew up on the quayside and three people, two men and a woman, alighted.

'That's Villiers and the woman calling herself Mrs Wheeler, sir,' said Hardcastle to Quinn, 'but I don't know who the other man is.'

'We'll find out soon enough, Mr Hardcastle.' Quinn signalled to his officers and a moment later the three arrivals were surrounded. Villiers and Mrs Wheeler were carrying briefcases and these were seized by the officers.

The unidentified man, however, attempted to make a run for it.

'Grab him, Marriott,' shouted Hardcastle.

In a matter of seconds, Marriott and Wood had sped the short distance across the quayside and seized the man by his arms.

'Not so fast, my lad,' said Marriott.

'What's this all about?' protested the man. 'Who the hell are you?'

'We're police officers, as if you didn't know,' said Marriott, and with Wood's aid escorted their prisoner back to where Villiers and the woman were being held.

'We'll take them back to London, Mr Hardcastle, and make use of your police station.'

'It'll be a pleasure, sir.'

'I'll interview Villiers first, Mr Hardcastle,' said Quinn, once they were back at Cannon Row, 'and you're welcome to sit in, but I'd be obliged if you were to remain silent until I've finished. After that you may question him. I may also have to involve MI5.'

'Of course, sir,' said Hardcastle, wondering when exactly he would be given the opportunity to question Villiers about the two murders. From what he knew of MI5, its officers did not seem possessed of the same sense of urgency as the police. 'Might I suggest that the fingerprints of Villiers and the unidentified man be taken immediately? I've a feeling that they might match some which are already in Mr Collins's possession. He found some at Flood Street that we think were Villiers's, but I'd like to make sure.'

'Certainly. I'll rely on you to arrange that?'

'Yes, sir.'

'On reflection,' said Quinn thoughtfully, 'I think it would be advisable if we were to await the result of Mr Collins's findings before conducting our interviews with them.'

'Very good, sir, I'll get Mr Collins on to it straight away,' said Hardcastle, and dispatched Marriott to make the arrangements.

It was near nine o'clock that evening when Detective Inspector Collins reported back to Hardcastle.

'We're in luck, Ernie.' Collins sat down in one of the chairs in the DDI's office. 'Sinclair Villiers's fingerprints match those that were found on the Morse code receiving apparatus seized by Special Branch. The prints of the other man match those I found in Villiers's car when I examined it down at Wandsworth, and they also match the prints I found at the scene of Reuben Gosling's murder in Vauxhall Bridge Road.'

'Got the bugger!' exclaimed Hardcastle, and rubbed his hands together.

'But we still don't know who he is,' said

Collins. 'His prints aren't in my collection.'

'Don't you worry about that, Charlie,' said Hardcastle. 'I'll sweat it out of him soon enough.'

'I'm sure you will, Ernie,' said Collins, nodding sagely.

'I'm going across to see Mr Quinn now, Charlie. It'd probably be best if you came with me in case he's got any questions.'

But Quinn was quite satisfied with DI Collins's report. 'I think we'll wait until tomorrow morning to start interviewing our prisoners, Mr Hardcastle,' he said.

'Is that lawful, sir? I mean, shouldn't they be charged with something?'

Quinn afforded the A Division DDI a bleak smile. 'I'm holding them under the Defence of the Realm Act and the Official Secrets Act, Mr Hardcastle. I can keep them as long as is necessary.'

It was ten o'clock by the time that Hardcastle reached home. There had already been another air raid warning, and the heavy drone of a Zeppelin could be heard overhead. But Hardcastle, like many Londoners, had become philosophical about the bombing, taking the view that if you were going to be killed there was nothing you could do about it. As the troops in the trenches often commented, *'If your number's on it...'*

'You're late, Ernie.' Alice was in the parlour

knitting socks and gloves and cap comforters for the troops. 'Been busy?' she asked, setting aside her needles and wool.

'As a matter of fact, I've been to the seaside,' said Hardcastle.

'That's nice, dear.' Alice knew better than to ask why her husband had been to the coast or what he had been doing there. 'I suppose you'd like a cup of tea.' She stood up and made her way towards the kitchen.

'No thanks. I think I'll have a Scotch. What about you? A sherry?'

'No, I'll have tea, love. If I have a sherry this late, I'll lay awake for hours.'

'You had one on New Year's Eve,' said Hardcastle.

'That's different,' said Alice, demonstrating a feminine logic with which her husband was loath to argue.

Hardcastle had no sooner settled with his whisky, and Alice with her cup of tea, than Kitty arrived home.

'Hello, Pa, Ma.' Kitty crossed the room and gave each of her parents a kiss.

Hardcastle leaned back in his chair and surveyed his daughter. 'My God!' he exclaimed, 'what on earth are you wearing?'

'It's the new conductorette uniform,' said Kitty. She smiled cheekily, pushed a leg forward and placed her hands on her hips in an exaggerated pose. Her skirt was knee-length over tight blue breeches, and she wore knee-high leather gaiters. 'It's been designed so that we can run up and down the stairs of a bus without having to hold our skirts up. Before we got this outfit, there was always some dirty old man sitting near the back of the bus hoping to get a glimpse of our legs.'

'Kitty!' Alice was appalled at her daughter's outspoken comments.

But Kitty only laughed. 'Anyway, I'm going to bed. I'm on early in the morning.'

'I don't know what the younger generation's coming to, Alice.' Hardcastle shook his head as their eldest daughter departed.

'It's the war, dear,' said Alice. It seemed that most deviations from acceptable behaviour these days were attributed to the war.

Hardcastle arrived at Cannon Row early on Friday morning, but Quinn was already seated in the DDI's office.

'We'll interview Villiers first, Mr Hardcastle.'

'Very good, sir.'

It was apparent, the moment that Quinn and Hardcastle entered the interview room, that Villiers was not going to make any admission readily. At least, not straight away.

'I'm a person of considerable standing with substantial means,' Villiers began pompously, 'and I'd like to know why I was detained in such a public fashion and brought here. It's a damned disgrace. I should've thought that you people would have had something better to do, especially with a war on. I should warn you that there'll be a matter of wrongful arrest and false imprisonment to be considered. I shall brief the finest barrister in the land.' He glared at the detectives with an air of righteous indignation. 'Who are you people, anyway?'

'I'm Superintendent Quinn, head of Special Branch, and this is Divisional Detective Inspector Hardcastle of the Whitehall Division who, of course, you've already met. And you can stop making speeches.' Quinn sat down alongside Hardcastle and coolly surveyed the prisoner. 'And in answer to your question, Villiers, you have been arrested on suspicion of contravening the Defence of the Realm Act and the Official Secrets Act.'

'Preposterous!' exclaimed Villiers. 'I demand the presence of my solicitor.'

'You'll have a solicitor if and when I decide you'll have one,' said Quinn mildly, secure in the knowledge that the statutes he had mentioned allowed such a denial of counsel. He opened a file and spent a moment or two reading through its contents. 'On Friday the seventh of this month, my officers seized Morse code equipment from premises at Bow Road where, incidentally, the dead body of Peter Stein was found.'

'I don't see what any of this has to do with me.' Villiers leaned back in his chair, an insolent expression on his face. 'And, as a matter of interest, I've never heard of this Peter Stein.

Are you suggesting that I murdered him?'

'I didn't say he'd been murdered, Villiers,' said Quinn. 'But you have been detained because your fingerprints were found on the Morse code apparatus and on various pieces of furniture in Stein's room. What have you to say about that?'

'Nothing,' said Villiers churlishly.

Quinn glanced at his file again. 'It has been established that a Frenchman by the name of Pierre Benoit had been receiving sensitive military information from your son, Captain Haydn Villiers, and that Benoit had been transmitting it by Morse code to the apparatus found at Bow Road. But this apparatus was originally at your house in Flood Street, Chelsea, until you decided to move it to Bow Road.'

'What makes you think my son had anything to do with this?' asked Villiers, avoiding the allegation that he had put the Morse code apparatus in Stein's room. 'He's an army officer, for God's sake.'

'He's admitted it,' said Quinn, closing the file. 'He is currently detained at the Tower of London following his arrest for espionage, coincidentally on the same day that Stein's body was found.'

The news of his son's arrest clearly came as a great shock to Villiers and his face showed it. 'My God! My son's been arrested?' he exclaimed. 'Why wasn't I told about this?'

'In wartime, Villiers,' said Quinn, 'the police

are under no obligation to tell anyone when we have arrested a spy.'

'A spy? What nonsense.' But Villiers decided not to challenge Quinn's comment any further. 'How did you know to find me at Shoreham?' Finally, his curiosity got the better of him.

'Your butler Henwood obligingly told us,' said Quinn, with just the trace of a smile. 'Incidentally, he obtained his position with you by way of a false reference.'

'I knew all about that, of course I did,' said Villiers defiantly. 'Did you think for one moment that I'd not checked on the rather amateurish reference he provided? Furthermore, I told him that I knew. And that gave me a useful hold over him. Consequently, he did everything I told him, otherwise I'd've handed him over to you people.'

'Not quite everything,' said Quinn. 'He kept a journal listing every occasion you went to Worthing. Curiously enough, on exactly the same dates that the SS *Carlson* docked at Shoreham. And Mrs Wheeler also took a cab to Shoreham on those dates. That's how we knew where to find you.'

'Henwood's a treacherous, ungrateful swine.' Villiers glared angrily at Quinn. 'I'll happily give you the reference he provided, and you can lock the bloody man up for as long as you like.' It was typical of Villiers's arrogance that he would readily abandon anyone who was of no further use to him.

Quinn turned to the A Division DDI. 'Do you have any questions for the prisoner, Mr Hardcastle?'

'Yes, sir. Why did you murder Reuben Gosling, Villiers?' Hardcastle posed the question mildly, but in such a way as to give the impression he had overwhelming proof that this was the case. To his surprise, it triggered a violent reaction, and eventually an admission of guilt. Of sorts.

'The bloody man was murdered because he was a traitor to our cause.' Villiers spat the words defiantly.

'Do you admit to murdering him, then?'

'No, I don't.'

'But you knew of it.'

'Yes.'

'And what cause is this that's so important that it was necessary for him to be killed?' asked Hardcastle.

'A homeland for the Jews.'

'But Reuben Gosling *was* Jewish. Why should he be murdered?'

'Because he disagreed with our aims.' Villiers took out a gold cigarette case and selected a Turkish cigarette from it. He fitted it carefully into a holder and took a lighter from his waistcoat pocket. 'Reuben Gosling threatened to denounce us to the authorities and he had to be stopped,' he continued, once he had lit his cigarette. 'It would have brought to nothing all that we've being fighting for, as well as leading to our arrests.'

'Perhaps you'd care to explain that more fully.' Quinn took over the questioning again; the subject had swung away from the murder back to matters political.

'You damned English only ever paid lip service to the establishment of a Jewish homeland,' proclaimed Villiers. It sounded like the beginning of a speech that he had made many times before.

'I'm Irish,' observed Quinn quietly, 'But *you* are English, are you not?'

'It makes no difference because I am first and foremost a Jew.' Villiers dismissed Quinn's observation as something he saw as a mere technicality. 'But the Ottoman Empire has made a promise that once the British have been defeated, they will establish a homeland for the Jews in Palestine. The Ottomans support Germany and that is why we were giving them information. To make sure that Germany would win the war.'

'If you didn't murder Gosling, who did?' asked Hardcastle.

'Isaac Gosling, Reuben's son.'

'Are you saying that Isaac Gosling murdered his own father?' asked Hardcastle incredulously. Patricide was a rare crime in Britain, and the DDI had some difficulty in believing Villiers's statement.

'Some things transcend filial loyalty,' snapped Villiers. 'Isaac Gosling made the fatal mistake of attempting to enlist his father to the cause, but Reuben Gosling was violently opposed to anything that might endanger this country. And he threatened to expose us to the authorities. He had to be got rid of.'

'Reuben Gosling sounds like a patriot,' observed Quinn.

'What's more, Isaac Gosling murdered Peter Stein,' said Villiers, ignoring Quinn's comment. 'The wretched man had also become a threat by his foolishness.'

'In what way?'

'Stein tried to sell some of the jewellery stolen from Reuben Gosling's shop and that would've brought suspicion on all of us.'

'And Isaac Gosling is the man who was with you when you were arrested at Shoreham.'

'Yes.'

'Why were you there?'

'We were proposing to go to Sweden.'

'Because you knew you were about to be arrested?'

'Of course. You people aren't as clever as you seem to think,' said Villiers arrogantly.

'We were this time,' murmured Hardcastle.

'Presumably it was the captain of the SS *Carlson* to whom you gave the information you had transcribed from the Morse messages you received from Benoit,' said Quinn, 'so that he could pass it on to the German embassy in Stockholm.' Quinn was guessing now, but he was fairly sure that that is what had occurred.

'Yes.'

'We know that Mrs Wheeler is *not* the woman she claimed to be,' said Quinn, suddenly changing the line of questioning. 'Where does she fit into all this?'

'Perhaps you'd better ask her,' said Villiers sarcastically.

'Oh, we shall,' said Quinn. 'Or is she just your fancy woman?'

For the first time since the interview began, a sardonic smile crossed Villiers's face. 'She was not an unwilling bed companion,' he said, 'and that was a bonus.'

'Perhaps you'd care to explain this document that was found in the briefcase you were carrying.' Quinn produced a small grey card from his file. The card bore a photograph of the bogus Mrs Wheeler, but the text was in German and the name of the holder was shown as Irma Glatzer.

'No, I would not,' said Villiers.

'Very well.' Declining to comment further on the document he had just shown Villiers, Quinn stood up. 'Sinclair Villiers, you will be charged with an offence against Section One of the Official Secrets Act.' He opened the door and addressed the Special Branch constable stationed outside the interview room. 'This prisoner is to be charged. Take all his belongings from him and place him in a cell. Then fetch the other male prisoner up here.'

'Yes, sir.' The constable took Villiers by the

arm and led him away.

'So far, so good, Mr Hardcastle,' said Quinn, a satisfied expression on his face.

A few minutes later, the man identified by Villiers as Isaac Gosling was brought into the room.

'Sit down, Gosling,' said Quinn.

'What makes you think that's my name?' asked the man, as he took a seat on the opposite side of the table to the two detectives.

'Your accomplice Sinclair Villiers obligingly told us who you are,' said Quinn. 'He also told us that you murdered your father on New Year's Eve, and Peter Stein at Bow Road on Friday the seventh of January.'

'The bastard's sold me down the river!' exclaimed Gosling angrily. 'But I didn't murder anyone.'

'Mr Hardcastle,' said Quinn, glancing at the DDI.

'It'll do you no good to deny it, Gosling,' said Hardcastle. 'Your fingerprints were found in Villiers's car and in various places in your father's shop. We also found your prints in Stein's room at Bow. And we found your fingerprints on the sash weight with which you killed your father; a sash weight that came from Stein's room in Bow. I'm quite sure that even further evidence will come to light.'

Gosling said nothing, confining himself to glowering at the detectives. But he was obviously resigned to the police having amassed more than enough evidence with which to hang him.

'How was it that you used Sinclair Villiers's car?' asked Hardcastle.

At last Gosling saw a way to wreak some revenge on the man who had informed on him to the police. 'Villiers told us to use it,' he said. 'And he knew exactly why we wanted it. He knew that Peter and I were going to murder my father.'

Hardcastle smiled a smile of deep satisfaction; Villiers had conspired with Gosling and Stein to commit murder. But how foolish of him to have lent his car to the murderers.

'And I suspect that you also were involved in passing information to the enemy,' said Quinn.

'I would never do that. I swear it on my mother's grave.' Gosling's denial was so vehement as to be credible.

'As a matter of interest your mother's still alive, and she's been interviewed,' observed Quinn mildly, without saying that Mrs Morgan had denied all knowledge of her son. 'However, you knew that Stein was receiving military secrets by Morse code from France. And you knew that he was passing that information to Villiers who sent it to the enemy via the captain of the SS *Carlson*, the vessel you were attempting to board when we arrested you yesterday.' Quinn knew that it was Villiers and not Stein who had been receiving that information, but posed the question to see if Gosling would confirm it.

'Stein didn't have that Morse code equipment,' said Gosling. 'It was Villiers who was receiving the information. But once he realized that the game was up, he put it in Stein's room so as to implicate him.'

'In that case, why were you trying to escape to a neutral country?'

'Villiers told me that the police were on to me about the murders and that if I didn't want to be hanged, I'd better get away.'

'Mr Hardcastle?' Quinn glanced sideways at the DDI.

'Why did you murder your father, Gosling?' asked Hardcastle. Although he knew what Villiers had said, he wanted to hear Gosling's explanation.

'He was going to peach on us to the authorities,' said Gosling, confirming what Villiers had told the detectives.

'And Mrs Wheeler?' Quinn raised an eyebrow. 'How well do you know her?'

'I don't know anything about her,' said Gosling. 'I'd never set eyes on her before today.'

'How did you know that you should go to Shoreham yesterday?'

'Villiers told me.'

'How? Did he send you a letter or telephone you?'

'No, I was staying with him and Mrs Wheeler.'

'So you had seen her before today.'

287

'Yes, but only for a few days. I didn't have any idea who she was.'

'Where was this that the three of you stayed?'

'A house in Godalming.'

Quinn pushed a writing pad across the table and laid a pencil on it. 'Write down the address.' Shaughnessy had reported that Mrs Wheeler had hired a cab at Godalming railway station, but there the trail had ended.

Gosling licked the pencil and scribbled a few lines on the pad before pushing it back across the table.

But Quinn returned it. 'And where were you living before that?' he asked.

Gosling hesitated for only a moment. 'I had a room in Wandsworth, over a butcher's shop in Wandsworth High Street near the brewery.' He wrote down the exact address.

'Not very clever of you, dumping Villiers's car close to where you lived,' observed Quinn.

Gosling just shrugged, doubtless thinking, too late, that he had made far too many mistakes to fool these Scotland Yard officers.

Quinn tore off the sheet of paper and handed it to the Special Branch officer stationed outside the door. 'My compliments to Inspector Strange and ask him to arrange a search of these properties forthwith. But before you do that, you can wait to take this prisoner back to his cell,' he said, and returned to his seat.

'Yes, sir.' The detective took the piece of paper and resumed his post.

'What did you do for a living, Gosling?'

'I was a butcher at the shop I told you about.'

'How very apt,' commented Hardcastle drily. He produced a silver necklace, a wristwatch and an albert and set them down on the table. 'We found these among Stein's belongings.' He added another albert to the collection. 'And this was in Sinclair Villiers's car when we examined it. Were they proceeds from your father's shop?'

Gosling gave them but a cursory glance. 'Could be,' he said. 'I told that stupid bugger Stein to chuck 'em in the river. We only took 'em to make it look like a robbery.'

Quinn opened the door. 'Take him away,' he said.

'Yes, sir,' said the SB officer, and escorted Gosling back to his cell.

'I take it that you'll wish to charge Gosling with the murder of his father and Peter Stein straight away, Mr Hardcastle,' said Quinn.

'If it doesn't create any problems for you, sir.'

'None,' said Quinn, 'but we'll have a word with *Fräulein* Irma Glatzer once Mr Strange is back from Godalming.' He paused at the door of the interview room. 'I suppose you'll have Gosling up before the beak at Bow Street tomorrow morning, Mr Hardcastle?'

'Yes, sir.'

'In that case,' said Quinn thoughtfully, 'I'd better come with you. I think it would be better if we sought a hearing in camera, just in case

Gosling decides to start talking about the espionage case that we have against Villiers and Irma Glatzer. The request will carry more weight coming from me.'

'But it'll only be an application for a remand tomorrow, sir.' Hardcastle thought that Quinn should have known that.

'Yes, of course,' said Quinn. 'In that case, I'll wait until the full hearing.'

'Very good, sir,' said Hardcastle, a little piqued that the Special Branch chief thought him incapable of making an application for an in-camera hearing himself.

SEVENTEEN

Hardcastle lost no time in charging Isaac Gosling.

The station officer drew up the charge sheet and recited the necessary words that were a part of such proceedings.

'Isaac Gosling, you are charged firstly that you did murder Reuben Gosling on or about the thirty-first of December 1915 at Westminster in the County of London, and that secondly you did murder Peter Stein on or about the seventh of January 1916 at Bow in the County of London. Against the peace. Do you have anything to say in answer to the charges?'

'No,' said Gosling.

'Turn out your pockets,' said the sergeant.

'His belongings have already been taken from him, Sergeant,' said Hardcastle.

'Very good, sir.'

'You'll be appearing before the Bow Street magistrate tomorrow morning, Gosling,' said Hardcastle. 'In the meantime, you'll remain in custody here.'

But between that little scene in the charge room of Cannon Row police station and Gosling's trial, other damning evidence came to light.

Having sent Detective Sergeant Shaughnessy and other officers to Wandsworth, Detective Inspector Strange took two officers with him to conduct the search of the house at Godalming where Isaac Gosling claimed to have stayed.

It was a small well-kept villa set back from a secluded road. The front garden was immaculately tended, despite it being the depths of winter.

There was a board in the garden stating that the property was available to rent. Strange sent Rafferty to the agent, a few yards down the road, to obtain the key and explain why it was needed.

'The house was rented by Sinclair Villiers on the fourteenth of November last year, sir,' said Rafferty, when he returned.

'That comes as no surprise,' said Strange. 'Open up, then.'

The inside of the house was neat and tidy, and it seemed that Villiers and company had been at pains to leave no trace of their residence. But, there again, they had not expected that police officers, skilled in finding evidence, would search the house.

Nevertheless, Strange was disappointed that he found nothing that was of evidential value, at least from a Special Branch point of view.

However, DC Rafferty, during the course of

his search of the front bedroom on the first floor, examined the top of the wardrobe. And there he found a Webley revolver. Using his handkerchief to take hold of the weapon, he ensured that it was unloaded before taking it downstairs.

'I found this on top of the wardrobe, sir.'

'I wonder what that was doing there,' said Strange.

'It could be connected with the murder that Mr Hardcastle is investigating, sir,' suggested Rafferty.

'Quite possibly. But if it is, the murderer obviously didn't think we'd be searching this place, or he thought he'd be in Sweden before we found it.' Strange looked around. 'Where's Sergeant Colter?'

'He said he was going to have a look round the back garden, sir.'

But at that moment, Colter came back into the house. 'I've found some interesting stuff out back, sir.'

Strange and Rafferty followed Colter into a garden given over largely to lawn with a clump of trees at the end.

'There's been a bonfire here, sir,' said Colter, pointing at a pile of ashes situated behind one of the trees. 'And there's what looks like some half burned fragments of material. It seems as though the previous occupants had set fire to some clothing. There's clearly part of a jacket lapel among it. I wondered if it had anything to do with the murder on A Division's patch that their DDI is investigating.'

'I dare say,' said Strange thoughtfully, 'along with the revolver that Rafferty found upstairs. There's a paper carrier bag in the kitchen, Colter; put some of that stuff in it and we'll see what the laboratory makes of it. And the revolver can go to Inspector Franklin, the firearms expert.' He thrust his hands into his overcoat pockets. 'I'm beginning to think we're doing A Division's work for them.'

It was five o'clock that evening when Inspector Strange returned from Godalming and reported the result of his search to Superintendent Quinn. Quinn immediately crossed to the police station from the Yard, and walked into Hardcastle's office without knocking.

'Good afternoon, sir.' Hardcastle stood up, surprised that Quinn was paying him a visit. In the past Quinn had always sent for the DDI whenever he wanted to see him. But that Quinn's prisoners were being held at Cannon Row had undoubtedly prompted his visit.

'Disappointing news with regard to Godalming, Mr Hardcastle. The house where Villiers and the others were living, not far from Charterhouse School, was rented by Villiers on the fourteenth of November last year. Doubtless it had been taken in case Villiers and company needed a bolt-hole. But, I'm sorry to say, Inspector Strange came back empty-handed. At

294

least, empty-handed as far as my interest is concerned. One of his men did, however, find a revolver that had been hidden, although not carefully enough. I've arranged for it to be sent to Franklin for examination. I suspect that it might have been used in the murder of Stein.' Quinn relaxed into one of the DDI's chairs.

'Mr Franklin already has the round taken from Stein's body, sir, and if we're lucky he'll be able to match that to the revolver Mr Strange's men found.'

'Strange also found some burned clothing in the garden that you may care to have sent for examination.'

'And Isaac Gosling was wearing good quality new clothing when he was arrested at Shoreham, sir,' said Hardcastle thoughtfully. 'I think it's probable that Sinclair Villiers provided the cash for that; I doubt that Gosling could've afforded such a suit.'

'Quite so. However, as I said just now, Mr Strange's search of the property revealed nothing of value to my Branch. It would seem that Villiers, Gosling and the woman merely kept the place as a pied-à-terre until they could escape in the *Carlson,* should the necessity arise. And it did,' he added, smiling.

'I imagine that the burned clothing was Isaac Gosling's cast-offs, sir?'

'He's already admitted that he was there, Mr Hardcastle, so I think that's quite likely.' Quinn gazed at the DDI, a slightly irritated expression on his face, as though rebuking him for not coming to that conclusion himself.

But Hardcastle sensed that the superintendent's irritation was not so much with him as with the fact that the search of the Godalming house had revealed nothing of value to Special Branch.

'I shall interview the woman now,' said Quinn. 'You may join me if you wish, but do not say anything unless I invite you to do so.'

Quinn and Hardcastle stood up when the bogus Mrs Wheeler was escorted into the interview room. She may well have been suspected of being a German agent, but neither man saw that as an excuse to abandon the conventional courtesies.

'Please sit down,' said Quinn. 'You are *Fräulein* Irma Glatzer, are you not?' MI5 had already confirmed that the document found in Sinclair Villiers's briefcase was genuine.

'That is correct.' The slender blonde was perfectly composed. The fact that she was in a police station, and must have known why, did not seem to worry her at all. 'May I have a cigarette, Superintendent?'

'Certainly,' said Quinn.

For a moment or two, Glatzer stared at Quinn. 'My handbag and all my belongings were taken away from me when I was arrested.' She seemed to accept that inconvenience as normal procedure.

Quinn crossed to the door and sent the constable to fetch the woman's cigarettes, and waited in silence until he had returned.

Irma Glatzer opened the small tortoiseshell case, took a cigarette from it and waited until Hardcastle offered her a light.

'Why are you in this country, Miss Glatzer?'

'I am a refugee.'

'From where?'

'From Germany, of course.'

'Whereabouts in Germany?'

'Hamburg.'

'Why was it necessary for you to seek refuge in England, Miss Glatzer?' Quinn knew that the German woman was playing a cat-and-mouse game with him, but he was a patient interrogator. And he had all the time it would take. 'You're no better off here than you would have been had you stayed in Germany.'

Irma Glatzer gave an expressive shrug. 'You would not understand,' she said. 'The Jews are not popular in Germany.'

'Why did you pretend to be Mrs Victoria Wheeler?'

'I did not want to be identified as a German, not when your country is at war with mine.'

'What made you select that particular name?'

'It seemed like a very English name.' She leaned forward to stub out her half-smoked cigarette in the tin lid in the centre of the table.

'You speak excellent English, Miss Glatzer. Where did you learn?'

'I had an English boyfriend in Hamburg. I've always believed that the best place to learn a language is in bed with your teacher.' She stared at Quinn with a half-smile on her face, but showed no sign of embarrassment at her admission.

'What was this boyfriend's name?'

'Leonard Wheeler. That's what gave me the idea for my English name.'

'Where is he now? Still in Germany?'

'I've no idea.'

'Why did you select Victoria as a first name?' Quinn suspected, not only that Leonard Wheeler did not exist, but that Irma Glatzer had undergone an intensive course in English at one of the language schools run by the German Intelligence Service.

'Why not? It was the name of your famous queen.'

'Do you have any questions for Miss Glatzer, Mr Hardcastle?' asked Quinn.

'The photograph in your house at Worthing, of a Scots Guards officer. Where did you get that from?'

'I found it in a second-hand shop.'

'So, your claim that the subject of that picture is your husband is not true.'

'No, it's not. I don't have a husband.'

'Thank you, sir,' said Hardcastle, deferring to Quinn.

'I think we've played this little game for long enough, Miss Glatzer.' Quinn, tiring of the woman's prevarication, opened his file again and took out a sheet of paper. 'This document was one of several seized from your house in Worthing on the evening of the day you vanished. Government scientists have examined it and found that it bore details, in code and written in invisible ink, of details of troop movements in France. There was also a document in your briefcase detailing the movement of certain Royal Navy ships in and out of Portsmouth harbour.' The SB chief did not say that that information was entirely false, and had been sent by British intelligence officers. 'I am satisfied, Miss Glatzer, that you are a member of the German Intelligence Service and that you were sent here for the express purpose of carrying out espionage on behalf of the German government. Do you have anything to say to that?'

'Das hat nichts auf sich,' snapped Irma Glatzer, her blue eyes blazing at Quinn. 'Daraus wird nichts.'

It was a response that left Hardcastle looking puzzled.

'She says that there is nothing in it, and it will come to nothing,' Quinn translated. 'In other words, we can't prove that she had anything to do with it. Furthermore,' he continued, addressing the woman again, 'you met the captain of the SS *Carlson* whenever his ship docked at Shoreham, and passed similar information to him for onward transmission to the German embassy in Sweden.'

Irma Glatzer just stared at Quinn with an unwavering gaze. *'Gott erhalt der Kaiser!'* she exclaimed vehemently.

Quinn did not bother to translate that. 'You are a brave woman, Miss Glatzer.' He stood up and opened the door. 'Take this prisoner back to her cell,' he said to the waiting SB officer.

'Are you going to charge her now, sir?' asked Hardcastle, once Irma Glatzer had been escorted from the room.

'Not until I have the Attorney-General's fiat, Mr Hardcastle.' Quinn spoke as though the DDI should have been aware of this necessary element of procedure. 'Then she'll be tried by court martial at the Tower of London and shot by firing squad.' It seemed to the Special Branch chief that the outcome of her trial was a foregone conclusion.

'It was bad luck for her, that she should have picked a name like Victoria Wheeler, sir, and having a photograph of a Scots Guards officer in her sitting room. Fortunately, Colonel Frobisher, the APM, was able to disprove her story, after which I confirmed it by visiting the real Mrs Wheeler in Esher.'

'Lack of planning,' said Quinn with a dismissive wave of his hand. 'Like carrying those papers with her that contained details of fictitious naval movements at Portsmouth. Incidentally, her fingerprints were found on the rather sensitive paper that she had written on. But she must have been mad to keep hold of her

300

identity document, much less to have given it to Villiers.'

'That was a bad mistake, sir.'

'In my experience, Mr Hardcastle, German spies make the most elementary of mistakes. D'you know that last year the Scottish police arrested a spy who'd just been put ashore from a German submarine off Inverary. He was walking along a quiet country lane when he was stopped and searched by a constable on a bicycle. The fellow had a German sausage in his briefcase, and you can't get those for love or money in this country since the war started. He'd been in Scotland for less than two hours. He was executed, of course.'

DS Shaughnessy reported back to Quinn some time after DI Strange.

'And I suppose you didn't find anything of importance in Wandsworth, either, Shaughnessy,' said Quinn.

'I searched Isaac Gosling's room thoroughly, sir, but all I found was a load of literature about the setting up of a homeland for the Jews once the war was over. I've been through it thoroughly and I can't see that there's anything seditious about it. And certainly nothing that points to espionage.'

'Very well, Shaughnessy.' Quinn sighed. 'Give it to Mr O'Rourke and ask him to cast his eye over it.'

'I interviewed the butcher where Gosling said

he was employed, sir. He said that Gosling was a good worker, punctual and cheerful. In short, he never had any trouble with him. He was very surprised to hear that he'd been arrested for murder.'

''Ere, what's going on 'ere, then?' demanded a flame-haired trollop as Isaac Gosling, an escorting constable and Hardcastle, swept past her. The girl was at the head of a queue of prostitutes in the corridor of Number One Court at Bow Street. It was a long-standing custom that these 'ladies of the night' appeared first in the calendar, and were only displaced when a serious charge was due to be heard.

Hardcastle stepped into the witness box as Gosling was directed into the dock by the constable.

'Good morning, Mr Hardcastle,' said the Chief Metropolitan Magistrate.

'Good morning, Your Worship.'

'Isaac Gosling, Your Worship,' cried the gaoler. 'Two charges of murder.'

'I respectfully ask for an eight-day remand in custody, sir,' said Hardcastle.

'Will you then be ready for me to take a plea, Mr Hardcastle?'

'Yes, sir.'

'Very well.' The magistrate glanced down at his register. 'Remanded to Monday the thirty-first of January.'

Hardcastle returned to Cannon Row aware

that the hard part of the enquiry now began. In his view, the preparation of a report for the Director of Public Prosecutions often presented more difficulties than the investigation itself. But that, he decided, could wait until Monday morning.

'Marriott!' Hardcastle shouted his sergeant's name through the open door of his office.

'Sir?' Marriott appeared, buttoning his jacket.

'What was the name of that woman whose telephone number you found in Sinclair Villiers's address book?'

'It was a woman called Simone Dubois, sir. I traced the telephone number with the post office and the address is in Eaton Square.'

'Simone Dubois? Sounds French, Marriott. We'll go and have a word, but not before we've had a lunchtime pint.'

The first person Hardcastle saw when he pushed open the door of the downstairs bar of the Red Lion was Charlie Simpson.

'Hello, Mr Hardcastle. Anything for me?'

'You don't waste any time in getting to the nub of the matter, I'll say that for you, Simpson. Perhaps you wouldn't mind if I got myself a pint first.'

'Allow me, Mr Hardcastle.' Simpson ordered pints of bitter for the two detectives.

Hardcastle did not usually pay for his beer in the Red Lion, but saw no reason why a Fleet Street reporter should not put his hand in his pocket. He would probably charge it to expenses, anyway.

'As a matter of fact, Simpson, I do have something for you. I promised I'd let you know when I'd made an arrest for Reuben Gosling's murder.'

'And have you, Mr Hardcastle?' Simpson took out his pocket- book and looked up expectantly.

'I arrested his son for the murder. Isaac Gosling appeared at Bow Street this morning and was remanded in custody for eight days.'

'Oh!' Simpson looked disappointed. 'And I suppose there was a load of hacks there writing it all down.'

'Wouldn't have done 'em much good,' said Hardcastle, taking the head off his beer. 'It was only a remand hearing; no names of the victims were mentioned. He's also charged with murdering a Peter Stein at Bow Road on the seventh of this month. Next appearance at Bow Street is on the thirty-first.'

'Thanks very much,' said Simpson. 'I reckon I owe you another beer.'

'Yes, I reckon you do, Simpson.'

EIGHTEEN

Although wearing traditional maid's uniform, the woman who answered the door of Simone Dubois' house in Eaton Square was middle-aged. In Hardcastle's experience, housemaids were always in their twenties; by the time they reached thirty, they had usually been promoted or had married and left service.

'Good afternoon, sir.' The woman paused. 'Oh, there's *two* of you,' she said, unable to keep the surprise out of her voice.

It was a comment that left Hardcastle in little doubt as to Miss Dubois' occupation. 'Yes, there are,' he said. 'Is Miss Dubois at home?'

'If you'd care to step inside, sir,' said the maid, 'I'll enquire if the mistress is at home. *Two* of them,' she repeated, half to herself, and shook her head.

Hardcastle and Marriott entered the hall as the maid disappeared through a door at the rear.

'She's no maid, Marriott,' said Hardcastle. 'If she ain't Miss Dubois' madam, I'm a Dutchman.'

'You know this Simone Dubois, then, do you, sir?'

'No, I don't, Marriott. But the name is too good to be true. Odds-on, she's a high-class whore.'

'Please come this way, gentlemen.' The maid returned within seconds and conducted the detectives into the room she had just left.

Simone Dubois was reclining on a chaise-longue, a box of chocolates on her lap, and made no attempt to stand up. Perhaps no more than twenty-seven, she was attired in a low-cut silk emerald green tea gown that matched her eyes, as did her silk slippers. Her chestnut hair, worn loose, tumbled around her shoulders. But at the sight of Hardcastle she sat up sharply. 'Oh my Gawd, it's you, Mr Hardcastle.'

'That's right, Poppy Shanks, it's me. And this here is Detective Sergeant Marriott. You've changed your name since you were a frequent visitor at Vine Street nick.'

'What d'you want?' The woman masquerading as Simone Dubois quickly recovered and glanced at Marriott apprehensively. 'I hope you haven't come to tell me I've been a naughty girl, Mr H.'

'I can't imagine why you should think that, Poppy.' Hardcastle cast his gaze around the opulently appointed sitting room. The furniture was of good quality, some of it apparently genuine antique, and the floor was covered in a thick pile Wilton carpet. 'You seem to have come up in the world, Poppy. Bit of a change from Shepherd Market. Getting too cold there, was it? Now it's winter.'

'I was getting nicked by them C Division rozzers too often,' said Poppy, and abandoning all pretence, added, 'but then I got set up here by a kind gentleman.'

'He wouldn't be a kind gentleman by the name of Sinclair Villiers, would he?' asked Hardcastle.

'Oh, you know him, then. Is he in trouble?' Poppy swung her legs off the chaise-longue and stood up. 'I think I need a gin. Fancy one, do you?'

'No thanks,' said Hardcastle, as Poppy cross-ed to an Edwardian satinwood cabinet and poured herself half a tumbler of neat Holland's. 'Your benefactor was unfortunate enough to have had his car stolen, a car that was used in a robbery and a murder.'

'Oh Gawd! How awful for poor dear Sinclair. When was this?' Poppy, holding her glass of gin, returned unsteadily to her seat.

'On New Year's Eve.'

'How dreadful. As a matter of fact, he spent New Year's Eve with me. Left the next morn-ing.' Poppy Shanks fixed Hardcastle with an unwavering, and slightly amused, expression. 'If only he'd stayed at home it might not have happened.'

'How did he get here?'

'In a cab, of course,' said Poppy. 'He's very discreet, is Sinclair. He doesn't like to leave his car outside all night. He says it might get me a bad name.'

'Bit late for that,' murmured Hardcastle. 'Does he visit you often?'

'As often as he can afford to.' She paused. 'Afford the time, I mean.'

'Come off it, Poppy. It's a copper you're talking to, and I know you've been on the game since you were seventeen. What's more, I'd put money on Villiers not being your only client.'

'What *do* you take me for, Mr H?' Poppy contrived, unsuccessfully, to appear coy and a little offended.

'Has Mr Villiers visited you since New Year's Eve?' asked Marriott.

'Yeah, he was here about a week later,' said Poppy.

'What day was that?'

'A Thursday. The seventh of January it was. I remember the date 'cos he reckoned he was going to stay the whole weekend and take me to a show on Saturday, but he only stayed the one night. Left here on Friday, about midday, I s'pose. I was real fed up when he got here and said as how his plans had changed, and he had to go to Worthing on urgent business.'

Hardcastle laughed as he and Marriott stood up. 'You just make sure you stay out of trouble, lass. We'll see ourselves out.'

'Well, sir, that takes care of the days that Reuben Gosling and Stein were murdered,' said Marriott, as he and the DDI made their way along Eaton Square.

'You think so, do you, Marriott?' said Hard-castle, stopping and turning to face his sergeant. 'Well, I'm not prepared to take the word of a tom who gives Villiers an alibi, even if you do. It all came out too pat; she'd been told what to say by Villiers.' He carried on walking. 'Not that it matters a damn,' he added. 'He'll be hanged anyway.'

With a sigh, Hardcastle pushed aside the report of the case against Peter Stein that he was writing for the DPP, and took out his hunter. It was five o'clock on Monday evening and he decided that he had done enough, apart from which there was another, more pressing reason why he did not want to stay late at work. He dropped the watch into his waistcoat pocket, crossed to the detectives' office and opened the door.

Much to his sergeant's amazement, Hard-castle announced that he was going home; Marriott had never known the DDI to leave that early on a weekday, and glanced at the clock.

'Don't look so surprised, Marriott. It's Wally's sixteenth birthday today and I've promised him his first taste of Scotch.'

'Are you sure about that, sir?' asked Marriott, who had stood up the moment the DDI had appeared.

'Of course I'm sure, Marriott. I do know when my son's birthday is.'

'I didn't mean that, sir. I meant are you sure it's his first taste of whisky.'

Hardcastle laughed. 'You might well be right, Marriott. There's no telling what these lads get up to at that office of theirs, but I doubt they can afford whisky.' Ever since the age of fourteen, Walter Hardcastle had been employed as a telegram messenger at the local post office. Regrettably, he now spent most of his working hours delivering telegrams to the loved ones of men killed in action, wounded, reported missing or taken prisoner.

'Give the lad my best wishes, sir.'

'Thank you, Marriott, I will.'

'Another three years and he'll be old enough to join the Force, sir.'

'Over my dead body,' growled Hardcastle.

The disruption to the tram service from Westminster to Kennington, occasioned by frequent alerts to Zeppelin raids, some of which were false alarms, meant that Hardcastle did not arrive home until almost six o'clock.

He hung up his hat, coat and umbrella and, as was his invariable practice, checked the accuracy of the hall clock against his hunter. Satisfied that it was keeping good time, he pushed open the door of the parlour.

Alice, Kitty and Maud were seated around the fire, the two Hardcastle daughters having managed to change their shifts in order to be at home.

But of Walter there was no sign.

'Where's Wally?' asked Hardcastle.

'He'll be here shortly, Ernie,' said Alice. 'He dropped by earlier on to say that he'd got some extras to deliver. He said something about there having been a lot of our lads killed and wounded at a place called Hanna in Mesopotamia a day or two ago.'

'Another pointless campaign, and for what?' exclaimed Hardcastle. 'They've put that General Townshend in an impossible situation trying to hold on to Kut. You mark my words, he'll have to surrender before the relief force gets to him.'

But before Alice could tell her husband to stop talking about the war, the door of the parlour flew open.

The Hardcastle family clapped and began to sing *Happy Birthday, dear Walter*...

Walter responded by sweeping off his uniform kepi and sketching a deep bow.

'Time for a drink to celebrate,' said Hardcastle, rubbing his hands together and crossing to the cabinet where he kept the alcohol. He poured glasses of Amontillado for Alice and the two girls, and turned to Walter. 'Well, Wally, now that you've reached sixteen, I think it's time you had a drop of whisky.'

'I'd rather have a brown ale, Pa,' said Walter. 'I don't much care for the taste of Scotch.'

For a moment or two, Hardcastle, holding a bottle of Johnny Walker aloft, was speechless, despite what he had said to Marriott. 'You've had it before?' he asked eventually.

'Once or twice, Pa. The last time was when I took a telegram to a retired colonel the other day. It was to tell him that his son, who he'd been told was dead, had only been slightly wounded and was in hospital in Hazebrouck. He insisted on taking me indoors and giving me a whisky to celebrate.'

'It seems Marriott was right,' muttered Hardcastle, a comment that had no significance for the family. 'Well, now, I think we might just have some birthday presents for you, Wally,' he added, glancing at the womenfolk.

Alice, Kitty and Maud stood up as one and left the room. Returning moments later, bearing parcels wrapped intriguingly in brown paper, they handed them to the sixteen-year-old.

'Golly!' exclaimed Walter, and spent the next few minutes opening his gifts and admiring them.

His mother had given him a silver cigarette case engraved with his initials; Kitty had found an accordion at Gamages, the department store in Holborn; and Maud had bought him one of Kodak's latest Brownie box cameras.

'Crikey!' Walter, usually the most talkative of the family, was able only to utter that single word. Crossing to his mother, and then Kitty and Maud, he kissed each in turn, murmuring his thanks.

'And now,' said Hardcastle, handing his son a carefully wrapped package, 'here is my present. And many happy returns of the day, Wally.'

Walter stripped off the paper to reveal a small leather covered box. Inside was a half-hunter pocket watch. Although the watch had been priced at six pounds, almost twice Hardcastle's weekly pay, Mr Parfitt, the jeweller in Victoria Street, had given him a generous discount. But it had still meant Hardcastle having to save for some months prior to the boy's birthday.

'Gosh, thanks, Pa.' Walter turned the watch over in his hands, examining every aspect of it before holding it up to his ear. 'It's super,' he exclaimed.

'This one,' said Hardcastle, producing his own pocket watch, 'was given me by *my* father on *my* sixteenth birthday, and has kept perfect time ever since. But be sure not to overwind it, Wally. That's a sure way to break the spring.'

'Gosh!' said Walter again, and shook hands with his father.

Alice had used up almost the whole of the week's ration to provide a magnificent meal, and Hardcastle produced a bottle of Rioja that had set him back a shilling, with which to round off the evening.

The next morning, Hardcastle decided that he would, after all, charge Henwood with furnishing a false character reference, and with obstructing police in the execution of their duty.

The Bow Street magistrate listened carefully to Hardcastle's evidence, pursed his lips and pronounced a verdict of guilty. He frowned when Hardcastle gave details of Henwood's previous conviction.

'Have you anything to say?' he asked.

'I'm very sorry, sir.' Henwood did his best to appear apathetic. 'But I was only defending my master.'

'I was considering a custodial sentence,' the magistrate began, staring fixedly at the ex-butler. 'However, I am informed that it is the army's intention to conscript you with immediate effect and that, in my view, will be punishment enough. You are remanded to await a military escort.'

It was three weeks after Quinn had interviewed Sinclair Villiers and Irma Glatzer that they, together with Captain Haydn Villiers, were arraigned before a general court martial at the Tower of London held in camera before Major General the Lord Cheylesmore.

Hardcastle, there at Quinn's invitation, but only as an interested spectator, was amazed when Sinclair Villiers was escorted into the courtroom. Gone was the arrogant Chelsea resident. Three weeks confinement in Brixton prison had turned him into a shuffling, round-shouldered, broken man. He had lost weight and his clothes hung on him as though they had been tailored for someone much stockier. His hair, once slicked flat with pomade, was now longer and comparatively unkempt.

By contrast, Irma Glatzer wore a grey tweed

costume with a flared jacket and a skirt the hem of which was at least six inches from the ground. Glacé-kid court shoes and art silk stockings completed the picture of a well-dressed woman, and gave the impression of a wealthy socialite rather than a German spy.

Captain Haydn Villiers was in uniform, but deprived of cap, sword and Sam Browne, the military bearing had vanished, and his face had taken on a greyish hue.

The indictment against all three defendants was that of committing a felony under Section One of the Official Secrets Act 1911: communicating information of use to the enemy. Predictably, each entered a plea of Not Guilty.

Quinn and the other Special Branch officers who had been involved in the investigation were called to give evidence, together with a number of shadowy figures from MI5.

Three days later, Sinclair and Haydn Villiers, father and son, and Irma Glatzer were found guilty.

Sinclair Villiers began an impassioned but rambling plea in mitigation from the dock about the need for a Jewish homeland, and what he described as the treachery of the British government in evading any commitment to that end.

But after five minutes, he was cut short by the president of the court. 'This is no place for political speeches, Villiers,' said Lord Cheylesmore curtly.

Irma Glatzer had nothing to say, but Haydn

Villiers once again protested his innocence.

After sentence of death had been pronounced, the prisoners were escorted to the condemned cells. The court adjourned and the witnesses made their way out of the gloomy chamber that had seen three more spies convicted. They would not be the last.

'A very successful outcome, Mr Hardcastle,' said Quinn, as he and the others left the Tower.

'Indeed, sir,' said Hardcastle.

'By the way,' Quinn added, 'Pierre Benoit, the Frenchman who passed on the information given him by Captain Villiers, was guillotined in Paris four days ago.'

'But I thought the French had offered him immunity if he cooperated, sir.'

'They lied,' said Quinn.

Within forty-eight hours the three convicted spies had also been executed. Haydn Villiers and Irma Glatzer were dispatched at the Tower; Sinclair Villiers had been hanged at Wormwood Scrubs whence he had been transferred immediately following his trial.

Waving aside the attendant rabbi, Irma Glatzer was the first to face the firing squad. She did so without displaying any trace of fear. In fact, there was an imperious lifting of her chin just before the volley of shots rang out.

Haydn Villiers, however, presented a pitiable figure. Gone was the sneering army officer who had told his MI5 interrogators that he was prepared to die for his cause, but who had believed that he would not have to. Semi-conscious and gibbering inaudibly, he was carried to his execution, and so incapable of standing was he that the officer in charge ordered that he be secured to a chair.

It was six weeks later that the trial of Isaac Gosling took place at the Central Criminal Court at Old Bailey.

Sir George Cave, the Solicitor-General, appeared for the Crown; Sir Frederick Smith, the Attorney-General, was otherwise engaged on matters concerning the war.

Gosling pleaded Not Guilty to the two indictments of murdering his father and Peter Stein. But once the evidence of the fingerprints and the footprint, together with Dr Spilsbury's testimony regarding the blood had been given, the jury took less than an hour to find him guilty.

The judge donned the black cap, sentenced him to death, and implored the Almighty to have mercy on his soul. To which the judge's chaplain added 'Amen'.

Three weeks later Gosling was hanged at Pentonville prison in north London. As was usual on these occasions, a morbid crowd surged forward to read the black-framed announcement that was posted on the gates. At the same time a black flag was raised over the prison.

In accordance with the regulations, Gosling's body was interred in an unmarked grave within the precincts of the prison.